CHRISTMASSY TALES

PAUL MAGRS

Contents

Stardust and Snow

My friend told me a story he hadn't told anyone for years. When he used to tell it years ago people would laugh and say, 'Who'd believe that? How can that be true? That's daft.' So he didn't tell it again for ages. But for some reason, last night, he knew it would be just the kind of story I would love.

When he was a kid, he said, they didn't use the word autism, they just said 'shy', or 'isn't very good at being around strangers or lots of people.' But that's what he was, and is, and he doesn't mind telling anyone. It's just a matter of fact with him, and sometimes it makes him sound a little and act different, but that's okay.

Anyway, when he was a kid it was the middle of the 1980s and they were still saying 'shy' or 'withdrawn' rather than 'autistic'. He went to London with his mother to see a special screening of a new film he really loved. He must have won a competition or something, I think. Some of the details he can't quite remember, but he thinks it must have been

London they went to, and the film…! Well, the film is one of my all-time favourites, too. It's a dark, mysterious fantasy movie. Every single frame is crammed with puppets and goblins. There are silly songs and a goblin king who wears clingy silver tights and who kidnaps a baby and this is what kickstarts the whole adventure.

It was 'Labyrinth', of course, and the star was David Bowie, and he was there to meet the children who had come to see this special screening.

'I met David Bowie once,' was the thing that my friend said, that caught my attention.

'You did? When was this?' I was amazed, and surprised, too, at the casual way he brought this revelation out. Almost anyone else I know would have told the tale a million times already.

He seemed surprised I would want to know, and he told me the whole thing, all out of order, and I eked the details out of him.

He told the story as if it he'd been on an adventure back then, and he wasn't quite allowed to tell the story.

Like there was a pact, or a magic spell surrounding it.

As if something profound and peculiar would occur if he broke the confidence.

If he told me, maybe I could pass the story on, he said.

But if he let me tell the story, could that possibly detract from the magic? Would it take away the power of the spell?

Sharing might even make the spell better.

It might spread that magic around the world.

It was thirty years ago and all us kids who loved that film then, and who still love it now, are all middle-aged.

Saddest of all, the Goblin King is dead.

Does the magic still exist?

I wanted to know.

So I asked him what had happened on his adventure.

And he told me about that Christmas, when he sang his duet with David Bowie.

I loved it and wanted all the details. How many other kids? Did they have puppets from the film there, as well? What was David Bowie wearing? I imagined him in his lilac suit from Live Aid. Or maybe he was dressed as the Goblin King in lacy ruffles and cobwebs and glitter.

What was the last thing he said to you, when you had to say goodbye?

He told me: 'David Bowie said, 'I'm always afraid as well. But this is how you can feel brave in the world.' And then it was over. I've never forgotten it. And years later I cried when I heard he had passed.'

My friend was surprised I was delighted by this tale.

'The normal reaction is: that's just a stupid story. Fancy believing in an invisible mask.'

But I do. I really believe in it.

And it's the best story I've heard all year.

*

When I was nine I sang with a duet with David Bowie.

It's true, it was almost Christmas in London and I met David Bowie and we sang.

I remember it was nearly Christmas because Grandma and I took the train up to London and it was cold and windy and all the leaves were down. There were decorated trees in the windows.

Tinsel and stars.

The air smelled smoky and maybe a bit like it was going to snow.

I'd won a competition.

I never usually went in for anything like that.

'People like us never win things,' Grandma said. 'It's all just the luck of the draw, and we're hopeless.'

But this time I had.

And this time it mattered because it was a competition to do with a movie I really loved.

You know the one. The one with the king of the goblins. It had come out the year before when I was eight and I still loved it. I'd seen it more than once.

I had the book and the record. I knew all the words.

I loved to sing, but only by myself.

Sometimes I recorded myself.

Singing, and telling stories.

When I was nine I had one of those huge ghetto blasters. It was almost as big as I was. It had two speakers and bits that lit up and graphic equalizers, whatever they were.

I used to love to record things, and I would make mix-tapes for myself.

'Don't you dare go recording me!' Grandma shouted. 'Don't you dare go bugging me in my own home!'

Why would I want to record her, though?

Grandma was interested in fashion. She loved to go into town and buy new clothes. They'd be clothes that were slightly too young for her. That's what Grandpa said. 'Look at you! You look like a fat Cher!'

On the day we went to London – the day of the special screening – Grandma was wearing her pink fur coat. It was her favourite thing in the whole world.

She also wore a colourful headscarf and spiky high-heeled boots.

On that day I was wearing a white shirt, a red v-necked jumper and check trousers. It was more or less what I always wore, but that day I was extra smart.

Because we were going to London to be with the other competition winners and some of the stars of the movie were going to be there as well.

Most of them were puppets.

But the big star of the show was David Bowie.

And he was actually going to be there.

'Huh, him!' Grandma said. 'He's a flash in the pan. He's overrated. Who cares about him?'

She didn't think David Bowie was anything special.

But I did.

And Grandpa did.

I loved my Grandpa. We did everything together. He used to buy me books.

He understood about David Bowie and the film in which he was the goblin king.

When the letter came and I found out I'd won, I dreamed that David Bowie would take me away, just before Christmas, far away to the land of the goblins, and away from Grandma and Grandpa.

But I didn't want to leave Grandpa.

'You're not the only winner,' Grandma said. 'Lots of kids must have won prizes. If it's a film show then they've given out loads of tickets, haven't they? Hardly makes it special.'

But it did, I thought.

It was just before Christmas in London.

And David Bowie was going to meet us there.

*

We caught the train. It was one of the old fashioned ones that you don't see any more, with the separate little compartments.

I was so excited I sang all the way there. I sang 'Greensleeves' because it was my favourite song.

'That horrible racket you're making is giving me a ghastly headache!' Grandma cried, tying her headscarf even tighter. 'Shut up!'

I hadn't even realized I was singing in front of her. I'd forgotten I wasn't alone with my ghetto blaster. That's how happy I was.

I didn't even much mind the crowds at the railway station when we arrived. Well, not too much, anyway. That kind of thing usually bothered me pretty badly. I hated being around a lot of people.

I kept looking at the time. 'Grandma, we're going to be late.'

She was queueing to buy a newspaper. 'Shush,' she frowned.

She didn't like to walk fast. She hated hurrying anywhere. She thought dashing about was common.

So we always ambled everywhere, but that was no good today, with the special film show starting at a set time. If we got there late to the place, they might even refuse to let us in, if it had already begun.

These were the thoughts going through my head as she took out the letter and looked, frowningly, at the directions and we headed to the Underground station.

I was struggling a bit with my ghetto blaster, especially on the escalators.

Grandma said, 'I don't even want to be here. I don't want to see that silly film – again! The only reason I'm even here is because your Grandpa isn't well, and he insisted.'

Also, he had offered to buy our tickets, and he had given Grandma the money for a new posh frock for Christmas. But I didn't point that out, because I didn't want her to lose her temper.

It seemed to take about a million years to get to the place.

We went on a Tube train and then a red bus and we almost got lost, and Grandma was getting angry.

It was freezing and starting to snow.

The ground was pretty icy underfoot. I stared at it as we walked along.

It was a funny kind of frost.

Glittery.

And the snow that was starting to fall… It was almost silver, wasn't it?

'Why can't this thing be somewhere centrally located?' Grandma was just about gnashing her teeth. 'How am I ever going to make it to the shops in time afterwards?'

She trod on my foot as we went down the high street of some place I didn't recognize.

I didn't make a fuss, even though she was in her spiky-heeled boots. It really hurt, actually.

When we got to the place eventually it didn't look like the right kind of building at all.

'It looks like an old school!' Grandma said, and she was right.

It was old-fashioned with turrets and tall windows and metal fences all around. The place was open, even though it was a Saturday, and we had to cross a schoolyard to get to the main doors. It was like a very fancy type of school.

'Is this where the special screening is?' she asked the man on the main door, showing him the letter I'd been sent by the competition people. She always put on a very haughty voice when talking to strangers.

The man was in a suit and he looked down at the letter carefully, then studied his clipboard.

'I'm afraid you're rather late,' he said.

My heart started hammering because I thought he was going to say we'd missed everything and we would have to turn round and go home.

'Well, that can't be helped,' said Grandma.

'It's okay,' said the man, and ushered us into the building.

The corridors were dark and wooden-floored. Behind a tall set of doors there was a large hall filled with kids and noise.

He opened the doors a little crack and we could see them all lit up by the giant screen.

The film had started and it was playing very boomingly.

I knew the story well.

We hadn't missed much.

The king of the goblins hadn't even come on yet.

But I'd missed the theme song, though, and that was a bit I really loved.

The man whispered to us that we could find seats right at the back. Would we be all right?

Grandma rolled her eyes and led the way into the noisy room.   We found seats next to some other parents and kids at the back, and they barely glanced at us as we sat down.

Grandma made me feel that everyone was looking at us, making a show of ourselves by coming in late.

We sat down and started concentrating on the film.

The most wonderful film in the world.

I felt rather than heard Grandma sigh.

How many kids were there? It seemed like hundreds. It really sounded like hundreds, when they started yelling and shouting out at the exciting bits.

It was all quite noisy, and that spoiled it a bit for me. But I stayed where I was. I wasn't going to miss any of this.

The film rolled on.

Brilliantly, sparklingly, wonderfully.

Just like it had the first three times I saw it.

There was something different.

Was it a clearer picture, perhaps?

It seemed like all the scenes in the land of the goblin king were covered in glitter.

The whole screen was twinkling and glittering throughout.

I wasn't sure it had been like that the other times I'd watched the movie.

And then I was sucked into the story again.

I mouthed the words to the songs under my breath.

I reached under my seat to press 'record' on my ghetto blaster and when one side of my C90 ran out, I turned it over.

Grandma tutted at my wriggling about in my seat.

And at last the movie finished.

The house lights came up and everyone was cheering.

'Absolute twaddle,' Grandma said, and pulled her headscarf back on and tied it tight.

*

They had puppets there!

The actual puppets from the film. There were puppet experts and special effects guys. There was a bit of a crush at the front of the hall, with all the kids shoving in to see.

From where we were you couldn't see all that much.

Just the tops of the biggest puppets' heads.

There were squeals and shrieks of delight, though, as the puppeteers made them do stuff. Move about and blink their eyes and shake their limbs.

The doors opened and even more puppets came in. Goblins and monsters. Trolls and the cute dog. They were mobbed by the competition winners.

'It's pandemonium in here,' Grandma complained to the adults nearest her. Her voice became rather shrill. 'Those kids are going wild. Can't someone get them under better control? My grandson is very sensitive and withdrawn. He can't stand to be around things like this.'

I felt ashamed that she was telling people about me, so I just stared at the shiny wooden floor and my tape deck.

And that's how I missed the moment when the doors opened again and David Bowie walked in.

But I heard the huge whooping cheer that went up, and the screams from the kids, and some of the grown-ups.

I could hear his voice shouting hello to everyone, but I couldn't see him.

'There he is!' Grandma jabbed me. 'You should look up and see! That's who you came for, isn't it? The great big star of the show? Stop looking at the floor and look! You're just as good and deserving as anyone else here!'

But at first I couldn't. I couldn't look up.

When I did sneak a look I saw that David Bowie was swamped by children. They had gathered round him and he was at the centre of a hurricane of kids and puppets. He was signing posters and records for everyone.

Then, all of a sudden, that man in the suit was standing with us.
He tapped my Grandma on the shoulder and addressed her by name.

'Yes?' she frowned.

'You're to follow me,' he said mysteriously.

Grandma grabbed my hand and dragged me away from the fringes of that noisy crowd.

We left the hall and followed the man down a corridor. Grandma's sharp footsteps were really noisy.

Had we done something wrong?

They'd seen me recording on my ghetto blaster. Maybe it wasn't allowed?

It felt like we were in trouble, when the man opened another door and sent us into a smaller room, behind the main hall. It was mostly bare, apart from some chairs, gym equipment and an old upright piano.

'You're to wait here,' he said, not smiling.

'Why?' Grandma demanded.

'You're the party who wrote in, aren't you?' said the man in the suit. 'About the boy?'

Grandma glanced at me and then glared at him. 'It was his grandpa who 'wrote in' as you put it. His grandpa wasn't well enough to come here today with the boy, and so I'm here instead. I've no idea what the old man said in his letter.'

'I see,' said the man. He looked at me and said, sounding more kindly this time, 'Well, you're to stay here. At Mr Bowie's own request. You won't have to wait long.'

'I should jolly well hope not,' said Grandma, watching him leave.

Then we were alone in this side room. She went to sit on a plastic chair in the corner of the room.

She took a flask out of her shopping bag and carefully poured herself a hot cup of tea. She sat drinking this noisily, smacking her lips.

Then she took out her Daily Mail and started reading it.

She didn't remove her headscarf.

I set down my ghetto blaster in the middle of the shiny floor and just stood there waiting.

I wasn't even sure what I was waiting for.

At Mr Bowie's own request?

Maybe I really had done wrong by recording the film on my ghetto blaster?

I took out the tape and swapped it for a blank one from my satchel. Luckily, I always carried a supply.

Was I really in trouble?

There was still a lot of noise coming from the main hall.

*

'If they don't get a move on soon, we shall have to go,' Grandma said loudly. 'I think they must have forgotten all about us. Really, it's not good enough. They have no right to get a young boy's hopes up...'

Just as she was talking the door flew open and...

David Bowie walked into the room.

I stared at him.

I gasped and held my breath.

He was in a silk pirate shirt and tight blue trousers. He was dressed just like he was on the screen, when he was the goblin king.

'You're Daniel, aren't you?' he grinned at me.

I stared at his jagged teeth.

Then David Bowie was striding over to Grandma. 'You must be Grandma,' he said, and confidently held out his hand.

She looked at him, and at his hand, and she didn't shake it.

She became flustered and went back inside her newspaper.

I cringed inside. I couldn't believe she was being so rude.

But nothing ruffled David Bowie. He just shrugged and turned away, leaving her to the Daily Mail. He strolled back over to me and I looked down quickly at the floor.

'Are you him?' he asked. 'Are you the one? You are, aren't you?'

I couldn't look up at David Bowie. I was so embarrassed about my Grandma.

I heard the rustle of her newspaper again. I heard her slurp her tea and tut loudly.

Then David Bowie sat down on the floor. He sat down cross-legged right in front of me so that I was looking down at him.

There he was.

One eye was slightly different to the other.

One of them had a bigger pupil than the other one.

His hair was cut shorter than it had been in the film.

But maybe that had been a wig, anyway.

He smelled nice. He smelled of soft ice cream.

Vanilla, that's what it was.

'You've got green eyes,' he said, looking straight at me.

'Y-yes,' I said.

'That's quite special, that. You must be part-wizard.'

He was looking straight at me as he said this. No one ever did that.

'Your Grandpa wrote me a letter, Daniel. I don't know how he found out how to write to me, or where to send it, but he did. Quite possibly it was magic. Does he do magic, your Grandpa?'

'No... but he's nice.'

'Well, he wrote to me and said... Mr Bowie, please look after my grandson Daniel at your special Christmas film show because I'm not able to be there. Daniel doesn't like big crowds and everyone being noisy and rowdy. Also, he can get a bit shy and withdrawn. Not everyone understands him, and he's had a bit of bother with bullies in the past and things like that. So he might need a special, quiet moment to himself. That's what he told me. Is that right, Daniel?'

I nodded.

'I like the sound of your Grandpa.'

Then David Bowie gasped. 'Is that a ghetto blaster? Is that yours? Do you record things?'

I nodded. 'Stories. Sometimes, songs.'

'Do you sing?'

I shook my head.

'Your Grandpa told me you liked to sing.'

Then David Bowie was reaching out and dragging my ghetto blaster towards him. 'Look at this! It's got graphic equalizers and everything. Whatever they are. Look, Daniel, why don't we just record our whole meeting, eh? Why don't I press record and then you'll have a tape as a kind of souvenir? Is there room on the tape that's in there now?'

I nodded.

I said, 'You have to press 'play' and 'record' at the same time.'

I watched David Bowie press 'play' and 'record' at the same time.

'Shall we sing together, Daniel? We could choose a song and sing it together, and then if you ever need to, you could play it back really loudly for yourself. Then it'll drown out any voices you don't want to hear, like bullies at school.'

Grandma tutted loudly.

David Bowie whispered to me, 'And it might drown out all the tuts, as well.'

I laughed at that, and stopped myself, in case Grandma heard.

'Is there a piano in here? They said there would be. Ah, there we are.'

Suddenly David Bowie was up on his feet and sauntering off across the room towards the battered upright piano.

He lifted the dark wooden lid.

'Come over here. What shall we sing?'

I wouldn't say it out loud. Suddenly I felt so shy I had to write it down. I took a piece of paper and a pencil from my satchel and wrote down that we should sing the song from the film. The one we'd just watched.

He grinned. 'Easy! But come and sit down here and help me. I need your help singing this, Daniel.'

The thing is, most people's voices sounded really horrible to me. I found them painful to listen to. But the way David Bowie spoke then, his voice was vibrating inside of me.

It made me feel calm and excited at the same time.

The piano was really old. The keys were yellow and some looked broken. He put his hands on the keys and when he tried a few chords one key went wobbly and made a dodgy noise. He laughed and moved his hands along the keyboard to find a bit that would play.

Then he started the song.

He played and sang to me.

When he got to the line that usually has 'little girl' in it, he sang 'wizard boy.'

And then he got me to sing with him.

He actually got me to sing out loud with him.

He made me feel brave and he freed my tongue.

'Hey, you've got a good voice, Daniel,' he told me, pausing between verses. 'You see, the magic will only work if we sing together. Because you're a green-eyed part-wizard. The magic will work only if you help me sing.'

And I sang all the louder after that.

We drowned out Grandma and her rustling newspaper and her slurping tea.

When we finished our song David said, 'Before I go, I'll write out the words of the song for you, because I changed them a bit then, and I think I prefer this new version. Do you have another piece of paper?'

I searched around in my satchel for a scrap of paper for David Bowie.

Then he said, 'Music's very important, you know. It's essential, in fact.' All of a sudden he looked very serious and incredibly wizardy. 'I'm going to do something with this music now.'

I stared at him. I had absolutely no idea what he was going to do next, and I was hanging onto every word.

'Can you see it?' David asked. 'The music is all around us. The song we just played and sang together. It's swirling and glittering around us in the air.'

I looked, and I could almost see it.

That was dust in the air, wasn't it?

This was just an old store room used for chairs and a piano and gym equipment and us being in here had stirred up all the dust.

It was dancing in great circles and loops in the air, with the last of the late afternoon sun slanting through the high windows.

'Can you see the music, Daniel?'

I concentrated hard on his words and then all at once I **could** see it.

Then it wasn't just old dust floating about.

It was like tinsel and glitter in the air.

Brilliant and silver. And it was more than that...

It was gold.

This was stardust.

'I'm going to make something out of it,' David said. 'Something rather special.'

'What?' I asked, looking straight at him.

'A magic face,' he said. 'An invisible magic face. Like the one I'm wearing now.'

I had no idea what he was on about.

'Here,' he said. 'I'll give you this one.'

He reached up with both hands and put them to his smiling face. He covered it and then it seemed like he gave a little tug.

His face came away in his hands.

I drew back slightly.

The face underneath wasn't smiling. It looked less certain, much less happy and confident. It blinked and looked worried.

He held out his former face in both hands and gave it to me.

'Here it is,' he said. 'My invisible face, do you see?'

I took it, very carefully.

It was light as a feather.

He looked uncomfortable and almost scared with his true face on show.

'Put it on, Daniel,' he told me. 'It's magic.'

And so I did.

It felt... strange.

Fine.

But strange.

Then David said, 'I always feel afraid, just the same as you. But I wear this magic face every single day. And it doesn't take the fear away, but it makes it feel a bit better. I feel brave enough then to face the whole world and all the people. And now you will, too.'

I sat there in his magic face, looking through the eyes at David Bowie and it was true, I did feel better.

After a while I put my hands up and started to take it off.

It was important. He would want it back.

But David stopped me.

'No, no,' he said, reaching out a hand. 'It's okay, Daniel. You can keep that one. You can have that one for yourself.'

I sat there breathing slowly, my eyes wide, staring at him.

I could keep it?

'I'm going to make myself a new one,' David said. 'A brand new face. Right now. It's what I always do.'

His hands were reaching out into the glimmering air, stirring that gold.

'I'm going to use all the music we created here today. You can watch me,' he said. 'Look!'

He held out his hands and moved his fingers very gracefully and slowly, as if he was swimming deep under the sea.

'Can you see the silver glitter and the golden stardust? It's all still here. It's dancing... dancing all around us in the air. It's a ballet. This room is filled with it. Watch this, Daniel.'

I watched as he started to make another magic face.

He drew strands of its glittery substance out of thin air, out of nothing at all.

Over his shoulder, across the room, I caught a glimpse of Grandma.

Her headscarf was poking over her newspaper.

She was watching us.

Just for a second. She looked over her paper to see what was happening.

I caught her eye.

A tiny flash of green.

She shook her head and looked back down.

David was drawing together all the gold into ribbons and he was moving now, walking into the middle of the room.

He stood over an anvil that only he and I could see.

'Come over here and watch, Daniel.'

He made me stand on a wooden bench so I could get a better view as he hammered away at that anvil.

He hammered and hammered the music into shape.

He moulded it gradually into the shape of his own face.

He worked like a true craftsman, perfecting and fashioning it and I watched it all.

He took his time.

Then, at last, he smiled.

It was finished.

He blew on it to cool down the new invisible face, then he took it in both hands and put it on.

And he looked so relieved and pleased. He smiled again.

He turned that brilliant, snaggle-toothed smile on me.

'Now we've both got invisible magic faces, Daniel. We can both see through them perfectly well and no one would know we're even wearing them,' he said.

Right then, I felt incredibly comfortable.

It was the first time I felt safe in my whole life.

It was magic. It was magic that really worked because he was a wizard. He was grinning at me.

'You have to wear it for as long as you want to, or need to,' said David. 'You see, I'm always afraid as well. Just like you are. But this is how you can feel brave in the world.'

We sat there looking at each other through our invisible masks.

Then suddenly my Grandma was folding up her newspaper noisily.

'Come on, Daniel. You've been ages. We have to get going. C&A will be closing soon.'

David ignored her and whispered to me, 'Just because people pretend not to see magic, doesn't mean it's not real. It simply means they don't have our eyes.'

I nodded.

He took the paper and started writing down the lyrics to the song in funny, loopy handwriting.

'Daniel?' Grandma was clopping over in her high-heeled boots. 'Are you listening to me? You've taken up quite enough time.'

'Oh!' David suddenly gasped, and jumped to his feet.

He went striding back to the door.

My heart lurched.

I thought he was leaving suddenly, without saying goodbye.

'I almost forgot,' he said, opening the door.

Then he fetched something from the corridor.

It was a large furry creature.

'What's that? A toy?' Grandma scoffed. 'We don't have room for that at home.'

It was the fox terrier from the movie. One of the heroes of the film. It was a life-sized version!

'He's yours,' said David. 'I brought him for you. Because he's brave and loyal and I thought you could do with his help.'

There was a blue silk scarf around the fox terrier's throat, which David carefully removed and then hung around my neck.

'There you go, Daniel,' he said, and passed me the furry puppet. 'That's everything you'll need.'

Grandma tutted. 'That'll be fun, carrying that thing on the Tube. With his dratted ghetto machine, as well.'

David looked her dead in the eye. 'Thank you so much for bringing Daniel all this way to see me. I know things can't be easy for you. It's been an absolute pleasure to meet you both.'

She wouldn't hold his gaze. She gulped and grabbed my arm. 'Come on, Daniel. I want to buy this frock. There's hardly any time left...'

Just before she dragged me away David Bowie reached out his hand and high-fived me.

No one had ever high-fived me before.

Then suddenly we were back out in that corridor.

There was less noise because nearly everyone had gone home.

'Grandma...' I said, twisting in her grip because I felt we had been rude and done it all wrong.

We hadn't said goodbye to David politely or properly.

He had given me these amazing gifts and I hadn't even thanked him.

'Shush,' said Grandma. 'You've had quite enough attention for one afternoon. It makes you go giddy.'

We were out in the dark, snowy yard and heading for the street before I realized he hadn't finished writing out the words to his song for me.

At least I had it on tape.

I had the whole thing on tape.

And I had the fox terrier in my arms as we sat on the bus and then the tube train into the centre of London.

I was wearing David's blue silk scarf.

And I was wearing his invisible face.

I wore it standing by the changing rooms of C&A's Ladieswear department as Grandma tried dresses on. It was warm and noisy and stuffy in that shop and my head was ringing.

After about a million years it was time for us to catch the train back home.

*

She hadn't found a dress that pleased her, and she wound up buying something that she wasn't quite sure flattered her.

Grandma sat in the train compartment looking flustered and cross. Shopping trips often went like this, with her never quite finding the thing she really wanted.

She had two spots of red on her cheeks like she was over-warm or felt upset.

I sat with my dog puppet, wearing my scarf and my magic face and I was absolutely beaming.

I was singing to myself. Quite loudly.

When the man came by to see our tickets he looked surprised at my singing and then he grinned at me.

'Merry Christmas! Someone's happy!'

He clipped our tickets.

Grandma tutted and he left.

Then she was brushing down her pink fur coat.

'Oh, look at this! Look at the state of my beautiful fur coat! It's got nasty stuff on it! It's got… glitter on it! Just look!' She glared at me.

It was true. In the smoky yellow light of the train compartment, Grandma was definitely glittering as she sat there opposite me.

'It's off that thing! That horrible fox thing he gave you. Just look at it! It's covered in glitter! Oh, who would give a child such a stupid, messy present?'

She scratched and rubbed at her coat in frustration.

It was weird about the glitter, really.

I wasn't sure where it had come from.

Maybe David had sprinkled it on the dog before he gave him to me?

But then… it had been falling through the air in that side room, hadn't it?

We'd created it by singing together, David had said.

We had sung together and because we were both wizards we had made the magic start working.

There was stardust as well as tinsel in the air.

I had seen it with my own green eyes.

'If you don't stop singing, Daniel, I'm going to grab that horrid fox off you and throw him out of the window!'

'No,' I said, and clutched my sparkling new friend tighter.

I stared back at Grandma through my invisible face.

She sighed and suddenly looked exhausted. 'You'll see eventually. When you'll get older you'll look back on today and think it was a real waste of time. You'll see what a boring, awful time you put your Grandma through. Going to see a daft puppet film you've seen before. Talking to that silly man. That popinjay! You'll be embarrassed eventually about all this. When you're as old as I am, Daniel, you'll see that dreams like this are daft. No one will even remember this Bowie person.'

'That's not true,' I said.

'You'll be embarrassed in the future. You sang with him! That awful song. You'll feel such a fool about all of this, you'll never be able to tell anyone about it. You'll be so embarrassed!'

She laughed then.

I just looked out of the window, watched the snow flurrying past and smiled.

Because after that I changed.

I never was that same boy again: the boy who wouldn't talk or look anyone in the eye.

After that I would sing at the top of my voice and I'd make up my own words for songs, just because I felt like it.

And I would look everyone right in the eye because I had to check out if they were wizard or part-wizard, didn't I?

That afternoon just before Christmas David Bowie had freed my tongue at last, and stopped me looking down at the floor.

He made me believe in the magic that's happening all the time.

You see, he really was a wizard.

*

And then it was over.

I've never forgotten it.

If nothing else, I once sang a duet with David Bowie. Like Freddie Mercury did, and Mick Jagger, and Bing Crosby and... Lulu!

And even now if I see anyone with green eyes, or just one green eye and one blue, I look at them and think – 'That's a wizard.'

Years later I cried when I heard he had passed.

I've not told anyone this story for years.

I used to tell it to people. I used to love telling it.

Then I started getting reactions like, 'That's just a stupid story. Fancy believing in an invisible mask. Fancy believing in the goblin king.'

But I do.

I really believe in David Bowie, and his invisible magic face.

I think you do too, don't you?

I've got my Fox Terrier puppet at home.

Some of the glitter has rubbed off his fur over the years, of course. But there's still some there.

He still looks like he could protect me bravely.

I still have the blue silk scarf David put around my neck.

And I still keep the magic face, of course.

This is it, now. I'm wearing it.

Look.

Snow in the Algarve

This is the Algarve, a part of Portugal that sits between the mountains and the sea. There are wonderful beaches, groves of orange and lemon trees and white houses nestling on the rolling hillsides. But did you notice the almond trees? This is the story of how they first came to be here, many centuries ago.

Back in those days the place was called Al Garb and it was ruled by the young Prince Ibrahim, from his palace in Silves, a historical city which you can still visit to this day. He was a handsome man with a moustache that curled at either end and who really seemed to have everything, even a genie. He wore silk slippers every day of his life.

He had even found his beloved - a Princess called Gilda, who was gorgeous, with long silvery hair that glimmered green like the Northern Lights. The Prince imagined that they were about to live happily ever after. However, there was a big problem. The princess had come in a ship all the way from Norway in the far distant, frozen north. It was a very different place to Portugal.

Prince Ibrahim couldn't get his head round the differences at all, no matter how she explained it. As weeks and months went by she seemed to grow paler and sadder. She looked at the golden sands of Al Garb and simply tutted in dismay. She stared at the azure seas with a heartfelt sigh. The balmy breezes made her irritable and the blazing sun brought her out in a heat rash.

'I hate it here!' Gilda burst out at last. 'Why can't it be more like Norway?'

The Prince was aghast to find she was so unhappy. 'What can I do? What can I change?' His kingdom of Al Garb was perfect in his eyes. He couldn't believe she didn't feel the same.

She grew quite miserable. 'I want blizzards and frosty mornings and Christmas and glaciers and everything!'

The Prince was rich and powerful and he would do anything for his Gilda, but what could he do about this?

He went to speak to the Princess' personal

physician, who had travelled with her all the way from the north. He was a great big bear of a man who didn't like the heat either and sympathized greatly with Gilda. In his heart he pined for the snowy lands and supposed that he'd never see them again now that they were settled in this southern, sultry country.

'I would buy anything, change anything, do anything for my Beloved,' cried Prince Ibrahim. 'Tell me what I must do! What does she miss most about her homeland?'

'She just says, 'everything!' when I ask her,' said the Physician, shaking his head.

'But what about you?' asked the Prince. 'You come from the same strange country. What do you miss, Physician?'

The Physician smiled fondly. 'Reindeer!' he said.

It took some minutes to explain to the Prince exactly what reindeer were.

He rushed to his genie to ask him to magically transform his stableful of Arabian horses into reindeer. 'No,' said the genie snappily. 'My magic is on the blink.'

So the prince had to do the best he could with what came to hand. He had his servants gather up a whole lot of twigs from the orange groves and these they tied to the ears of the Arabian horses and tried their best to make them look like antlers. They didn't, very much, and the horses weren't very pleased with this arrangement at all.

'There – reindeer!' announced the prince.

The Norwegian Physician didn't look too impressed and neither, unfortunately, did the Princess, who burst into tears at the sight of the pathetic reindeer with their antlers hanging down.

'Oh dear. What else can I do?' asked the Prince.

The Physician thought hard. 'What about – snowmen?'

After he had explained what snowmen were the Prince quickly summoned the many seamstresses of Al Garb and bought all of the ermine fur that could be found in his entire kingdom. He made the ladies stay up all night long, running up onesies in white fur, and when they were finished he made the servants dress up. They were extremely hot. Still, they had to do what their master commanded, of course. They stood sweating as the Prince called his beloved down to the courtyard.

'Look – Snowmen!' he proclaimed.

She took one look at those furry monstrosities, burst into tears, and ran away.

By now the Prince was becoming desperate. 'What else do you have that's so special in your Norway?'

The Physician clicked his fingers. 'Why, SNOW!!' he yelled. 'The thing that would remind her of home the most and make her happiest of all would be if you could make it snow here in Al Garb, your Excellency.'

The Prince looked at him in disbelief. 'Don't you think I've already thought of that? But my genie's magic is on the blink, and even if he could make it snow, it would surely melt in an instant!'

'But, Excellency, I have a plan… and it might

just work. On our journey from the north we stopped in many lands before we came to Al Garb, and in one I discovered the most wonderful trees. The tree of the Almond.'

'I have never heard of these trees,' mused the Prince. 'Tell me more.'

'We must fill all of Al Garb with almond trees, Excellency. We need hundreds of them, and they must be planted all around the palace and the city of Silves, and on all the hillsides hereabouts.'

The Prince was mystified. 'And what will we do with that many almonds?'

'It isn't the nuts that we need,' said the Physician. 'No, what I am thinking of is something else. But it will be expensive and difficult and will involve lots of hard work, carrying and planting the trees and watering them every day... It will involve much effort and expense.'

Prince Ibrahim snapped his fingers. 'A piffle, if it will only make my Gilda glad at heart. But are you sure it will work?'

'Oh yes,' said the Physician.

All of the palace servants were put to work, and many of the kingdom's other subjects, too. Almond trees were sourced from many lands and brought to Al Garb. The Prince watched as they were planted in every available patch of earth.

'Just wait till spring, your Excellency,' said the Physician.

Prince Ibrahim was quite impatient, and his beloved grew more miserable and cantankerous with every day. When Christmas came Ibrahim brought out once more the rubbish reindeer and the terrifying snowmen but none of it amused her.

Yet eventually the spring came and when it did...

The Physician threw his hands in the air and laughed joyously. 'It's here, your Excellency!' He ran through the palace waking everyone up.

'What? What?' cried the Prince, jumping out of bed and running to the window.

The almond trees had all burst into white blossom.

'See?' beamed the Physician. 'The blossom is

the most brilliant, frothy, foamy, wonderful white! It's like candy floss! It's like frothing cream! It's like icy, white, fabulous... SNOW!'

'Is it really?' echoed the Prince excitedly. 'Is that what it looks like?'

Every almond tree had woken up at the very same time. The palace, the city, and every hill in Al Garb was alive with fragile blossom: stirring and glimmering brightly.

'Like sugar!' the Prince howled. 'Like silk! Like cream!'

Princess Gilda got out of bed and pulled on her dressing gown and went to the balcony to see what all the fuss was about. What she saw then made her eyes pop out and her heart light up with joy.

'IT'S SNOWING!' she cried, as a flurry of light breezes rushed through the whole of Al Garb, stirring the almond blossom and shaking the branches so that it floated away and coated the hillsides. White flowers carpeted the kingdom so softly and beautifully that Gilda could hardly wait to rush out and walk in it all.

It was enough like Norway for the Princess Gilda to feel like she was at home for the rest of her days and so he and her Prince could live happily ever after.

And every spring since then, there has been snow in the Algarve.

Miss Baumgarten's Trolls

'Look, Class 6,' she said. 'You have to stand out, you know? You have to do something quite different. And you know what all the others will be doing, don't you? The usual Christmas rubbish. Dopey Nativities and the same old boring fairy tales.'

We were shocked by this. We'd never heard a teacher talk like this before. Dopey Nativities..?! Christmas rubbish?

Miss Baumgarten always said things the other teachers never did.

Right now – last thing on a November afternoon when it was purple and yellow and stormy outside – she was sitting on Mrs Hellist's desk and strumming her twelve string guitar. The noise was huge and warm as she tuned up.

We were transfixed by Miss Baumgarten.

Everything she did was surprising and just a bit wrong.

Also, she looked like Barbra Streisand, had a perm, wore a poncho, and carried this guitar everywhere she went.

'Before we sing the Joni Mitchell song again, I want to sound you guys out about an idea I've had for this class's Christmas show this year...'

We were hanging on her every word. It had been like that for two weeks now, since she had started standing in for our regular teacher. Mrs Hellist's lessons were usually so predictable and dull. She liked to fill up the board with stuff she was copying out of a book, and we had to race to keep up with her. The best scholars and writers were those who could write as much and as fast as she could. She'd finish lessons looking red in the face and worn out. Perhaps that was why she was taking so many weeks off school?

Lessons with Miss Baumgarten were quite different. We never knew what was coming next.

She strummed her guitar and la-la-la'ed for a while and thought deeply and then she started explaining her great idea to us. And how we were going to be doing an interpretation of a play by a Norwegian called Henrik Ibsen for our holiday spectacular.

*

No one I knew had ever heard of Henrik Ibsen, and no one thought Miss Baumgarten's idea sounded very Christmassy.

'When is it?' Mam asked, flipping the pages of our kitchen calendar.

'The last Monday before the holidays.'

She didn't look keen on coming. Last year she had gone to the concert with Dad, and the year before, but he wasn't around any more, of course. She wasn't sure it was the kind of thing Brian would be into.

'I don't want to face all those questions and looks,' she sighed, pursing her lips and writing 'school concert..?' in pencil on the calendar. 'All those nosy teachers and other parents and everyone will be looking and judging. They'll see I've got a different man with me.'

I didn't say anything. As far as the kids in my class were concerned, the news was already out. I had gone through weeks of being elbowed and hissed at. 'Hey, is that bloke your new dad? That fella with the green Cortina? Is that your dad now? The bloke with the big beard?'

I kept my head down and didn't say anything and, of course, this made them ask all the more, and laugh about it. 'What happened to your real dad, then? Did he run away? Did he die or summat? Who's this fella with the green car?'

Brian had moved in with us at the start of autumn.

It was weird and I wasn't used to it yet at all, but I wasn't going to talk about it with anyone at school.

'Is it going to be worth coming to see?' Mam asked, 'This concert thing? You wouldn't mind if I didn't come to see you, would you? I'm not going in there by myself. I can't do that.'

Mam hated going anywhere by herself, especially when there were people there. She could do the shopping down the town precinct by herself, but that was because she knew where she was going and what she wanted and it was all quick and easy. She went every day to get our food for that day, since we didn't have a fridge (Dad took it.)

'The thing you were in last year wasn't worth seeing,' she laughed. 'What were you again? Stood at the back?'

'A sheep,' I said.

'You had that paper mask on. You couldn't even see it was you.' She laughed, fetching down pans to start the tea. Findus Crispy Pancakes, beans and mash.

'I made the mask myself,' I said.

'You were still just a sheep,' she said.

'But it's not just the plays,' I pointed out. 'It's a whole evening of festivities. There's a Christmas raffle, and carols and Mr Robertson does a kind of comedy routine and makes everyone laugh…'

'Oh, god, yes,' she shuddered, as the pan began to sizzle. 'Well, you know. I'm not sure. I might not come to this one. We'll have to see.'

*

Miss Baumgarten began rehearsals in earnest.

She clapped her hands loudly, and looked very businesslike, standing at the front of the school hall. 'We must be very serious about this,' she said. 'If we're going to do this, then we have to do it right. And so all your gym classes are going to become rehearsal hours from now until Christmas.'

I felt like cheering. I could have run to the front of the hall and kissed her.

Gym classes with Mrs Hellist were awful.

She'd had us doing forward and backward rolls and I just couldn't.

She prodded my bum with her platform boot. 'Come on, you lazy lump. You can do it!'

The whole class was standing round us. They'd got past doing these rolls straight away. They were already onto vaulting over apparatus and climbing up the walls. I was crunched over in the middle of the shiny floor and everyone was looking and I was, like she said, a big fat lump. Her boot prodded at me and she hooted. 'You have to try harder! You're making no effort!'

Miss Baumgarten hated gym classes. 'You're not lab rats! You're individuals! That stuff is no good for you! It's no good just doing things other people tell you to do! You must learn to express yourselves! That's the most important thing!'

And so, while she was in charge that winter, gym classes became Music and Movement.

'You'll see, Class Six,' she grinned, dashing to the record player. 'You'll see how all this will feed into our Christmas play, and will enrich your performances.'

She put on a record she had brought from home. The needle hissed and the large speakers crackled.

A kind of jazzy music started up.

She clicked her fingers to the beat.

'Can you hear it? Can you feel it?'

All of Class Six stood there frozen, staring at her. We were in our sandshoes and shorts and T-shirts and didn't know what was expected of us.

'Now, you must MOVE!' she cried, flinging out her arms and swaying on the spot. Her perm bobbed about and her flowery maxi-dress floated out around her. 'MOOOOVE, Class Six! Express yourselves, children! Dance just how you want to!'

She had her eyes closed as she demonstrated and we stared in amazement.

'Think of Kate Bush! Think of Mick Jagger! DANCE like them, children! Do whatever comes into your head! Just let your bodies do their thing…!'

Some of the girls were already moving. Some of them did dance stuff in classes after school.

The taller boys – Andy, Chris, Colin – they were pogoing like the Sex Pistols and making each other laugh.

'That's it! That's very good! Do more of that!' gasped Miss Baumgarten.

She dashed over to the boys and this startled them.

They were expecting to be told off for being silly, but she was full of admiration.

'I love it! How creative! You're dancing punk rock-style to the sounds of Duke Ellington! How fantastic!'

She clapped her hands busily. 'Look, everyone! See how these boys are interpreting the music? See their spasmodic, jerky movements and their leaping about! You see? Can we all do that? Do we all want to try that..?'

Yes, we did.

She dashed over to the record player and started 'In the Hall of the Mountain King' again, and then we were all jumping up and down like Sid Vicious, even the girls.

It got hot and sticky in the school hall pretty fast.

Even Miss Baumgarten was leaping up and down and twitching her arms. 'Everyone! Do it like this! Like this!'

We still weren't sure whether we were doing it right. Some of us were giggling and stopping to breathe and clutching our sides. Chris went running around the room doing his monkey walk because he was getting carried away. When Miss Baumgarten saw that she cried out again, 'Oh, how wonderful! How do you do that, Christopher? Oh, let me try...'

And that was when Mr Robertson came walking through the school hall with his pile of signed registers that he was delivering to each of the classes.

He was already frowning at the noise. The jazzy music was bad enough, but what was all that laughing and carrying on? And the noise of thirty kids jumping up and down on his polished floor?

He marched out into the hall and simply stared. He went a bit red and his eyes bulged out. He didn't look cross, though. He looked flabbergasted.

Miss Baumgarten noticed him, and stopped doing her monkey walk and dashed over to the record player to turn the volume down.

'Hello, Mr Robertson! Aren't the children doing brilliantly..?'

'Erm,' he said.

'Carry on, everyone!' she cried out. 'Keep expressing yourselves! Keep on dancing!'

'What is it supposed to be?' asked our headmaster, looking worried.

'Peer Gynt, by Henrik Ibsen,' she told him, grinning sweatily. 'With music by Grieg. We've decided we're going rather highbrow for our contribution to the end of term spectacular. What do you think..?'

*

Mam said she'd ask Brian about the old clothes.

'What do you need again?' she said. 'Just any old, raggy clothes?'

'It's for being a troll,' I said.

Brian was watching telly. He was sitting on the new settee and drinking a mug of tea. He looked alarmed when Mam pushed me towards him.

'David's got a question for you, Brian.'

I took a deep breath. I felt a bit strange talking directly to Brian because he'd never said anything directly to me in the whole time he'd been living with us. 'Uh, do you have any old clothes I could have for being a troll?'

'Huh?'

'It's for his school play,' said Mam.

'Uh, no.'

'You must have,' said Mam. 'You brought over that whole rack of clothes when you moved in. You've got more clothes than I have…'

He just glared at her and went on drinking his tea.

Mam said to me, 'You'll have to ask your dad and his lot when you see them at the weekend. They'll have some old rags you can have, they're bound to.'

Mam still didn't see the relevance of us kids dressing up as trolls for Christmas. She thought we should be doing something more traditional. I pointed out that maybe Ibsen's Peer Gynt was traditional in Norway.

'But we're not in Norway, we're in Newton Aycliffe,' she said.

*

At school Miss Baumgarten went through the music cupboards and brought out every spare instrument she could lay her hands on. We were all supplied with maracas and bongos and recorders and anything else she could find. I had a triangle.

'The idea is just to make lots of noise,' she told us. 'Cacophony is the watchword here. Think about being noisy, dirty, bad-tempered mountain trolls...'

So we stood in the main hall and made as much noise as we possibly could.

By now we were getting pretty good at expressing ourselves.

'That's wonderful!' she gasped, clapping her hands. 'That's so marvelous! Just listen to yourselves!'

Then she encouraged those of us who weren't blowing into recorders or trumpets to moan and shout as loud as we could, just as we imagined Norwegian trolls might do as they lollopped about in the mountain passes.

So we did that and the main hall became even noisier.

'And now incorporate all your fantastic movements!' Miss Baumgarten shouted over our hullaballoo. 'Remember how you moved in time with the music? Remember how monstrous and awful you were? Do that again, Class Six! And make music at the same time...!'

She dashed over to the record player and on went 'The Hall of the Mountain King' again, but this time it was the Grieg concerto. It was a very spooky piece of music, we all thought, and it made us get right in the mood for being extremely noisy trolls, jumping about the place.

This time not only Mr Robertson but several of the other teachers emerged from their classrooms to see what was going on. They simply stared in amazement.

Eventually Mr Woods – our old teacher, who had a moustache, footballer's hair and who always wore a tracksuit said – 'We're doing a spelling test. Do you think you could pipe down a bit?'

'Not yet, Robbie dear!' Miss Baumgarten shouted happily. 'We've just got a bit more rehearsing to do! Go on, Class Six! Keep going! Keep moaning and groaning! Keep lumbering and shaking and rolling about! You're doing fantastically well..!'

*

At the end of the school day she read us a chapter from 'The Hobbit' and then took up her guitar and got us to sing 'Look What They've Done to my Song, Ma.'

When we were being taught by Miss Baumgarten we didn't have to put our chairs up on our desks and stand with our eyes closed as she intoned a prayer about being glad we made it through another day. Miss Baumgarten didn't believe in prayers like that.

Then it was time to go home.

It was darker and the streetlamps were on, leading the way down the long school drive, past the hills and waste ground, and down to the Burn. Swathes of mist were rolling up from the stream and it was like being somewhere completely magical, as Miss Baumgarten said.

'Look, we walk into the mist and we could be walking anywhere, couldn't we? The mist comes down and takes us to... Narnia! Or Middle Earth! Or perhaps back in time to Roman Britain..?'

She marched along fearlessly and a gang of about twenty kids went with her.

One of the reasons we thought that she was so great was that she lived on the same estate as us. All the other teachers got into their cars at the end of the day and drove off to some place else. Darlington or Aycliffe Village, somewhere posher. Mrs Hellist lived on a farm, which is why her land rover was skirted with thick mud, and so were the wellies she wore to drive in.

But Miss Baumgarten lived on our estate of blocky, black-bricked council houses. She lived in one of the maisonettes with her 'fella', Tony. The kids who walked along home with Miss Baumgarten heard a lot about Tony and his looks, his job at the electronics factory, his family in Italy and the holidays they went on together.

Miss Baumgarten breezed along through the mist in her winter cape and we hurried along beside her, like her protectors. Her own private goblin horde.

'Well, we don't really do Christmas in a big way, of course,' she was telling us. 'But Tony and I like to mark the day by exchanging smallish gifts. Tokens of affection, really. But they are always very silly things. This year, for example, I've bought him The Incredible Hulk Annual, because he enjoys that show so much. Also, he's started doing body building and the results are beginning to show.'

We all pictured the mysterious Tony's muscles and in my imagination he was green, with a moustache like Mr Woods.

One of the girls suggested that we all sing 'Look What They've Done To My Song, Ma,' as we walked through the thickest of the fog, over the wooden bridge and up the long tarmac path to our estate.

On the bridge we paused and Miss Baumgarten insisted we all look over the edge into the churning brown waters.

'This is one place trolls traditionally live,' she said. 'Under bridges like this. Now, every time you pass from one side to the other you must ask the troll permission, and sometimes pay a toll to the troll. And when you first step onto the bridge, you might hear him shouting from underneath: 'Who's that trip-trapping over my bridge?' And then he'll jump out! All hairy and hideous...!'

*

'Giving kids nightmares,' Mam said, after I told her I'd dreamed all night about Miss Baumgarten's goblins and trolls. 'What does she think she's doing?'

'I don't mind having scary dreams,' I told her. We were sitting at the breakfast bar with weak coffee and jam on toast.

It was still misty through the picture window that looked out upon the Burn and all the dark skeletal trees. We'd just watched Brian go off in his duffel coat to his job in the same factory Miss Baumgarten's Tony worked at.

'You should try talking to Brian more,' Mam told me. 'You never said a word to him when he sat here having his coffee.'

I looked down at my toast. I never knew what to say. I was a talkative kid. Everyone knew that I would and could talk to anyone. I wasn't shy. But I did feel shy when Brian was there. More than shy. He'd stare at me with a huge frown on his face. He'd stare and say nothing and then look away.

'He's really nice when you get to know him,' Mam said.

'I like his mam and dad,' I said.

'Well, that's good,' said Mam. 'Because we've been talking about it, and we've decided that we'll be going to their house for Christmas Day. Brian would prefer it that way. This was the house that we had Christmas in with your dad, and he's not comfortable with that.'

'Why's he not comfortable with that?'

'I don't know. He just isn't. It's a man thing.'

'But he's living here and Dad lived here, and so why would he mind having Christmas here if...'

'Stop asking questions!' She started gathering up our plates and cups. 'It's time you went off to school.'

It was, as well.

I didn't mind going off to school in these days of Miss Baumgarten and rehearsals for our dance interpretation of Ibsen.

The end of year show was taking over all of our days.

*

We couldn't rehearse in the hall on Friday because there was painting going on. This happened every year: Mr Morley supervised a team of all the best artists from each class in the school. This hand-picked squad worked with him, mixing poster paints and following his instructions as he laid out huge sheets of brown wrapping paper on the parquet floor.

The paint had a very particular, dusty, chemical smell that I loved. We mixed the pasty colours and the smells blended with the pine scent of the Christmas tree that had just been set up at the front of the hall. The tree was huge and it took some careful arrangement, getting it standing up straight in its bucket. Mrs O'Connor, the school secretary was watching over a small group of the best-behaved girls, who were putting baubles on evenly-spaced branches.

Mr Morley, in his shirtsleeves, frowning at a book of Disney characters, hunkered down on the floor, sketching jumbo versions of characters from The Jungle Book and Alice in Wonderland. We gathered round him to watch, agog as he worked his usual magic, swirling his pencil in rough circles at first, and then fixing on details and bringing the cartoonish faces to life with just a few darker outlines. He instructed us on which colours and left us to get on with it, moving on to the next giant character.

This was one of my favourite things every year.

Mr Robertson put on a record of carols and he went to watch the Christmas tree's progress, and then the cartoon characters coming to life. You could see him beaming with pride, his chest puffing up. Mam always said he reminded her of a pixie in an old Enid Blyton story, like someone who lived up a tree. I think she was thinking of the Enchanted Wood, perhaps and the stories about the Faraway Tree.

'You're all doing very well,' he told all the volunteers as we worked that afternoon. I think most of us were just glad to get out of ordinary classes. 'I reckon this year's Christmas Spectacular is bound to be the best one yet, don't you, everybody? What with the little ones giving their Nativity, and the Pantomime from the second years and then Year Four's 'Alice in Wonderland.' And... erm... whatever it is that Miss Baumgarten is planning.'

I straightened up from painting the bright orange stripes of Sher Khan the tiger. 'It's an improvisational dance piece based on Henrik Ibsen, Mr Robertson.'

He nodded at me, 'Oh, yes. That's right.' He blinked. 'And how are you getting on in your studies, young man? Since your parents' separation and all?'

I was aware of all the Christmas decoration volunteers staring at me. 'Uh, all right, sir,' I said. I didn't have a clue what I was supposed to say. I obeyed Mam's usual rule that, if anyone from outside asks about personal stuff, tell them nothing. It's none of their business.

'Good. You're a good lad,' the headmaster said. 'That's... uh, a very effective tiger you're painting there.'

I went back to the orange stripes and thought about how much I'd love to be painting the black outlines on these characters, once all the coloured paint had dried. That was the true moment of magic. But that was the moment Mr Morley kept for himself. He had the steadiest hand, he said.

*

There was one really good speaking role in our Ibsen Spectacular and I was desperate to have it. Miss Baumgarten typed it out on the school secretary's typewriter in her lunch break and then ran off several copies on the machine in the staff room. The copies from that machine came out with pink and purple smudgy ink and the smell could make you feel high.

The character was called The Crooked One and he was an evil, wormy, snakelike being who challenged and tempted the hero, Peer Gynt. Andy was already cast as the hero because he was the tallest in the class and that was no big deal because the part was boring, really. At least it was when compared with The Crooked One.

Those of us interested had to stand at the front of the hall and give a little bit of the speech. Miss Baumgarten sat in the middle of the school hall floor with the rest of Class Six and watched as us Crooked Ones auditioned.

'Brilliant! Brilliant!' she cried out, after each and every try-out.

If we were all brilliant, how was she ever going to choose?

She nibbled her pencil and ruffled her curly hair and consulted her notes. She asked the rest of the kids and got us Crooked Ones to wriggle and slither and hiss our evil speeches again.

This could be it, I thought. I could have this fantastic speaking part and be the star of the show. I could paint my face green and make my hair stick up with sugar water. There was already talk of how the Crooked One's costume was going to be a bright green sleeping bag zipped right up to the neck (it was an old camping one belonging to Miss Baumgarten's live-in boyfriend Tony.) Turned inside out and fastened right up it would make a perfect serpent skin.

My heart was racing and my head was filled with images of my starring role in our show. Mam would have to come and see, and even bring Brian with her. They'd have to take their places among all the other, rowdy parents of Woodham Burn kids and see me do this fantastic show.

'Vicki Williams,' Miss Baumgarten said at last. The name burst out of her and she beamed happily, as if she had just worked out a solution that should have been obvious the whole time.

'Me..?!' squealed Vicki, jumping up and down loudly on the hollow wooden blocks of the stage. 'I'm the Crooked One?'

'You gave the most convincingly evil reptilian speech!' laughed Miss Baumgarten. 'Now you're the villain of our piece of experimental theatre! Cheer, everyone! Everyone, give Vicki a huge round of applause!'

On the walk home that night I didn't fancy joining the usual tribe of suck-ups around Miss

Baumgarten. I dashed on ahead, and then dawdled over the wooden bridge.

It was frostier that night and the tall reeds in the ice fringing the stream were stiff and white. I listened hard to the gurgling water and tried to imagine a troll calling out from under the bridge.

Miss Baumgarten and the third year girls caught up with me and she said, 'Hello, there. You shouldn't hang around here too long, in case the troll comes out and eats you up.'

The girls around her giggled at this, but something had robbed me of my appetite for her usual whimsy.

'Are you disappointed not to be the Crooked One, David?' She asked me straight out, and I blushed.

'No, I'm fine… I probably couldn't have learned all those lines anyway…'

'I'm sure you could have,' she said kindly. 'But you must see, Vicki will do a wonderful job. And how often do you see really good parts for villainous females, hmm?'

I stared at her. What could she mean? I was a Disney fan. All the best villains were female.

'And you will make a marvelous troll,' she said. 'Your improvised troll-dancing is really quite wonderful.'

The girls giggled and she smiled kindly and they all moved on, gliding away with her cape flapping along behind them.

I was going to be one troll amongst a whole tribe and class of trolls. There was nothing special about that whatsoever. Not now.

*

Mam said, 'Isn't it great? We've decided – we're all coming to see your school play!'

We were having our tea on Monday night. Pies from the bakery with peas and mash. There was something funny in the mash. Onion or something, it didn't taste the same as usual. 'What's in the mash?'

'I talked about it with Arnold and Anna, Brian's mam and dad. They're very keen to come along and see your show. And there's Anna's sister visiting, too, Katy, from Holland. So you'll have quite a crowd!'

I felt excited and worried at the same time. I really liked Brian's parents, but what were they going to make of what we were trying to do in our show?

'They know it's not a traditional Christmas thing, don't they?' I said.

'I've explained to them all about it,' said Mam. 'How you're going to be a troll and everything, and how they probably won't even recognize you in your make-up and your ragged old clothes.'

In the end we were using some clothes Dad had left behind, in the bottom of the wardrobe. An old woolly jumper and some jeans. Mam brought them downstairs and dumped them on the smoked glass coffee table.

'Well, he clearly doesn't have a use for these. He cleared everything else that was his out of the house, so I suppose you might as well have them.'

I was in two minds about it as we set to work with scissors, cutting holes in his jumper and jeans to make them more like the kind of thing a troll might wear.

'He really is a bloody troll, your father,' Mam said, attacking the fabric. 'Shall I get an old lipstick and we could put, like, blood on them as well?'

'Okay,' I said, though that sounded more like zombies than trolls, but she was enthusiastic.

'Do you remember?' she asked, splodging and dabbing blood on my stage outfit. 'The day you came home from school and he'd taken all our stuff away?'

I nodded. It hadn't been so long ago. I wasn't likely to forget.

'Him and that bloody useless Uncle Eric of yours. They didn't even warn me. Just turned up with a van. I didn't know what was going on. They were straight to the point: 'We've come for all my stuff. I'm out of the hostel now, and in my own flat in Durham. So I've got room for my furniture.' Well, I said, 'Our furniture. Your family's furniture.' But they just got to work and they took everything. The three piece suite. The fridge. The record player and all the records. 'It isn't *our* house anymore. We aren't a family anymore.

You saw to that, Mary.' That's what your Dad said to me, and they took everything but the beds and that bloody wall unit he bought me for my birthday. Well, the only reason he didn't take that thing is because it still hasn't had all the instalments paid, and now I'll have to finish paying for it myself. And that was your Dad. He left you with nothing to sit on when you came home from school that night.'

I remembered. It had only been a few months ago.

'Have you told him about your Christmas play? He isn't thinking he's going to come, is he? Because if he turns up at the same time as Brian, there'll be war on. Brian will kill him, probably.'

I shook my head. Dad wouldn't be coming to the Christmas Spectacular, I was sure.

Mam brightened up, holding up the gory stage outfit I'd helped her create. 'It'll all be good, you'll see. You'll have a bigger and happier family than you've ever had. A better family than that rough lot of your father's. Now, go and try on your troll outfit.'

*

'No, no, no,' said the headmaster. He waved his hands, looking perplexed. He was standing by the serving hatch at the very back of the school hall. 'It really won't do, you know. You can't do it like that.'

Miss Baumgarten looked up sharply from the piano and all us kids stopped what we were doing to look at Mr Robertson as he advanced on us.

His attention was fixed on Vicki Williams, who was lying flat on the stage, hissing and wriggling inside our teacher's sleeping bag.

'Stop that for a second, Vicki. The headmaster's got notes.'

He sighed and puffed out his chest. 'Well, it's obvious, isn't it? Can't you all see? I was standing at the back of the hall there and I was picturing what it was going to be like when the whole place is filled with parents on the night of the concert. They're all be standing up and pushing and shoving and trying to get the best view. They're loud and not quite the genteel theatre audience you might ideally like, actually.' He rolled his eyes and put a finger thoughtfully to his lips. 'So, the big problem is this. The Crooked One can be acting her heart out, wriggling away on the floor of the stage. She can give an Oscar-winning performance down there, but no one out here is going to see or hear a single word of it! They're all going to be jumping up and shoving each other out of the way, shouting, 'What is it? What's happening? I can't see it!'

Miss Baumgarten looked stricken. She jumped up from the piano and dashed over to the middle of the stage. 'You're quite right, Mr Robertson. Oh, how could I have been so silly?'

She helped Vicki Williams gently to her feet. 'Did I do something wrong, miss?' asked Vicki.

'Oh, no, you're doing a tremendous job,' our teacher told her. 'It's just that the headmaster thinks that the Crooked One should probably deliver her villainous speech standing up from now on.'

Mr Robertson nodded, smiling. 'Yes, indeed.'

'And how does the rest of it look?' asked Miss Baumgarten hopefully.

'Ohh,' he said. 'It's… erm… quite interesting. Yes, very interesting. I do think the zombies are very effective when they all come on.'

'Trolls.'

'Trolls, are they? Well, they're very good. Very frightening. I think it'll get lots of laughs on the night.'

'Laughs?' Miss Baumgarten frowned.

'But I do think you probably need to shave about fifteen minutes off the running time. None of the rest of the classes are going over twenty minutes with their performances. We need to keep a strict eye on timings to make sure everyone gets their moment to shine!'

Miss Baumgarten nodded and pretended to listen to what he was saying. Later she told us, 'I'll take his point about the Crooked One, but we're not cutting a thing! Not a single moment!'

In the classroom, later, as we folded up our ragged costumes, some of the boys were telling Vicki Williams that her inside-out sleeping bag was stinky.

It was, a bit.

*

It was exciting, going back to school after tea in the evening. All the windows were lit up and there was music coming out of the main entrance as we arrived.

Mrs O'Connor the secretary had a table in reception where she sold raffle tickets for the hampers that she made up every year. They were filled with tins and packets of fancy biscuits and bottles of drink, all wrapped up in colourful cellophane with bows. Mrs O'Connor had been on a special course to learn how make things like that, and she and the headmaster were very proud of the raffle prizes. They looked like the fancy goods that came down the conveyor belt at the end of The Generation Game.

School that night smelled of aftershave and perfume and cigarettes. The adults brought a whole new lot of smells into the school hall, along with a lot of noise. There was jocular, booming laughter over the Christmas carols.

I had a big family group with me. Everyone had dressed up in their smart clothes. Brian's mam and dad were in coats and hats and scarves. His Dutch aunt was fat and beaming and red-faced, in her belted raincoat. She didn't seem quite sure who she was here to see, but she was happy to be out anyway.

'Are you nervous?' Mam asked, a few times on the way there. We walked up the Burn and the school drive: it wasn't worth all of us cramming into the car.

'Of course not,' I said, though I was beginning to wish our show was less improvisational and that we had more lines and actual things to do in it. We'd had such a good time going over it again and again we had become quite used to the whole troll and goblin thing. Now I was wondering how it would come across to the invited audience, and whether they'd get the point of what we were trying to do.

'He's not nervous, are you, lad?' scoffed Brian's dad, as I showed them all into the hall and they took their seats somewhere in the middle of the crowd. 'There's nothing to be scared of!'

'Break a leg,' said Anna, Brian's mum. 'That's the right phrase, isn't it? That's what they say?'

'That's right,' said Mam. 'And he'll be brilliant, you'll see.'

*

I went off to be with the rest of Class Six, and found that I was just in time for Miss Baumgarten's inspirational pep talk and moment of meditation.

'Now, just you remember, all of you,' she told us. 'That audience out there, all those parents, they've seen these shows before. Year after year. The same old rubbish. Kids dressed up as shepherds and angels and donkeys. They don't know it yet, but they're desperate to see something new and exciting. They're all craving something with a bit of novelty and some innovation. And you lot...!' Her face was shining. She shook out her permed her, rolled up the sleeves of her purple mohair jumper and hugged herself hard. 'You splendid lot, you've been a credit to me. You've done me and yourselves really proud. I hope you realise that.'

By now we were all in our troll outfits, with garishly painted faces. Vicki Williams was over-warm, zipped into her sleeping bag.

We nodded. 'Yes, miss.'

Because we did realise that we'd pleased her. We'd leapt at the chance of doing something different and new.

We'd done everything we could to please Miss Baumgarten.

She was crying! She was actually wiping way a tear! 'Come on, Class Six! Join me in song to warm up your voices...'

She fetched out her twelve string guitar and, just before we started singing 'Look What They've Done to my Song, Ma', we could hear the whistling and applause from the main hall as our headmaster took to the stage. His microphone whined and hissed for a moment and then he launched into his usual patter, welcoming them warmly to our school for our annual Christmas spectacular.

'And do we have some surprises in store for you tonight...!' he promised all our parents warmly, and they laughed.

Their laughter sounded like a tidal wave coming down the decorated hall and corridor to our classroom, where we were waiting to go on. The boys were nudging and elbowing each other. Some of the girls were laughing. Vicki Williams had turned a strange colour and someone kept letting off.

'Remember, Class Six,' Miss Baumgarten said. 'Remember that sometimes audiences don't understand truly innovatory and special experimental art. Not at first.

'Sometimes you will be met with silence, confusion and even hostility.

'But you must still go on! The show must go on! You must be brave when you're experimental like we are!

'We must all be brave together..!

'And they will learn from us. We will expand their horizons beyond the petty and narrow world they know.

'Now… off you go!

'And you just make sure that you all become the most wonderful trolls and goblins that the world has ever known…!'

The Everlasting Match Girl

Toaster wasn't made out of wood, so the legend didn't strike terror into his heart the way it did the others.

'What on Mars is the matter with you all?' the sun bed frowned. 'I thought you had more gumption than that! What could be so scary about a little girl?'

The cocktail cabinet clattered her doors at him. 'You wouldn't understand. You're not make of cherry wood or teak or mahogany like some of us are...'

Oh, snobbery. Toaster really disliked snobby people. Snobby Servo-Furnishings were the worst of all. Just because he was made out of metal and glass, somehow he was less important than Earth antiques made out of genuine polished wood. Well, Toaster the sun bed knew his value. He knew he was unique. These old hat-stands and lamps and chairs had really got above themselves. The City Inside could be such a snooty place, he was finding.

'Well,' he said, deciding to laugh off their fears and objections. 'Don't worry. I will protect you all, if that evil little ghost-child scares you! If we see her as we make our way through the city, I will fight her to the death…!'

The other Servo-Furnishings didn't join in with his laughter…

*

He was new to the City Inside, having lived for many years on the lonely prairies of Mars. So only now, for the first time in his very long life, Toaster was meeting other Servo-Furnishings and learning about their lives and traditions.

It was certainly an eye-opener. All these years he had been servant, protector and educator for the Robinson family. He expected no reward, nor even any loyalty. He was their robot sun bed and he was glad to be of service. He harvested crops and he baby-sat the children. He could turn his clunky, clamp-like hands to anything. But now he was meeting the sentient furniture of the City Inside, he was being told that he had been much too subservient. He had never stood up for his own rights.

'Servo-Furnishings are people, too!' he was told, at the first meeting he attended.

'Are we?' he asked. He felt the light bulbs inside his glass chest fizzing at the very thought of being described as a person: as an equal to the Robinson clan he worked for. 'Well, I never...'

For the first time in his life he had friends amongst the serving class. Cherry, the cocktail cabinet, she was abrasive in manner, but she was glamorous and fun to be around. Arthur the hat-stand. Beryl the armchair. These were his closest acquaintances amongst the furnishings he grew to know over those first few months living in Stockpot Tower, at the heart of the City Inside.

He knew his owner, Lora, dreamed about returning to the crimson plains one day. He did, too, but in the meantime he was making the most of living in this extraordinary city, with its pillars and towers of green glass and its vast over-arching dome.

That Christmas it snowed actual scarlet snow and it made walking around difficult for one on clunky robot legs, but still something stirred in Toaster's glass chest. A strange longing. A nostalgia, perhaps, for inclement weather back on Earth, in a much earlier life he only dimly remembered.

Christmas was coming, and he could feel the approach of the season with a bittersweet fondness spreading in his chest.

When he heard about the carol-singing, he leapt at the chance to take part.

*

The others still had misgivings. Arthur, Beryl, Malcolm and Cherry. They gathered in the laundry room in the basement of Stockpot Tower. Here they were allowed to gather together for their meetings. The building's superintendent didn't mind letting them have the room, though he was as wary as the next human about letting Servo-Furnishings meet in large numbers.

'Here, you're not plotting revolution in there, are you?' he chuckled uneasily, as ambulatory furniture filled up the low-ceilinged room. 'I'll lose my job if it's discovered I joined in with subversive activities!'

Toaster and the others laughed at this, but they were aware that the Authorities were very wary of Servo-Furnishings that became keen on fighting for their rights as individuals.

'All we're doing is rehearsing our singing,' Toaster assured the building's Super. 'We're going carol-singing! What do you think about that?'

The grizzled old man was tickled by the thought. 'Wonders will never cease! You think you've seen it all in the City Inside... and then there's something goes and tops the lot. Carol-singing Servos!'

Then he left them, still chuckling and shaking his head.

Ella – a narrow lectern surmounted by a carved eagle – eyed them all beadily and called the meeting to attention. 'We'll start with 'Ding-dong

Merrily on High,' she said, tapping her own head with her conductor's baton. Then a host of scratchy, unpracticed, reedy voices joined in with hers on this first song, and then a selection of other festive classics.

Toaster – who memory banks were deeper and more capacious than anyone's present – realized that the Servos were avoiding the more overtly religious Christmas songs. He thought that was probably wise, given the broad mixture of cultures at large in the city. Also, some humans might be discomfited at the thought of mere furnishings lifting up their voices in celebration of a god meant exclusively for human beings? Toaster mulled this over as he joined in with 'Jingle Bells' in his throbbing, electronic contralto. The issues were so very complex... Even with a brain the size of his – a brain the size of the great Martian Prairies themselves – he couldn't hope to figure it all out. So was going to put all the metaphysical thoughts aside and simply sing.

But after the meeting in the laundry room, as everyone was preparing to return to their owners' apartments, he caught a whisper of gossip about the Match Girl again.

'Some say that she had a particular grudge against sentient furniture...'

'I heard that too! My owner has a book about serial killers in the City Inside... one hundred years of brutal deaths in the premier city of Mars... and I had a flick through...'

'Oh dear, you didn't?'

'I did, and I found that reports of her evil misdeeds go right back to the beginnings of this city. This is no natural little girl. She's been killing folk at Christmas for a very long time...'

Toaster barreled over to where Maude and Beryl were gossiping. 'Are you still going on about the Everlasting Match Girl?' he sighed.

Beryl jerked at the mention of the name. She reeled backwards on her castors. 'Shush, Toaster! You're not even supposed to say her name aloud.

That's how you summon up her spirit. It's how she latches onto her victims...!'

'Oh, rubbish. I'm not sentimental,' Toaster wheezed. 'You lot are terrible! Silly old gossips, with nothing better to think about! Look – there's nothing to be scared of out there in those city streets. Not for us. We'll all go out on Christmas Eve and sing our songs and have a lovely time. There's absolutely nothing to be frightened of.'

The lady Servos looked only partially mollified by his brave words.

*

Days passed and Christmas drew closer. It was interesting to see how differently the season was celebrated in the city, as opposed to the small town on the Prairie that Toaster and the Robinson family were used to. He stared out at the green pinnacles and the red snow and his mechanical heart thrilled at the sight of the city inside the dome. His owner, Lora, might wish that they were back home, but he was glad he'd had the chance to see a place as grand as this.

Two days before Christmas Eve he was stopped on his way to the garbage chute by Beryl, who was taking her family's recycling bags.

'What are you doing carrying a heavy load like that?' he frowned. Beryl was an elderly armchair, with sagging springs and musty fabric. She wasn't built for the kind of carrying tasks that her owners gave her these days. It was clear that she wasn't exactly a prized possession in her family. 'Let me help you,' added Toaster, hoisting up some of the plastic bags for her.

'Thank you, dear,' she said. 'Have you seen this?'

She indicated a certain story in the previous evening's edition of The City Insider. Toaster had indeed read the piece in question. He read all the city's newspapers each evening, filling up his databanks with as much information as he could glean, as was his habit. 'You're referring to the murder of the jewellery box.'

'I am,' said Beryl, worriedly.

'It'll be opportunist thieves,' he said. 'It was a jewellery box! Of course it was thieves! There's nothing mysterious or spooky about that. If the silly Servo hadn't been out by herself in the city streets, she'd have come to no harm...'

'She was running away from home,' said Beryl. 'Many of us are unhappy in the homes of our owners. We dream about escaping into the wilderness...'

'Yes,' Toaster said. 'I do know. But I've seen some of the wilderness out there, beyond the dome of the City Inside. It can be a harsh and dangerous place. You soft furnishings wouldn't last a day out there, some of you...'

Beryl laughed softly. 'I don't suppose I would!'

'I don't mean to offend,' said Toaster. 'It's just that I've had experience and adventures. I know what life is like out there...'

'Yes, indeed,' said Beryl. 'And you'll protect me, won't you, Toaster? When we go out singing on

Christmas Eve? If any robbers or… murderous ghosts come and try to take me away..?'

She was gently teasing him, he knew. They reached the disposal hatches and he smiled at her. He didn't mind that she was gently ribbing him. He liked Beryl a lot. He liked most the Servos he had met here in the city. For the first time in his life Toaster was starting to feel as if he had a kind of community outside of his human family.

*

Christmas Eve came and Toaster was word perfect, of course. Even if he said so himself, he thought he was in fine voice.

He asked his owner, Lora, if she minded if he slipped out for a couple of hours in order to sing with his friends.

She was busy and her mind was clearly elsewhere. She didn't even remark on how unusual it was, that her sun bed wanted to go out carol singing. She simply waved him away, and off he went.

The Servo-furnishings each left their apartments at the appointed time. They took the elevators and escalators down to the market hall on the ground floor of Stockpot Building, and gathered at the agreed place. Everyone was wrapped up warm against the snow and the wind, and they'd all brought extra lighting. Cherry the cocktail cabinet had been fitted with colourful fairy lights, which looked fabulous reflecting off her mirrored interior. Everyone praised and petted her.

'She always has to go one better,' muttered Beryl, who was covered in an unflattering rubber sheet in order to prevent the wet snow harming her upholstery.

'Are we all ready, then?' asked the bossy Ella.

And then they were setting off. They were walking out into the city streets as a group. They weren't going about business for their human owners. They were going out of their own accord, simply to enjoy themselves. It was really quite remarkable, Toaster thought. And he tried to put last night's terrible dream out of his mind.

He'd been plugged into the mains for a couple of hours in the middle of the night, when he was sure he wouldn't be needed.

He didn't often have dreams… but when he did they were usually quite strange. Toaster felt – quite illogically – that when he had dreams it was because the universe was trying to tell him something. And last night was no exception.

He was dreaming that he was carol singing in the snowy streets… and in his dream the red snow was very deep and it keep on falling all night… The canyons of the streets were deeper and darker than they even were in real life. And somehow, after a few songs in the brightly-lit districts, he had become separated from his fellow Servos. He was wandering lost in the city, and in some of the darker, more obscure alleyways.

'Toaster…' he heard a high, childish voice calling his name.

'Who is that?' he asked tetchily. 'Who could possibly know my name..?'

'Too-ooasss-terrr…' came the voice again. It was mocking him.

'Hello..?' He clanked and clumped crossly through the drifting snow. 'Who is it..?'

And then he heard a noise that struck fear into his electronic heart.

'Heeee heee heeeeee heeee…'

It was the most awful laughter and it floated all around him. Whoever it was… it was as if they were surrounding him. He was lost in the city.

'I can't feel fear. I don't have emotions like that… I am built of metal and plastic and glass…'

But he did indeed feel emotions. He knew just how it felt to be afraid.

Then his charging period came to an end and he was relieved to unplug himself.

He put the dream quite out of his mind…

It only came back to him as they started to sing their first song on Christmas Eve. A shudder went through him as they stood outside a department store window singing 'Ding Dong Merrily…'

A crowd of humans were soon gathering to listen and watch. They were astonished at the spectacle of Servo-Furnishings behaving so extraordinarily. 'Look! Look at this! Whatever will they think of next?'

Some coins were tossed onto the slushy pavement for them, though the Servos had no real need for money. They were doing this just for fun.

They all exchanged glances with each other. Beryl looked delighted at the attention they were getting from the crowds of shoppers.

But Toaster couldn't enjoy the moment fully. Not quite. He felt haunted by the memory of last night's dream.

'Heeee heeee heeeee...'

Somehow he knew he had heard the voice of the Everlasting Match Girl...

*

'Well, Toaster? What do you think? I'd say our evening has been a resounding success, wouldn't you?' Cherry the cocktail cabinet was even more full of herself than usual. As their small party took a little break from singing she was pouring them all small drinks in dainty glasses.

'What a lovely surprise, Cherry!' Arthur groaned. 'So thoughtful! So clever!' She had stashed away drinks that would appeal to them individually: teak polish, liquid paraffin, green, slippery oil.

'Yes, indeed,' agreed Toaster. 'I think we've all acquitted ourselves rather well.'

It was close to ten o'clock and they had been singing for several hours, moving from street corners to shop fronts, never staying in one spot for more than two songs, just in case the Authorities took any notice. Even Toaster had to admit, the possibility of being interrupted by the police had only added a little frisson of adventure to their evening...

He sipped green oil happily and gazed fondly at his fellow Servos.

They were under an old verdigrised copper lamp at the corner of the park. After a few moments of self-congratulations and cheers Toaster realized that the lamp above their head was winking at them and trying to catch his attention.

'What are you lot doing out by yourselves, then?' it asked.

'Oh!' cried Beryl. 'You poor thing! You're stuck in one spot. How long have you been here?'

'Me?' asked the streetlamp. 'From the beginning, I suppose. I'm Lily. Lily Marlene. Since they first laid out these streets and built these tall houses and set out this park. I guess I've been here as long as the City Inside itself...'

The lamp's amber light flickered and she grew dim for a few seconds' reminiscence. The Servo-Furnishings clustered beneath all sighed in wonder at her venerable age.

'We've been out carol singing, Lily!' boasted Ella, the eagle-headed lectern. 'We've organized ourselves and set out alone and sung all evening...'

The streetlamp stuttered and then brightened in amazement. 'How wonderful for you all. I'm glad that life is improving for our kind in the City Inside...'

Toaster was struck by a sudden inspiration. 'Tell me Lily, if you've been here so long, you must know an awful lot about this city and its history and legends...'

'I know enough,' agreed Lily.

'Then what about this story of the Everlasting Match Girl, eh? What about that?'

The streetlamp dimmed down for two, three, four seconds, and then flared irritably. 'What about her?'

It struck Toaster straight away that the lamp was talking as if the Match Girl was real. Also, she seemed shifty all of a sudden, like she didn't really want to talk about it.

'It's just a hokey fairy tale, isn't it?' asked Toaster bluffly. He was aware of his wooden friends shrinking away from the lamp.

'A fairy tale?' cried the lamp. 'Oh no, no, no. She's quite real. Or rather, she used to be. I saw her myself, once or twice. And even these days... on these dark, snowy nights... when there are fewer human beings about... sometimes you see a little flickering, a tiny guttering flame… and you know it's her. She's passing through the city streets, looking for shelter… But no one ever takes her in. No one ever gives her a home. She's doomed to sit on doorsteps or on benches here in this park. All she has for comfort and warmth is her packet of Everlasting Matches…'

Toaster scoffed at this. 'A fine story. And what about…' Here, he lowered his voice fractionally, 'What about the other things they say about her? That she hates Furnishings. The rumours that we've all heard say that she's a killer… she hates anything that isn't human…'

The streetlamp flickered wildly and Toaster and the others realized that this was the way Lily Marlene roared with laughed. 'Oh, why would she hate the likes of you? Or me, for that matter? Why would a poor little creature like that waste her time hating us?'

Toaster had to admit that he didn't know. 'These were just the stories we've been hearing…'

'Servo Furnishings always go gossiping and spreading tittle-tattle,' chuckled the streetlamp.

'But what about the murders?' Beryl the armchair burst out. 'That jewellery box… and the others.'

'Escapees,' sighed Lily. 'Those Servos who run away from home always come a cropper. You know that.'

The small choir muttered amongst themselves at that.

'Now I suggest that you all get yourselves home to where you belong,' said the streetlamp. 'For it's late and, even if there aren't ghosts of evil little girls with grudges haunting these streets, there is still plenty of danger you might encounter out here…'

They passed their glasses back to Cherry and they all thanked the lamp, and offered her the compliments of the season. Lily bade them a firm farewell. 'You've a long trek back to Stockpot Tower,' she told them. 'I suggest you start walking!'

'She's right,' said Ella. 'Come along, everyone. Perhaps we can finish our evening with a few songs outside our own tower. Wouldn't that be a splendid way to round off our adventure?'

All the Servos agreed with her and they set off on tired, squeaking castors and wooden feet for home.

Only Toaster and Beryl lingered at the back of the crowd. Beryl was exhausted and much slower than the others. Toaster kept pace with her, and told her he didn't mind at all, lagging behind. 'You're a proper gentleman, Toaster,' she told him.

As they took a short cut through a rather rough neighbourhood a few jeers rang out from drunken youths. Their small and strange-looking party was taunted by young humans, but the Servos kept their heads up and ignored them.

'What's this? A walking junk heap! What's going on here, then?'

'Why are you taking no notice of us, eh? You lot have got above yourselves..!'

'Look at the state of them! They should be chopped up for firewood, the lot of them!'

'Oh dear, Toaster,' whispered Beryl, nudging closer to him as they made their way through these shabby streets. 'We should have gone back the way we came. This is a horrible place...'

'Never mind,' said Toaster steadfastly. 'Just ignore them, my dear. They won't do anything to harm us.'

Toaster couldn't be quite sure that was the case, though. He prepared himself mentally to fight anyone who came forward to menace them. The sun bed packed a fairly lethal electric charge and could zap the life out of any attacker. He would only use this power as a last resort, of course.

'Keep walking, everyone!' cried Cherry. 'Ignore these ruffians!'

The streets were more crowded here. It was chucking-out time at the pubs and dizzy-looking specimens were reeling about on the snowy pavements.

'Oh, why did we come this way..?' moaned Beryl. 'Why did we come out at all? What was the point of it? What were we proving to ourselves?'

Toaster looked down at his armchair companion. She looked so disheartened and soggy, for the snow had gone through her polythene sheeting. 'Why, Beryl, didn't you enjoy yourself this evening? I heard you singing! You loved it! I'd never heard you sounding so wonderful.'

She smiled at him. 'You old flatterer. And of course, you're right. The singing part was marvelous. It's just this bit… being away from home… being amongst these people…'

'They're only human beings,' he told her. 'They're friends to Servos. They won't do us any harm…'

But Toaster was wrong about that.

The choir of friends was accosted shortly after he'd tried to comfort Beryl.

A group of belligerent young men set about Cherry, convinced that, since she was a cocktail cabinet, she'd be carrying drink that they'd be interested in. 'I've nothing for the likes of you!' she shouted at them.

The other Servos tried to defend her, but the boys were too strong.

'YACK! What's this..?!' They were soon spitting out the green oil and teak polish that Cherry's cabinet was stocked with. 'You're trying to poison us!'

There was an unmistakable feeling of threat in the air.

'Leave this to me,' said Toaster. He shouldered forward through the crowd. He extended his telescopic legs so that he towered over the drunken boys.

'Oh, do be careful, Toaster...' whispered Beryl.

But it was too late. Toaster strode forward with lightning flickering angrily in his glass belly. He hated to see anyone being picked on. Especially when they were friends of his. He wouldn't defer to human beings simply because of who and what they were. He would challenge anyone who he thought was behaving badly.

'What are you doing?' he said to the young men in his most booming tones.

They glanced at him and were unimpressed. 'What are you supposed to be? A sun bed?' For some reason the boys found this hilariously funny. They fell about themselves on the cold, slushy pavement. 'A sun bed! A talking sun bed!'

Toaster glowed with suppressed fury. 'Yes, I'm a sun bed. A super-intelligent sun bed from Planet Earth. I've more intelligence in my tiniest little glass bulb than you lot have got between you.'

It really wasn't like Toaster to be so braggardly, but his patience was fast running out this evening. He deeply resented having to defend his friends against these inebriated primates.

'It's all right, Toaster,' said Cherry. 'You don't have to fight for my sake. I really wouldn't want you to… to electrocute them, or anything…'

Toaster chuckled and raised up his metal hands. Vicious blue sparks were spitting out from both clamps and arcing between them. There was a deadly buzzing that sounded quite threatening.

'Y-you wouldn't hurt humans,' one of the boys shouted. 'You'd be in proper trouble then. The Authorities would come after you… They'd take you to pieces…'

'Let them try,' said Toaster, inching closer and grinning in their faces.

One of the less drunk boys was tugging on his mate's sleeve. 'Oh, come on. Let's just leave them. They don't have any booze, and they won't have any money... let's just go...'

There was a still moment just then, as everyone glared at each other.

And then...

'Look...!' Beryl's voice rang shrilly in the midnight air. 'Just look...!'

Toaster caught the queer tone in her voice and knew at once something most peculiar was happening. He turned from the scene of confrontation to see what it was...

All at once it was as if time had slowed down...

Even the crimson snow seemed to be falling slower...

As the Everlasting Match Girl came walking towards them across the snowy street.

There was no doubt in Toaster's mind that it was she.

She looked exactly as he had pictured her.

She was small and hunched and wearing rags. She had some kind of hood over her head, so that her features were shrouded.

Her hands were cupped about a tiny flame, which she managed to keep alight even in the swirling snow.

The Match Girl was shuffling towards them.

All the Servos and the rough boys had stopped what they were doing. The tense air between them was frozen. If anyone had asked not one of them would have remembered what their confrontation had been about.

All eyes – electronic and organic – were fixed on the little Match Girl and her tiny, golden flame as she approached.

Then they could hear her.

'Heee heee heeeee...'

Toaster tried to move. He tried with all his considerable might to shift his clumpy feet. He

wanted to defend his friends. He wanted to run away.
But sick, heavy dread fixed him to the ground.
Something transfixed him. Some weird and ancient
power.

He heard Beryl whispering, 'It's her, isn't it…
It's really her…!'

Just a few feet away from their party the
Match Girl stopped.

She reached up with one withered hand and
took down her hood.

Everyone gave a gasp of horror.

This wasn't the face of a human girl.

The creature was bald. Its flesh was dark
purple and ridged.

The worst thing of all was her eyes. They
were spiraling and mesmerizing. They were pink and
green and gold… and as they span round everyone
stared into their iridescent depths…

'You mustn't fear me. I can tell that you do. I
wouldn't harm Servo-Furnishings. I couldn't hurt you
if I tried… I'm a ghost. I'm a Martian Ghost. I'm all

that's left of the people that were here… long, long before your people arrived. But you mustn't fear us.'

'That giggling…' gasped Beryl. 'That terrible giggling…'

'It isn't laughter,' said the little girl. 'How do you think we all died? How do you imagine we became ghosts? Your humans changed our world. They created a wholly new atmosphere for your humans to breathe. They introduced all kinds of elements and chemicals that we couldn't breathe… and so when you hear us going 'Heee heee heeeee…' you must realize that we aren't laughing… We're trying to breathe… We're only trying to breathe your terrible air…'

'Oh my goodness,' said Toaster. 'That's awful.'

The little girl fixed him with her spiraling eyes. 'It doesn't matter now. What's done is done. And my kind… we still survive… as ghosts, you'd call us. Flitting about on our tattered wings…'

Her cloak shifted then and the Servos gasped, because it wasn't a cloak at all on her back. They were wings, like a moth's. They were chocolate brown and indigo. Dusty and scaly and wonderful to see as they opened out and unfurled behind her.

The drunken boys took this moment of distraction to run away, yelling and hooting with dismay.

'The humans will bring policemen, perhaps,' said Cherry. 'They don't like anything different and strange in their streets...'

'I will go,' said the Match Girl, still holding up her tiny, unquenchable flame for them all to see. 'I will leave you all to return to your homes. I just wanted you all to know that... we are watching. The Martian Ghosts are still here and we are watching you all. I wanted you to know that I am not dangerous. I didn't kill anyone. You needn't fear me. Only humans harm Servo-Furnishings. It is humans you must beware. I just wanted to tell you... I was happy to hear your singing tonight. I followed you around the city blocks and listened to you all night. I flew above you, blotting out the stars... didn't you see me? Didn't you hear my wings above you?'

The Servos admitted that they hadn't.

Toaster had heard something, he thought. All evening he'd had a strange feeling of being watched by alien eyes.

'I loved your singing,' said the Martian Ghost. 'And I think you are all very brave. Take my blessings, and go home now. It's so very late.'

The Everlasting Match Girl smiled at them. Her mouth was wide and filled with tiny, pointed teeth. It was an almost frightening smile, but by now they had all stopped being scared of her.

'Goodbye,' Toaster said, and stood back as she flung out her marvelous wings and took to the sky again.

The choir watched her tumbling upwards through the falling scarlet snow and they kept on watching until she was completely out of sight. The brilliant golden light of her everlasting flame stayed for a moment, and then was gone.

'Come on, everyone,' Toaster told them all. 'It's midnight. It's Christmas! Time we all were home.'

Fester and the Christmas Mouse

1.

I suppose this is meant to be like a Christmas story
kind of thing. Paul's saying I should write one for his
readers. Like, maybe think about some nice things
that happened in the past and do a story about it.
Probably to publicize his bloomin' book. Well, it was
my book, really, of course – The Story of Fester Cat.
It's all about me and I wrote all the words and there'd
be no book without me, and no Christmas story
either. So, here goes.

This is from when I first started realizing
what Christmas was all about and stuff. When I saw
that those two dafties who'd adopted me – Paul and
Jeremy – made such a big fuss about Christmas and
all. They put a big tree in the front room. Massive, and
it was all cluttered up with decorations they brought
down from the attic in big boxes. There were
decorations going back years, from different houses
they'd shared and places they'd lived in separately

before they'd known each other. The tree was like all the Christmases they could remember and it was pretty good, yanking at the decorations and scritchy-scratching my claws on the trunk when they weren't paying attention. Hoiking down that duck-wearing-a-headscarf or the robin made with real feathers and giving them a good mauling.

Not that I maul anything much with my one and a half teeth. But at least they aren't sore these days, after all that dental work I had. There was a big operation, did you know? I went to the hairdressers on the Stockport Road and Mr Joe kept me in overnight in his strange cat hotel and when I woke up my mouth didn't hurt like it used to and I could crunch up biscuits and stuff no bother.

There's a lot of decent food around this place at Christmas. Part of the thing of looking forward to it is knowing there'll be crispy bacon and slivers of smoked salmon and bits of roasted offal and, eventually, when they have their dinner, steaming cuts of succulent turkey flesh. They set me a place at their table and I sit there properly, with the fire blazing away, and that's how we round out the day each Christmas, before they watch all the TV shows and I doze clutching my Santa mouse to my chest. (They bought me a toy mouse in a Santa hat. I kind of hugged it between my paws to look like I appreciated it and was caring for it, but I was planning to eviscerate it later, but maybe not on Christmas because ripping little animals to pieces isn't very festive, apparently.)

Anyhow, the story is about a Christmas mouse. But it wasn't a toy mouse. That Christmas it was a real mouse who was causing a fuss round at ours and getting in the bloomin' way and stuff.

2.

He wasn't really any good at talking. I guess it was because he was just a baby mouse, but even if he could have made himself understood, he was so frightened all the time I don't think I'd have known what he was on about. He kept going 'Gleep! Gleep!' the whole time I knew him.

Christmas that year was so cold and, as a result the basement mice had got a bit cocky. I'd been watching my feeding station in the kitchen pretty vigilantly. There were holes and knots in the wood of the floorboards and the little devils would come shinning up the pipes and the brick walls and stuff, just to get into our kitchen and the first thing they went for was my Smorgasbord of cat food. I suppose they must have been really starving to risk everything like that. Cos I was watching a lot of the time. I'd sit on the kitchen table, right on the corner edge with my shoulders hunched, hiding between the piles of papers and letters and books and the heaps of crockery and the vase of pink lilies. Waiting and watching and ready to pounce.

They must have been really starving down there in the cellar to send up the youngest one of the family. 'Gleep! Gleep!' he went in that tiny bloomin' voice.

I first saw him on Christmas morning. I was bounding down the stairs with Paul at six a.m. It was our usual routine, of course. Every single morning I'd lead him round all the things he had to do to make the house properly habitable – putting on the lamps and opening the curtains on the darkness of the street and the garden. He'd open the front door and I'd sit patiently while he fetched in the milk and I'd sniff the air for the morning news. Those mornings were very fresh but through the clean frost I could smell the trains that had gone by in the night and the cars that had slithered past on the slushy road, and the pin-pricky footsteps showing that the family of foxes from the embankment had all been out hunting in the dark.

We went bounding down the stairs and Paul was telling me about the treats I'd be getting. Remember last Christmas? It'd be all the same marvelous stuff. I'd get the hot roasted heart of the turkey again, and I'd try not to let it roll away under the table this time. I was drooling with anticipation as we went downstairs and there, right at the bottom, I heard this 'Gleep! Gleep!' and Paul with his human hearing didn't notice it, of course. Nor did he see that dark little huddled form, no bigger than one of my paws. It was crouching and panting in the muddle of shoes under the hat stand. Gleep was hoping to stay in the shadows and he would have gone unnoticed, but my eyes are pretty keen, and I spotted him at once, and I jumped on him.

'Gleep!'

Paul saw straight away what was happening. 'Fester, don't!'

I think he thought I'd swallowed little Gleep down in one go.

Don't think I hadn't thought about it!

I might be thoroughly at home and domesticated and all that, but I still have the instincts of a hunter and a killer! Oh, yes. But I was looking forward to my salmon and stuff and I wasn't going to spoil my appetite on a pesky little morsel like this. Also, he tasted a bit like the damp cellar did, kind of vegetably and dark.

He was going 'Gleep! Gleep!' inside my mouth, scared out of his wits, I reckon.

'Fester, let him go! Spit him out!' cried Paul, like a dafty, sounding scandalized I was doing something as horrible as what nature intended on Christmas morning.

He insisted I spat out the little mite, even though all I was doing was a bit of safekeeping and making sure he never ran away.

Pffftttt.

I relinquished Gleep and he shot across the floorboards, seeking shelter inside one of Jeremy's leather shoes. Paul hurriedly picked it up and carried it like it was something special or precious to the front door, which he quickly unlocked.

'Ungow!' I shouted at him, because I realized what he was going to do. 'Ungow!' You can't! You can't just empty that shoe into the front drive. You can't just shove that tiny gleeping thing into Chestnut Avenue at six in the morning on Christmas bloomin' Day!

'Sssh, Fester,' he said to me – a bit tersely, I thought. 'No, you can't have him to chew on. I'm rescuing the poor little fella.'

I could hear Gleep shouting his own name, sounding all frantic and shrill. Paul emptied him out under the hedges and then he brought the shoe back inside.

'Ungow!'

'Shush, Fester. You've got fancy cat food and stuff for breakfast. I'm not letting you eat a little mouse like that on Christmas morning.'

'Ungow!'

But I wasn't shouting cos of that. He should have known that. I was shouting because Gleep was stuck out there now. I don't think there was a way back into our cellar from the street outside. Not even for someone as tiny as he was.

He was stuck out there. He was separated from the rest of his family and he probably didn't have the wits in his tiny head to think up a way to get back. So he was completely doomed. Unless I did something to bloomin' well help him.

3.

This was in the days before I became a house cat and stopped going out so much. I was still youngish and I never thought twice about skipping out of doors and perambulating the whole neighbourhood. Up and down Chestnut Avenue checking out all our other local cats and seeing what was what.

So, a little after breakfast on Christmas morning I left Paul with his toast and a glass of Prosecco and I was off down the street. 'Keep off that road, though,' he warned me. He had been a bit funny about me and the road out front since he saw me rolling about on the warm tarmac one afternoon in the late summer, sunning myself.

Out I went, to hunt through the undergrowth between the hedges and the houses.

'Gleep?' I called. 'Gleep...?'

It was such a bloomin' foolish noise. That mouse was so tiny and insignificant and silly that he didn't even have anything sensible to say.

'What are you doing, Fester Cat?'

Suddenly I could hear the snarky, snickering voice of that old Bessy. I sighed. Of course she'd have to be there. Of course she'd have noticed I was up to something interesting and she'd start being all sarcastic about it.

'Happy Christmas, Bessy,' I said, carrying on about my business.

Bessy was once a member of our household. Paul and Jeremy let her move in for a while because the big old bruiser looked like she was beaten up and destitute. Once through the doors she proceeded to eat them out of house and home, and thought that she could call all the shots. She bullied me out of my favourite beds and perching spots and life wasn't the same around ours until she decided one day – quite out of the blue – that it was time for her to move on.

Bessy with the great big bollocks. Bessy with the bad attitude.

'If you're looking for that mouse,' said Bessy, chuckling, 'Then you're too late. I already found it.'

'What?'

'That damp-smelling baby mouse?' She examined her claws and rolled her bright green eyes. 'Is that what you're looking for?'

I had to tell her that it was. 'You haven't eaten him, have you?'

'Hardly! I'm not that hungry.'

You could never tell with Bessy. She was sly and liked causing bother. 'Where have you taken him?'

She considered this. 'I suppose you and those dafties round yours are having turkey for dinner, then?'

'You could be, too,' I burst out. 'You're the one who moved out. You were living with us last Christmas. You could have stayed...'

'Nah,' she shrugged her big shoulders like she was wearing a very luxurious coat instead of a ratty old thing. 'I got itchy paws. I prefer living rough.'

'Ungow,' I said. I didn't point out that when I lived rough, as one of Bessy's street gang, it wasn't just itchy paws we had – it was itchy bloomin' *everything*. 'Look, will you tell me where Gleep is?'

'Why should you care about some little mouse? He's not even a gobful. He's just a scrap of a thing. Not really a living creature at all.'

'I want to take him home,' I burst out. 'Down to the cellar.' And I felt like biting my tongue. You should never tell Bessy what you really want because she'll find some way of turning it against you.

'Bring me the turkey's heart,' Bessy said. 'And I'll get you your stupid little mouse.'

'But the turkey won't be cooked for hours yet,' I gasped. 'Gleep can't wait that long to go home. He'll freeze out here!'

'Gleep, is it?' snickered Bessy. 'Do you always go round naming animals?'

I frowned at her and felt my lip go up in a snarl round my single tooth.

'Some salmon then,' she said, salivating and looking stupid with hunger. 'Bring me some of that lovely salmon. I know they'll have some. I can wait for the heart. And then I'll take you to your awful mouse.'

4.

Bessy was chuffed as muck. She wolfed down what I brought her and reeked of salmon all day because she had it all round her mush and didn't clean it off. Her habits were as mucky as ever, it seemed.

We were stopped in the street by Whisper and Three-Legged Freddy from next door. 'Who's got the smoked salmon then?' yowled the Siamese. I've never really liked her much. I've always found her a bit bloomin' insinuating. She was weaving around like she wanted to mug us both.

'I can smell something nice – huff huff,' sighed Three-Legged Freddy. He was going round in circles on the frosty path. He'd been doing that a lot with his damaged leg and since his stroke. His fur was all in clumpy tatters and he looked like he'd been out drinking stagnant water or something.

I wished I'd brought them something from our fridge, too. It seemed unfair that only Bessy had got fed, when she didn't deserve anything.

'I'm on a rescue mission,' I told them proudly.

'He's got it into his head he's gonna rescue a cellar mouse and reunite it with its family,' Bessy scoffed. 'I think Fester's gone a bit doo-lally in his old age.'

'I wouldn't mind a mouse as a pal, huff huff,' mused Freddy. 'It would be nice to have a pal you could just – you know, huff huff – *eat*, kind of thing, when you got bored with playing or having the same old conversation.'

'Can we go past?' I say, doing the ritual thing of asking if it's okay to cut across their little span of the world in front of their house. Can we cross their front garden to next door? Freddy and Whisper are flattered by my lovely manners and they let me pass. They glare at Bessy. Actually, not many round here are that fond of Bessy. She keeps causing rows, is the problem.

'Is this where you brought him?' I ask Bessy, looking up at the minister's tall house. It's the next house in the terrace and here lives the oldest, most venerable cat in our avenue.

'Might have,' Bessy shrugs. She's decided to be unhelpful again.

5.

Minutes later I'm in the back garden there, in the long grass and under the frozen hawthorn branches. I nod good morning to the cats from the last house in the terrace – Rowan and Scooby – who don't appear to know much about my kidnapped Christmas mouse. I believe it when Scoob says he doesn't know anything – he always looks as if his mind is on loftier things. But Rowan – through she's sweet and sometimes affectionate – has a look about her that says, 'I could have seen him, or I might not have done. I might have eaten him and forgotten all about it. Why would I tell you anything?' I've seen Rowan go after birds and leap a mile into the trees after squirrels almost bigger than I am.

Off they go for their own Christmas breakfast indoors – they've got a cat flap. Bessy watches them with her usual slow, envious eyes.

But the person we're out in the frosty garden to see is the king of cats round here. It's Smokey. He sits regally, like a great mound of soft white and charcoal fur, beside a small pond. It's frozen solid and he's peering at the dim shapes of frogs and fish like he's a human watching morning cartoons on the telly. Are they real frogs and fish frozen down there, I'm wondering? Or just the vague shadows and memories of fishy things from the summer?

'Good morning, Fester Cat,' he rumbles pleasantly. 'Merry Christmas. Ungow.' Those huge amber eyes look on me with fondness. I know Smokey's always had a soft spot for me. He looks more askance at Bessy, who's sucking on her claws and between her stinky toes and pretending like he isn't even there, or she couldn't care less. Her usual way.

I explain about Gleep, being as brief as I can.

And I tell Smokey something I haven't told anyone yet.

'Gleep was after food in our house because the mice are all desperate, down in the cellar. He's too young to forage. He's really tiny. It's because his dad's dead and – little as he is – he's the best at climbing and getting through gaps and stuff.'

'How do you know so much about his family circumstances?' asks Smokey.

'We found his dad's body,' I sigh. 'Just a few weeks ago. It was under our boiler, in the kitchen, all curled up. He'd been there long enough to dry out completely. When Paul picked him up in a tissue he weighed nothing at all.'

'Dessicated mouse,' laughs Bessy. 'Yum. Fry him up with breadcrumbs. Dip him in salsa. Cover him in sour cream and jalapenos and cheese.'

'Ignore her,' Smokey frowns.

'The boys – my boys – put out some poison, a little while ago. I tried to tell them – ungow! Don't! – it's nasty stuff to have about the place. But I think they learned their lesson. Paul was upset when he found that tiny, dried-out mouse. It was the thought that, as he was dying, that mouse went to the boiler for warmth. He went right under the metal box that houses the flames – the pilot light kind of thing. It's red hot down there. Too hot, really, but the father mouse must have been shivering and losing his sense of what was cold and hot as the poison went through him. He was all curled up like he was asleep.'

Bessy chortles. 'Honestly, Fester. Christmas has made you all sentimental and stupid this year. Since when did you care about something like that? Don't you hunt them? Don't you crunch them up and swallow them in one slippery go?' She eyes me nastily. 'You're the one who had all his gums fixed. Don't you chomp them to death by the dozen?'

I have to admit that I don't. I like to catch them, yes, of course, when instinct kicks in and when I see them gadding about the place. But I just pop them in my mouth and walk them about a bit, as a warning. Then I return them to the door at the top of the cellar steps. I nudge them through the little gap in the wood so they can make their journey home down the wonky stonework of the steps.

Smokey laughs to hear this. 'You're a soft-hearted thing, Fester Cat.'

This reminds Bessy of her hunger. 'He's promised me the turkey heart if I bring back his baby mouse alive and unharmed.'

'Well then,' says Smokey. 'Then you better had, hadn't you, Bessy dear?'

6.

But as usual Bessy leads me a merry dance. We hop over the garden fences and through the hedges.

'Where are you taking me?' I keep asking, jumping after her tail. She's just enjoying herself, the mangy old besom. She's pretending like it's how it used to be, when she ruled our little gang and we all lived rough and I followed her around like this.

We pass by the back of my house, scooting over the Beach House roof and taking a breather. At the back window I can see a shape watching us. A silhouette with tufted, furry ears. I'd know those sharp, black beady eyes anywhere. Panda never misses a trick. He knows I'm running about in the frosty morning. It's still not even fully light and Panda can spot me from miles away, scampering about.

'Ugh, the stupid Panda,' Bessy snickers. 'You know, I never believed he could really talk. I always thought it was one of the boys doing his snooty voice.'

'Which just shows how much you bloomin' know,' I snap.

Then she's got us tiptoeing along the fence. My balance isn't as good as hers for this kind of thing. I had that ear infection and my fence-walking skills went to pot. It turns out we're here to have a word with the squirrels.

'Hellooooo!' bellows Bessie, into the trees, eyeing the dark masses of the drays in the upper branches. The squirrels are there, listening – we can both sense it. Brave as they are, they sensibly keep their distance when Bessy's abroad. I've seen her grab a squirrel or two in the past and it isn't pretty.

'Halloooooo!' she tries again. 'Have you seen Fester's friend? He's lost a mouse. A baby mouse. I had hold of him for a while, but I'm not sure where I put him... Have you seen him? He goes, 'Gleep!' It's all the foolish thing can say.'

The bravest squirrel is the one with no tail. He lost it in a terrible scrap when he was much younger. He's lean and angry and behaves like he's got nothing left to lose.

'I saw a mouse, yeah,' he nods, wringing his hands together and cracking the knuckles, like he wouldn't say no to a punch-up. 'It wasn't an outdoors mouse. He was all over the place. Didn't know where he was, or who he was meant to be. It was at the front of your house, Fester. I said, come and live with us squirrels.'

'With the squirrels?' laughed Bessy. 'Why would he want to do that?'

'It's not a bad life. Better than skulking about in corners and trying to get adopted by humans,' Derek shrugged. 'Anyway, he wouldn't. He sat there quivering. He wanted to get back to the cellar.'

'Of course he bloomin' does,' I sighed.

7.

As Christmas Day lightens briefly and all the scratchy hedges and bare trees are revealed along the embankment I realise how impossible this is. We'll never find the tiny thing. I'm going along, sniffing stuff, trying to pick up the mildewy, widdly scent of a frightened cellar mouse. I'm even calling out, 'Gleep! Gleep!' which sounds so silly.

Bessy is amused by the whole thing.

We even approach the railway lines and take a look at the foxes, padding about. 'They wouldn't bother with a mouse,' Bessy says. 'Hardly worth their while.'

There are amazing smells coming from all the houses. Intermingled with the woody scents of open fires there comes all this reeking steam and smoke from the roasting flesh of birds. Different kinds of birds – geese and ducks and turkeys and chickens. It could fair drive you into a tizz. We spot the dirty orange fur of the foxes. They stop tumbling and playing their daft games and sit up, alert and keen and they make strange noises low in their throats. Yes, I think it's best if Bessy and I back off through the crackling grass to Chestnut Avenue…

The boys will be wondering where I am. Their house is lit up – every window a different colour – pink and golden and green and blue. There's disco music blaring out of the kitchen as Paul cooks dinner. He'll be roasting the giblets and the heart and the turkey neck with thyme and wine for gravy…

'You know what you must do, Fester Cat,' says Bessy, with solemn greed.

I nod, hurrying home. They let me in the back when I yowl at the step: 'Ungow!' (I've never felt comfortable with the cat flap.)

In the kitchen, as is traditional, Paul presents me with the heart. It's a bit hot and yes, it ends up rolling about a bit on the bare boards. Cue much bloomin' hilarity. But then I've got the grisly, gorgeous thing in my mouth and I'm running out of the kitchen and down the hall with it. 'Unngoowww!'

It's a huge sacrifice.

But here you are, Bessy. It's the greatest gift I could ever give.

'Thank you, Fester Cat,' says she, looking moved. 'I'll enjoy that. And thank you, not just for that.'

I give her a suspicious look. 'What else?'

'For running about outside with me. For being in my gang again and following me around. It was a bit like old times, wasn't it?'

Then Paul's found us, chatting like this. 'Bessy!' he goes. 'Have you come back for Christmas?'

But she grabs her heart and off she pops. 'I'll see you later, loser,' she snickers at me, and is gone.

'But what about bloomin' Gleep?' I shout, as she bounds away, back out the door.

8.

For the rest of the day I'm worried sick, though I pretend not to be for the sake of my boys. I pounce about the living room when we're all together, jumping on the chairs and into their laps. I let them stroke me and pretend to fall asleep, even doing a bit of singing to show I'm content. They've bought me the most ridiculous bloomin' present – it's a furry blue snake on an elastic string that bounces and dances and thrashes about. It's supposed to look as if it's alive and I'm meant to go daft trying to catch it. But I can see it's only a toy – it's obvious what it is. But to make them happy I do some jumping and scampering, for a few minutes at least.

Then I flomp down in front of the fire, hugging last year's toy mouse – the one in the Santa hat. Letting my dinner settle, contemplating the flames as they twerk about in the hearth.

'He looks distant and thoughtful,' Paul tells Jeremy. 'He looks like he's worried about something…'

Jeremy tells him he's being daft. Paul's always over-dramatizing things, especially when it comes to my world, he says.

The two of them drift off to the settee and all their human telly stuff, which I'm never all that interested in…

And after a little while, I reckon I can hear singing outside.

It's not carolers or anything like that. The time for that is finished and Christmas has come and is on its way out again. No humans are traipsing about in all the cold and singing tonight…

I jump onto the dining table, tiptoeing through the rubble of blue china and glasses and tangled streamers and remains of crackers, and I poke my head through the curtains at the street beyond.

There's a special cat *passeggiata* happening tonight.

I have to be out!

I hop down from the window sill and rush to the hall, and I'm doing a whole lot of scratching at the front door. The heavy purple curtains are pulled across to keep out the freezing drafts. I carry on shouting 'Ungow!' until the two dafties know that I need to be outside.

'Are you sure, Fester Cat?' Jeremy asks, unlocking and unbolting everything.

I'm bloomin' sure.

Off I dash into the frost, down the front drive and into the Avenue.

They're all waiting for me, under the trees. It's rare that you ever see them altogether. If they are, it's because there's a fight on and everyone's crowding to watch and spit. But here's Smokey and Rowan and Scooby, and Three-Legged Freddie and Whisper, and even Ralph and a few others I don't recognize, from further afield round our way.

They're all singing together. It's a proper cat jamboree for Christmas night.

It's not a song like any of you humans would recognize, of course.

Bessy! Bessy's with the rest of them, puffing out her impressively fluffy chest and singing with gusto. She winks one of her green eyes at me and looks as if she's chewing something. Maybe she's still got that roasted turkey heart, working it round like a gobstopper? Her manners were always bloomin' awful.

'Come and join us, Fester Cat!' shouts the venerable Smokey, over the wobbly noise of the others. 'Come and sing-sing-sing!'

And so I head over the road to join my fellow cats from Chestnut Avenue.

Peace on Levenshulme.

Good will to all moggies.

I've just taken up my place amongst them and started to sing like mad, when Bessie turns to look down at me.

'Got a present for you!' she snickers and, before I can react, spits something at me.

A wet little hairy thing that lands at my paws. For one horrible moment I think she's coughed a furball at me. It's the kind of thing she'd do.

But then I look at what's wriggling at my feet on the pavement.

Ungow!

'Gleep!' goes Gleep, looking deeply worried.

Bessy looks smug.

She's been carrying him around in her mouth all day long. 'He's been warm, anyway,' she shrugs. 'He was in no danger.'

I can hardly believe her.

I get to the end of the song and make my excuses to the others. I've got to get this mouse home to the rest of his family before he freezes in a coat of Bessy spit.

'Happy Christmas!' the others all go, as I hold Gleep tenderly in my toothless jaws and hurry home.

Much later that night, after I've snuck down into the basement and back, and there's been a shrill reunion in the dark, between the boy, his siblings and his frantic widowed mother, I return to the fire. It's there that I realise Bessy only held him trapped in her huge mouth all Christmas so that she could spend most of the day with me. That's what she really got out of the whole thing. The poor old giant-bollocked dear must have been lonely.

Well, tonight no one's lonely round our house, and that's good. I can remember Christmases not so long ago when things were much less settled. Everything is better than ever tonight.

Ungow!

Baubles

'Don't knock it Robert,' she told him.

Aunty Jessie was getting cross as she clip-clopped across the piazza di San Marco clutching her useless sun hat, swinging her bag and scattering the evil pigeons as she went. 'We can't help the time of year,' she went on. 'It's cheap, all right? That's all that matters.' Robert took a last look at the towers, domes and scaffolding, and followed her across to the arcade of shops. They were glowing with coloured crystal and glass, beckoning to her through the fog.

That's all she wanted to come for, he found himself thinking. The shopping. The shopping and the Italian men. Outside an expensive café a mini orchestra had started to play. 'We Are the Champions'.

He hurried after his aunty knowing that, by the time he caught up with her, her mood with him would have changed. It always did. They were best mates really. Otherwise, how could they work together? How could they come on holiday together.

*

Back at home in Whitby, they even had rooms next door to each other in the Christmas Hotel. They were high in the attic, far from the paying guests.

When Robert had been down on his luck and, after a new direction for his pitiful career, it had been Aunty Jessie's suggestion that he join her in the fishing town and become an elf, one of Santa's happy little helpers in the Christmas Hotel.

The Edwardian hotel looked out blearily across the wet black rocks of the shore and the crumbling priory. It was filled mainly with pensioners and run by an evil-looking woman with grotesquely swollen legs, whose idea of fun was to celebrate Christmas every day of the year. The ancient visitors lapped her sales gimmicks up.

All summer Robert had waited on, ran around and been a general kind of servant, all dressed as an elf in a skin-tight green costume and a red hat. The outfit had shown off his packet something chronic:

his festive little holly sprig, Aunty Jessie had laughed, something else to cheer up the old dears.

Hard work in the Christmas Hotel, pandering and present-wrapping, all summer long. Then came autumn and meagre, rather begrudged bonuses and the determination in both nephew and aunt alike that they had to get away on holiday. Away from the churning froth of the North Sea and the keening, kamikaze gulls. Time to fly on some cheap airline to Italy and hopefully catch the last of the sun.

They took the kind of flight where you have to pay up for even a glass of water and the stewardesses sell things like aftershave and bikinis up and down the gangway.

*

They'd been in Venice for a day. It was misty and the drizzle was warm. Like dishwater, as Robert put it: dropping on them slowly as they sat in pavement cafes, traipsed foggy, perplexing alleys, and minded their steps on slippery humpbacked bridges. 'Well, I think it's downright romantic, seeing it off-season and autumnal,' Aunty Jessie announced just this morning as they embarked on their exploration of the Left Bank. 'When it's foggy like this, you never know who you might end up bumping into, coming around the next corner.'

Aunty Jessie was coming up to fifty. Robert had to admit she'd kept herself nice. She was slim and still, as she put it, with-it. She'd bought a caseful of patterned summer frocks. She was here, she said, to take in the culture: the music, buildings and paintings. All Robert had seen her looking at was the men.

Having bruschetta and a glass of the local pink Pinot Grigio in an off-licence last night, she'd told him: 'I've finished with those chat-and-date phone lines. Never again. All those fellas want to know is what dress size you are, and are you still pretty, have you got your hair done nice. And when it comes to them, they don't want to tell you anything. Well, then you go to meet them in some godawful wine bar — a place too young for both of you — and he's sat there waiting and he looks like Worzel Gummidge. Oh, no. Not for me. No more shooting in the dark.'

Once she'd thought that she was bound to find someone, working in a big hotel. Some millionaire with a rakish glint in his eye as she brought his fried breakfast. Someone with cash to spend on a smart, mature person like her; who couldn't believe his luck, meeting her in Whitby, where he'd come to spend an unseasonable Christmas. She wouldn't mind if he was eccentric.

But no one at the hotel had caught her eye. More to the point, she hadn't caught theirs.

Robert and his Aunty Jessie sat at the high stools of the off-licence bar for a couple of hours, drinking the pale, murky wine served to them by a bloke who looked like Harvey Keitel. They talked about love like they never really had before. The conversation was an eye-opener for both of them.

They drifted out, bought peaches off a fruit stall gondola and sat on the steps of a white stone bridge. The evening mist and dark came down and they talked about their ideal men, and how sick they had become of turkey, tinsel, and all the blazing blue Christmas puddings.

'Look at him,' Robert suddenly said, laughing and pointing at an old man strolling by the closed-up front of a church.

'He's ancient,' his aunt said, wiping peach juice off her chin.

He had a huge white beard and a scarlet face. He was a skinny old thing in a checked sleeveless shirt and Bermuda shorts.

'It's Santa Claus!' Robert laughed, choking. 'On holiday!'

They both laughed until the old bloke was out of sight. 'He must wear special padding at Christmas time,' Aunty Jessie said, and then shuddered. 'Oh, don't talk about Christmas to me.'

*

'But who could afford all this? And how would you carry it back in your luggage?'

They were looking at the coloured glass objects in the shop windows.

Twisted, sculpted glass with crimson and aquamarine seeping clouded and frozen in spirals and whorls like ink dropped through water. The two of them gazed for an hour or more at jewellery and vases and bottles and, finally, a whole tree of blown glass that teemed with life-sized and haughty-looking parrots.

It was as they were studying the glass birds that Robert glimpsed a familiar figure inside the shop.

'Don't look now,' Robert hissed. 'But there's Santa again.'

Santa was having something carefully wrapped in green tissue paper. His Bermuda shorts showed off his pale, hairless legs and sandals. He looked affluent and pleased with himself, scratching at his magnificent beard.

'Oh, no,' said Jessie. 'Let's ignore him. God, I hope he didn't hear us laughing at him last night...'

She was blushing as the old man came out of the glass shop, struggling with his precious parcel and the awkward door. Aunty Jessie looked away, but Robert was watching.

Santa fixed them with a genial frown, his feathery eyebrows pulled together. He waited until Aunty Jessie met his glance.

Then he said, 'Ho, ho, ho!' and she gasped.

The old man moved off into the narrow, bustling arcade and soon he was lost to them amongst the brollies, damp fleeces and shopping bags.

*

They had tiny cups of bitter, gritty coffee at a table by their hotel.

'The canals smell of damp wool,' Robert said, staring at the milky green water. He looked at his despondent Aunty Jessie and sighed. A litre of wine at lunchtime in the Peggy Guggenheim museum hadn't been such a good idea. The sour wine had tasted like rainwater, like tears, and as they'd trooped around, dutifully taking in the surrealist pieces (nightmare interiors by Ernst and Magritte, driftwood assemblages knocked up by Picasso), Robert had watched his slender, nervy Aunty Jessie sink into a deep depression.

She bolted back the rest of her espresso like medicine, pursed her lips and told him: 'Don't you ever turn out to be like me, Robert.'

'How do you mean?' He'd found he was watching the gondoliers again, as they rested on the opposite side of the canal. Larking about in a foreign language, shoving each other, lazing in the afternoon sun as the cobbles gave off wreaths of warm mist.

'I was your age in the Seventies and I thought I had it all in front of me. I was like one of Pan's People off *Top of the Pops*. That's what I looked like. And I called it sexist at the time, the way all the blokes looked at me and tried to chat me up. I just breezed through and then it was a decade later and I was a housewife for a bit. Poodle perm, batwing mohair sweaters, negative equity, the lot. And by the time I'd got myself out of all that, I found I'd turned into a little old lady, like this...'

'You're not a little old lady...' he murmured. One of the gondoliers was climbing back aboard his boat and Robert was watching him: the curious, wiry strength of him, the overdeveloped calf muscles.

'I may as well be,' she said. 'And who has looked at me during this holiday, eh? Who has looked my way?'

Robert's heart went out to her, because his Aunty took such a pride in her appearance, and it was a shame if no one paid her any attention. But he had seen men looking, in the Departures lounge at Stansted, and in that shop in Pisa.

'Them?' she gasped. 'They were perverts. I don't want perverts looking at me.'

*

It was a strange city, and not for the reasons they expected.

Not because of the weird, overlapping sounds of the canals at night, or the fog that slipped down and swapped all the streets around so that nothing was in the same place as before. And not because of the thought of ancient ballrooms, casinos and bordellos sunk underwater, preserved somewhere beneath their feet, with monstrous fish drifting about through gilded rooms, under chandeliers bearded with lichen and weed.

It was strange because it seemed empty to Robert and Jessie. They were here together, but they were both looking for other people. There was a sense of something here for both of them, but neither knew how to find it.

'We may as well be invisible,' Aunty Jessie said. 'We're like ghosts in a city that's sinking...'

Robert didn't like it much when her thoughts went morbid and lurid like this and she told him all about it. Each night, when he knew she was sleeping, he slipped out of their shared hotel room and went hunting around the Academia bridge. There were men hanging around, sure enough, smoking fags and following him when he attempted to lead them a merry dance.

But they didn't play the rest of the game like they were meant to. They had some other cryptic purpose, knocking about the woolly-smelling canals in the dark. Robert couldn't figure it out.

Their holiday was taking a bleak, sour turn and reluctantly Robert had to put it all down to sex. We're on what could be a romantic trip, he thought: that's why. All this romance is just like rubbing our faces in it.

*

They ate in a trattoria with a courtyard out back. Their waitress kept pinching Robert's cheek and his ciggies and came over to gabble at them in Italian, as if they understood every word.

'She's very insinuating,' Aunty Jessie said, flicking her menu. She had come up in terrible bumps from insect bites and was itchy, dizzy and cross. 'She's much too familiar. I don't like her.'

Aunty Jessie considered herself to be a very fine waitress and took great interest in how others behaved on the job.

'I think they're all ex-prostitutes, those who run this place.' Robert was studying the plastic lobsters on the walls and the mirrors with disturbing clowns painted on. Everything was garlanded with fairy lights. 'They're all retired and they've set up a co-op and now they're raking it in.'

'I must say, their bread buns aren't very fresh,' Jessie sighed.

The waitress was back. She wasn't that helpful with explaining the menu. 'Oh, lasagna, tagliatelle, spaghetti... is all the same.' Then she was nudging Robert with her bony elbow. She was wrinkled from the sun, but very pale and her dyed black hair had gone thin on top. 'She your mama, yes? Your lover, no?'

'Oh no,' said Aunty Jessie.

'No, no,' said Robert. 'My aunt. Just my aunt. My friend.'

The waitress didn't understand and passed him a rose. 'Che bello,' she told him, and ruffled his hair.

Aunty Jessie was looking aghast, but not at him.

'What's the matter?' At a table in the ramshackle courtyard of the trattoria, Santa Claus was wearing a pink linen suit and sitting hunched over by guttering candlelight. He was polishing off a dressed crab and beaming to himself.

'He's following us about,' Aunty Jessie said, transfixed by that formidable beard.

'Never,' Robert laughed. 'It's a small town, really. Like Whitby. You're bound to bump into people again and again...it's like maze with everyone going round...'

She shook her head, looking grim. She fiddled fearfully with her long dark hair. 'No. He's a pervert. He's a Santa Claus pervert and he's coming after me.'

Robert had to laugh.

*

The old man finished his dinner and paid up just as they were going. He didn't make it obvious and neither of them noticed him casting sidelong glances their way, but somehow he timed it so he was leaving the noisy, shabby trattoria just as they were.

Their waitress was hugging Robert goodbye and Aunty Jessie was hissing, 'told you!' as Santa squashed by, grinning.

They took the dark back alleys to their hotel. Aunty Jessie had them scooting along, shooting backward glances all the way, until Robert lost patience with her.

It was true, though. The bearded man in the pink linen suit was ambling after them, all the way to their hotel.

They'd been lucky, managing to get a room with an arched window at water level, right on the Grand Canal. They had a pedestal table and wickerwork chairs, where they could sit to watch vaporetti chugging past.

'He must be staying in the same hotel,' Robert told her.

His aunt was getting far too jumpy. She had two high spots of pink on her cheeks.

'It's the way he went 'Ho, ho, ho,'' she said, coming out of the en suite, brushing her teeth. 'It sent a chill right through me...'

*

The next morning they were sitting at their window and waving at the vaporetti, trying to get the passengers to wave back.

'Well! The cheeky devil!' Aunt Jessie burst out suddenly. Robert looked and saw why. It was Santa, up on the top deck of the passing water bus. He was waving both arms at her energetically, grinning his head off through his beard.

It was Jessie's idea that the two of them split up for that morning and do some exploring alone. She felt Robert may be tiring of her nerviness and want to get away.

Jessie found herself drifting about not too far from the hotel, since she'd come without her map. It was a cautious exploration, with her clothes sticking to her.

She sat right out on the front of the bay, where the choppy Adriatic came up to the front of the newsagents and bistros. She sat a table and ordered a coffee and then she saw the two waitresses from last night's trattoria ambling along the prom, carrying between them what looked like a big bag of leftovers, a huge doggy bag, one handle each. It was as if they had been working in that tatty restaurant all night and were only now setting off home on aching feet, looking even more ancient in the lemony-grey morning light.

Jessie had a kind of future-shock then. One of her sudden, horrible glimpses of what might be in store for her. She often tortured herself like this. In these queer flash-forwards, she never saw things going well for herself. She saw herself as a real old lady (really, she knew she wasn't one yet) and she was still grafting away at the Christmas Hotel. And Robert was still with her, twenty years and they were still finishing their backbreakingly festive shifts and struggling home together at the end of them, just like these two gamey old birds — who had noticed her by now, and were waving at her as she sat under her awning, blowing on her coffee.

They were jeering at her really; two wizened old death's head crones, knowing that her life might as well be over already and it was always going to be the same.

She gulped her coffee and refused to wave back. They moved on, out of sight. And then Santa was pulling up one of the aluminium chairs, scraping it on the cobbles and seating himself heavily at her table.

Jessie narrowed her eyes, deciding to treat him, if not with contempt, then at least as an hallucination.

Sunspots. Fever. Malaria from her insect bites.

'Ho, ho!' he said.

*

'Go away,' she hissed, mustering the nerve to swear at him.

He looked hurt in an exaggerated way, an operatic way. 'You treat me like exactly the kind of man who you don't want to meet. But look at me! I'm perfect! I'm doing everything to catch your eye.' He laid a bunch of bedraggled, wilting anemones on the table. Their petals were like wet rags. 'Is it my age?'

'No, no,' she sighed. 'I'm just not used to being pursued across a strange city by...'

He chuckled. 'Pursued...!'

'It's very disconcerting.'

'You act as if I appall you. Am I so grotesque?'

She relented for a second. 'I don't even know you.'

He twinkled at her. 'Are you sure?'

She pulled a face savagely. 'You're so bloody jolly and good. Every time we've seen you on this horrible holiday, you've looked so... well... happy...'

'Is it really a horrible holiday you're having?'

She realised her mistake. 'No, not really. It's fine, actually.'

He leaned forward conspiratorially. 'You know, Jessie... you've got me all wrong.'

'I have?'

'I'm not the man you think I am.'

'You're not.'

'I do have my darker side.'

'You do?'

He nodded happily. 'If I really was the man you think I am, don't you think I could have solved all the world's problems? Conquered famine, and hunger and disease? Oh, but I'm too selfish for that.'

Her eyes were swimming in the dappled light from the sea. She tried to snap out of it: 'I don't know what you're talking about.'

'If I was the man you thought I was I'd be a very powerful, magical old man, very remiss in my duties, leaving the world so mixed up and sad. I'm too selfish to use my powers to put everything right.' He stroked his luxurious side-whiskers and beamed at her. 'You were quite right about who I am. But I'm a very limited, selfish, and sexy kind of Santa Claus. Nothing to do with your preconceptions. Nothing to do with Christmas.'

She snorted. 'I've had Christmas coming out of my ears.'

She was staring at him. Could she think of Santa as an erotic object? It seemed perverted, almost.

He whispered, 'I promise, you'll only have Christmas when you want it. Only the bits you like. If you come with me.'

She flushed. 'Come with you where?'

'I know you think your life is over. That it holds no more surprises for you. All I can say is, if you carry on in your regulated life, sticking with your nephew and living in a hotel where every day is necessarily the same... of course that will be true. Your life will be smooth and predictable till the end of your days.'

He produced another present for her then. It was wrapped in tissue paper. She took it like an unexploded bomb and unwrapped it in front of him. It was the glittering blue bauble he had bought in the glass shop yesterday.

'You can walk across the surface of your own life forever,' he said softly. 'Round and round the same old world. Or...'

She looked up sharply, despite herself, wanting to know now what the alternative was.

'Or you can come inside. Into your own life.'

He really was a cheeky old thing.

Now he was getting up to leave. And she found herself disappointed.

'Meet me tonight,' he said. 'On the bridge by the hotel. One o'clock. Bring the glass.'

'Why?' she asked, bracing it in her fingers like a crystal ball.

He was gone.

I've never been given a magic object before, she thought.

No one's ever promised to take me out of my life.

I wouldn't have to stay for long.

And If I didn't like it, I could come back.

She got up and started putting her things into her bag; purse, and then the glass bauble, which she dropped and smashed on the wet cobbles. She gave a short, anguished cry.

She picked up the pieces, careful not to cut herself. She put them all into the tissue paper, wanting to cry with shame.

The glass was so thin. It was like blue spun sugar.

Well, now she'd just have to go and meet him.

To explain. To apologise. For being so clumsy and hopeless. So dangerous and out of control of her life.

*

After a long day spent alone Robert was full of pasta and wine. He was nodding off as he watched black water pushing against the steps up to their windowsill. He was mesmerized by the reflections of light on the waves.

Aunty Jessie's complaints from across their room had quietened to murmurs. He managed to block out her twittering and drift off.

Then he awoke with a jerk in the dark. The hotel room lights had been dimmed right down and it was much quieter.

He looked over at Aunty Jessie and made out the rigid bump of her, lying under a single white sheet. She even slept tidily.

He stood stiffly and woozily, grimacing as the wickerwork creaked beneath him.

I'll have just once more round the block, he thought. Just a little scout around in the dark before dawn. Get some of that muggy air into his lungs on their last night in town. Might get lucky this time.

There wasn't a peep out of Aunty Jessie. He took his key and slipped out into the corridor.

Dreaming of a White Christmas

He was drawn to the steps of the Academia bridge.

For a while, no one came past. Then, one or two late stragglers came and went and left Robert to his business. He smoked and watched the sudsy clouds passing over the moon.

He stared at the bridge.

There was his Aunty Jessie. She was standing there like a sleepwalker, in full view of anyone who cared to look.

She tricked me, he thought. She must have slipped out of the hotel before even I did.

There wasn't much space between her and Santa Claus.

They were in hushed, urgent conference.

Aunty Jessie looked flustered and hot, even in her loose nightie. Santa was chuckling at her, lifting up his great beard, rippling his fingers in the humid air. Uncertainly, Jessie was joining in with his echoing laughter.

When Santa snapped his fingers, Robert could hear the click.

A solid transparent sphere shimmered around both figures on the bridge. It looked brittle and faintly blue, like Murano glass.

Aunty Jessie stared at the old man in wonder and he was laughing again. The glass started to mist over and it was harder for Robert to see them. He realised that it was snowing *inside* the bauble. A perfect, miniature snowstorm was raging just inside the sphere.

Santa had taken Robert's aunt and trapped her with him in a bubble of winter.

All around them in that hermetic space, silent clots and specks of snow were whirling, and colliding with his Aunty Jessie's overheated flesh.

He's doing it, Robert thought suddenly, to prove that he is real.

Santa's doing it to prove it all true.

Aunty Jessie was frozen in that moment; aghast, awhirl. Her breath was crystallizing. Robert could see his aunt's gasp of amazement hanging in front of her and it was like a large white question mark.

Santa bent forward to kiss her. He'd be melting the flakes on her face, her eyelashes.

Then he reached up and pricked the bubble from within. It burst like soap and the glass and the hectic blizzard melted in an instant.

The hot wet air of the Venetian night came flooding back.

'I'll catch my death,' Robert heard his aunty say.

Santa was peering over the side of the bridge, down to the canal, where a great dark shape had drifted up and was waiting for him.

'Time for home, Jessie,' he said, in an unexpected accent.

Jessie let Santa lead her down to the gondola. He nodded to the boy in the boat-necked jumper, who was bracing his slight weight on the slant of the gondola's stern. Robert stared as the boy doffed his yellow straw hat at Jessie, revealing his nascent horns, their rounded nubs poking out of close-cropped hair. Reindeer, Robert realised. The boy had cloven hooves.

He watched his aunt rubbing her arms, though she must be warmed through again by now. She was stepping aboard. She looked dainty as she sat down in the cushions, hugging her knees as Santa joined her.

The gondolier shoved their small boat away from the crumbling shore. As they went sailing off into the dark, Robert heard his aunt come out of her trance with a gasp.

It wasn't really like her, taking off like that.

The Christmas Hoover

Once again Ruth scanned the recipe from Good
Housekeeping. All the ingredients were laid out on
the kitchen table, even the tinned chestnuts (murder
to find). Actually making the Chestnut Rissole
Surprise seemed impossible now. It was ten o'clock
on Christmas Eve and she couldn't concentrate
because of the noise Desmond was making as he
smashed up the Hoover.

Desmond had been keen to help tidy the
house before tomorrow's arrival of their Christmas
guests. Hoovering had become one of his jobs round
the house, since the new device they had bought in
October was actually too heavy duty for Ruth to carry
about, which mortified her. It was a very swanky
model, and Desmond had done all the online research
necessary before they made their purchase. It was
top-notch but awkward and heavy.

She paused, listening to him bash the thing about in the hallway. Really, she thought, they were cursed when it came to vacuum cleaners. It seemed that they bought one almost every year. A new one would arrive, full of promise. Its ailing forebears would be sitting around the house, having seen it all before. Desmond would never throw them out, in case they suddenly started working again. Ruth was sick of tripping on festoons of tubing.

She was just about to return her attention to this business of the Chestnut Rissoles for Desmond's vegan sister, Claire, when there came an almighty outburst. Desmond was bellowing and the Hoover was being thrown out of the front door. Ruth knew she'd have to leave her safe haven, where Barry Manilow crooned in the gentle steam of parboiling parsnips. She tottered reluctantly to the hall, where she had a view of Desmond in the driveway. He grabbed his axe and then he was smashing their deluxe new Hoover into splinters, on the very spot where he usually chopped firewood. He was shouting and swearing for everyone to hear, too. Which hardly seemed very Christmassy.

Now the vacuum cleaner was shattered and lying in pieces on the drive. Its dusty, fluffy, cat-hairy innards lay exposed in the snow. The brown paper bag of its heart slowly collapsed.

Ruth didn't say anything. Best leave Desmond alone with the thing. She returned to the kitchen and went back to assembling the vegetarian option. At the same time she was thinking about a story.

In a wild and wonderful Christmas story, she thought, our ruined Hoover would lie outside on the ice and slush of our front path. It would stay there as the night deepened. It would leak some lint and bits of fluff and try not to despair too much. At midnight tonight there would be a visitation by some kind of household appliance fairy. The whole thing would be observed by the various snowmen, Santas and Christmas ducks from the tree in the dining room, who would naturally have awoken in the night.

The Christmas toys and baubles would watch the Appliance Fairy bringing the Hoover back to life. The Hoover would be like Cinderella submitting to the ministrations of her Godmother. He'd gaze down at himself. He'd pull himself together with hardly any effort. Pulsating and glowing, his various panels would click into place around his fully-functioning and decongested parts. His cables and tubing would flash out like lassos. They would accomplish this easily, with no snarling or tangling for the first time ever. All the penguins and angels would applaud.

Now it was time to set off and fly about the rooftops of Manchester. The snow had been bad. He could suck up the excessive drifting and leave just enough snow to keep the place decorative.

Ruth finished off the Chestnut Surprises quickly. She had no time for messing about. They had become a bit burgerlike and simple, but who cared? She was busy thinking about the Christmas Hoover as she got on with the rest of her jobs. Sprouts to be peeled. Stuffing to be stuffed.

Tonight the Christmas Hoover would sweep up over the kebab shops and back gardens of Levenshulme and Fallowfield and over the frosty trees of Victoria Park. He'd soar over the orange towers of the Palace Hotel and the pointed eaves of the Town Hall and streak above the solemn dome of the Central Library. He'd swing about the Arndale Centre and then swoosh up the frozen canals. Then he'd zoom down the neon bunting of the Curry Mile and the crisp blankness of Platt Fields Park. Chugging along on his tiny motor.

Not clapped out yet. Through the purple wintry clouds: their Hoover moonlighting far away from home.

Longer than any lead would stretch. He'd be turning end over end. No one to push him around. Deciding for himself where he wanted to go.

She wondered where he'd end up by the early hours. Snowmen melted, didn't they? Reindeer returned to their stables in the far north. Fairies dissipated in a shower of tinsel.

Ruth decided to leave the dinner preparations as they were. Everything else could wait. Time to get the sherry out. Pour two schooners, and maybe invite Desmond back inside. Tell him it was okay that he had destroyed their Hoover in a fit of Yuletide pique.

It'll be okay, she decided, because their Hoover would come shuffling back up the gravel of the front garden in the dark hours before dawn.

He would know their house already had loads of broken things that might get mended one day. He'd sit by the door on Christmas morning and cough politely, waiting hopefully to be let back indoors.

The Fabulous Animal Jamboree

1.

Deidre was flattered by Maude's invitation, but she was nervous, too. 'What if it doesn't even happen anymore? What's if it's all a false hope?'

Maude drew herself up as far as her glass case would allow. 'It had better not be.'

It was very late at night. Once the museum was empty of human beings and the lights were low, it was the usual thing for Deidre to hop over her little barrier and toddle along the hallways to visit her friends. In recent weeks the Dodo had become quite pally with Maude. Maude had been kept in storage for a good many years and only recently had the museum authorities rediscovered her, dragged her out, and put her proudly on display in a case at the top of the stairs.

'What's a Tigon when it's at home?' Deidre had asked, the first time she happened by. She squinted at the Maude's information plate.

Maude was resplendent with pale gold fur and the faintest, most elegant stripes. She held her head proudly erect and crossed her hefty paws, sprawling comfortably in her cabinet as all the stuffed animals came by to examine her. 'My mother was an African lioness and by dad was a Manchurian Tiger,' Maude announced.

'A Mancunian Tiger?' asked Deidre. She was sometimes slow on the uptake. 'Hey, chuck, you've got all the animals coming by to see you. You're causing quite a stir. And they're all mad jealous of you. You're so much more glamorous than that humdrum lot. All those plain old monkeys and boring bears.' The Dodo gave a honking laugh.

Maude had become quite fond of her new friend. The Dodo was squat, waddlesome, foolish and slightly pretentious, but she was frank in her admiration of the Tigon. She had taken to visiting Maude nightly, filling her in on who was who in the museum, and the little bit she had gleaned about the world outside its dark, castle-like walls. She was pleased to show off her knowledge to Maude.

'I suppose an awful lot has changed since I was put in that cupboard,' Maude sighed. '1949 it was...'

Deidre squawked. 'That's yonks ago! So much has changed! Almost everything!'

Even if the city's buildings and people had altered completely, and the way that humans lived, and even if the museum and all its displays were different, Maude was sure that the Christmas Jamboree must still happen every year. That couldn't be changed about, could it? One night she cut through Deidre's chatter with a question: 'Did you ever go to the Annual Fabulous Animal Jamboree?'

'What? The what?' blinked the Dodo.

'Paris on Christmas Eve!' Maude growled, astonished that the bird didn't seem to know what she was talking about.

'You'll have to explain,' said the Dodo.

'Really? You've never been?' Maude's golden eyes were wide with amazement. 'The annual gathering of all the most fabulous stuffed beasts in the world? The rarest and preferably extinct creatures from all over the globe converge on Paris for a great big knees-up. It was always the event of the year. And you've never even heard of it...?'

Deidre hung her head. 'I've never been anywhere. Not since I was stuffed and put on my little podium.'

'We'll have to do something about that,' Maude said fiercely.

2.

'You have to be rare to be invited. Or preferably extinct. And naturally you need to be well-preserved...' Maude was explaining this business of a party in Paris. 'It's all very glamorous. It's chic, in fact. And it's a wonderful place to be at Christmas. Oh yes, in the Natural History Museum in the Jardin des Plantes on the Left Bank. Away from the main parade of animals there's a special hall kept dimly lit, so as not to fade the colours of the extremely rare

creatures. And here there are amazing specimens…
very few of whom still walk the earth…'

Deidre was listening to all of this, agog.

'And it was this collection of extinct animals
who started issuing annual invitations to all the rare
beasts in all the museums and collections, worldwide,
to gather in Paris during the festive season…'

'It sounds magical,' said the Dodo.

'Oh, it is. To see these creatures, squeezed out
of existence by calamity or brutality, all bounding
their way happily to Paris by any means they can
find… it's quite something. And for that night all
animals are equal and best of friends. Even the
Tasmanian Tiger is less snappy than usual…'

'Best of friends like we are, Maude,' said
Deidre rather dreamily. 'Because in real life, had we
ever met, I'm sure you'd have made short work and
an easy feast of me.'

Maude stared solemnly with her gold glass
eyes at Deidre's plump breast and belly and chunky
thighs. She could almost imagine she was starting to
salivate. If she'd been the Maude of old, trapped alone

in her tiny cell at Belle Vue Zoo where she was never quite fed enough, she'd have gobbled up Deidre in two deft bites. 'I'm sorry,' she purred. 'But I'm sure you were very delicious.'

Deidre shrugged her stunted wings. 'I don't have any memory of being alive or what I was like. But if I close my eyes very tight I can picture all my flock scrambling through the undergrowth, screaming and panting like mad. I can hear the guns going off and I can smell… roasting…' She shuddered. 'All of which is quite bizarre because hardly any of this body you see before you is actually the real deal. My feet once belonged to some old turkey. I'm mostly made of sawdust and wood. My feathers are goose and swans down. My face is papier-mache and yet… and yet… My beak is real. This daft old honking thing.' She could feel a tear forming in her false eye. 'I know I am a true Dodo in my soul.'

3.

The thing worrying Maude was: did Deidre actually count?

If they went all the way to Paris, would she be turned away for not being real enough?

The Tigon nipped out of her glass case one night – very carefully, so she didn't actually shatter anything and make a mess. She padded through the museum halls to consult with one of the oldest of the revenants in the whole collection. They called him Stan, and he was a T Rex towering two stories high. He was frozen forever in an attitude of ferocious attack (which he actually found rather taxing. All that constant attitude.) Visitors to the museum loved to take selfies with him, and so it was imperative he always looked his most ferocious.

Maude had paid him a number of visits and they enjoyed the camaraderie of high class carnivores. The instinctive rapport of those who had once shared the topmost point of their respective food chains.

'Hallo, there!' he roared down the airy gallery, spying Maude's approach.

She greeted him fondly and wasted no time in explaining her quandary.

'Oh, I see,' mused Stan. 'Well, I think you're quite right to worry. I only ever attended a couple of those French shindigs and I never felt quite welcome. Not that they could complain, though. I mean, you can't get more extinct than me, can you? But I'm not exactly what you might call stuffed. And the Parisians can by so snooty. There were raised eyebrows about my being fossilized and not being in actual possession of any of my original fleshly-parts, as it were… Well, I didn't mind. I don't bruise easily. But poor old Deirdre might be upset by them. I'd hate that to happen to the poor old duck. She'd be mortified…'

Maude nodded her shaggy head. 'Perhaps it's best if I stopped encouraging her? Maybe I should never have started her off on these mad thoughts about Christmas in Paris..?'

*

The next night Maude was woken at dusk by Deidre. 'How are we going to get there anyway?'

'Oh, well,' said Maude, feeling shifty. 'That's to do with magic. You know that giant spider crab downstairs in the main hall?'

'Eric?'

'He can do magic. Any sort. He was always a dab hand. Back in the old days he did amazing things at Christmas. One year he turned us all invisible. We caught the train and then the ferry and another train. It was a hoot! And then another year he cast a spell so that we could fly all the way to Paris! That was the best. Can you picture it? Dozens of stuffed animals, streaming through the starry night...'

Deidre's eyes were gleaming.

'Another year he commandeered a Manchester tram and hypnotized the driver. We climbed aboard and then the whole thing took to the air and soared through a blizzard...!'

'It all sounds wonderful,' said Deidre.

Maude gulped. She was only making the Dodo worse. She was getting her hopes up.

4.

Somehow, no matter how much magic was involved, Deidre didn't think she'd be able to fly all the way to Paris. She couldn't picture herself floating over the high, dark gables and turrets of the museum, let alone going any further. Just the thought of her stumpy, fluffy wings flapping away made her feel bilious and tired.

She imagined the way Maude would fly. She'd be magnificent and lithe, bounding through the clouds. I'd only hold her back, Deidre thought unhappily. No wonder the Tigon looked as if she was having second thoughts about these Christmas plans.

That night Deidre wandered about the museum, visiting a few old friends and seeking out their opinions.

The British woodland creatures thought she was being a fool. Badger threw up his clumpy paws in horror at the thought of venturing as far as the continent. Rabbit threw up a number of sensible objections. Fox threw up a stuffed Robin he'd eaten.

Deidre went to ask the painted faces from Ancient Egypt what they thought. 'This Maude person is dragging you into something rather dangerous,' one of them said. Deidre looked up at the calm, beautiful faces and sighed. This room was one of her favourites in the whole museum. She was standing before a cabinet of delicately painted faces recovered from sarcophagi. They were so unfathomably old and wise they made Deidre's papier-mache head spin.

'Do you really think it'll be dangerous?' the Dodo frowned. Of course, failing to recognize danger was the downfall of her whole silly species. A wave of sadness crashed over the Dodo.

The Egyptian faces gazed down on her with great compassion. But what could they say? How could they help her? They couldn't imagine wanting to leave the museum and travel elsewhere. They loved being on display here and seeing the variety of faces that came to inspect their own. And it was a thousand times better than being in a nasty old tomb, any day.

Next Deidre shuffled down the hall to visit Brute, the dead dog from Pompeii. He was curled up like he was perpetually trying to scratch an itch. From within his overcoat of once-molten lava she could hear his voice quite clearly: 'Are you crazy, woman? You must go! You must get out! You must have fun! Enjoy yourself, lady! Dance and jump and skip about!'

This outburst stiffened her resolve.

The rest were too timid.

What was the point of being able to come to life anyway, if you weren't prepared to do anything with it?

'I really want to go to Paris on Christmas Eve,' Deidre told Maude. 'But I might as well tell you right away – I can't fly. Look. These wings are rubbish. And I'm a bit heavy. No matter how much magic is involved.'

Maude grinned. 'I'd already guessed that. Don't fret. We'll ask Eric the spider crab to do something a bit special...'

And so the following day they waited impatiently for the visitors to file out of the building and for closing time to come. Outside the early evening traffic plied headlights through the snow that had started to fall on Manchester. As the indoor lights went out and the museum staff bid each other festive farewells and locked up all the doors, Maude, Deidre and the others perked up.

It was Christmas Eve.

'Who will come with us to Paris?' Maude bellowed at the assembled stuffed creatures.

They quailed at her ferocious teeth and her outrageous plan.

'What, none of you..?' she roared.

It was a tradition which very few remembered. It had been a long time since anyone had left the museum on Christmas Eve.

'You disappoint me, the lot of you,' scoffed the Tigon. 'Look at Deidre, here! She's not scared! She's never been anywhere and she's brave enough to come with me to France tonight! She's not even real! She's a facsimile Dodo! And she's not ashamed..!'

Deidre looked abashed, but very pleased with the idea of her own courage.

5.

'Christmas Eve again already?' Eric gave a horrid, scratchy yawn. 'They come round faster and faster. Oh, it's you, Maude. Off to Paris, are you? I thought you might. It's been a long time, dearie.'

The spider crab squinted his jewel-like eyes at Maude and then Deidre and cackled with glee. 'Really? You're taking her with you? Will they even let her in? Won't they turn her away at the door?'

'Ssssh, of course not,' the Tigon snapped. 'Don't be unkind, Eric. It doesn't become you.'

He muttered, 'You're right. I've become tetchy over the years. People don't even ask me to do magic stuff for them anymore, in case I turn on them capriciously and do something nasty. It all comes of being on display so much. I feel over-exposed.' His cabinet was unique in that it could be seen from both inside the hall and from outside in the street. He was supposed to be an exotic enticement to passersby, which he found wearying.

'Time's getting on,' Maude said softly. 'And we need your help.'

'Time can do strange things on Christmas Eve,' he mused, and then he swiveled his eyes to study her carefully. 'I know what you want. I know which spell you want me to cast. Oh, that's a lovely idea. Oh, yes, dearie. I don't mind doing that one at all…' His skinny limbs twitched and his armoured body began to judder and emit a pinkish-golden glow…

'Oh, crikey! Oh, help!' Deidre gasped, clacking her beak. 'I'm not so sure now, Maude. Is this going to be safe? Is this going to work out as we want it?'

But Maude wasn't listening. She was busy submitting herself to the workings of Eric's particular sorcery. There was a rushing and a sparkling noise in the air all about them and they both felt that a transformation was starting to take place...

Maude was patting her friend's wing with her paws. Deidre was aware of the comforting weight of her claws. And then the claws were gone and Maude was patting her hand. Her hand? Why, they both had actual hands. Warm, fleshy hands with blood – real blood- running through their veins.

It was strange and unknown, this whole sensation of being human and being made of actual flesh. To Maude it was a long-ago feeling, filling her with nostalgia and glee all at once. To Deidre it was wholly novel and queer. She had never been made of flesh and blood.

All at once the two of them were sitting side by side in an aeroplane, with a stewardess helping them to fasten their seatbelts. There were only moments until the plane took off for its Christmas Eve flight to Paris.

Deidre turned silently to look at Maude and saw that she was wearing a fluffy hat and dark lipstick and she made rather a handsome older woman. She was saying to the stewardess, 'My friend has never flown before. She's rather nervous.'

The stewardess smiled. 'No problem, madam. It's a very short hop. We'll be at Charles de Gaulle in just over an hour. You'll hardly even notice the journey.'

'Wonderful,' said Maude, eyes sparkling.

6.

It snowed over England and the Channel as they flew. Flakes whirled past the dark windows. Deidre grimaced, sitting back and gripping the armrests for dear life, completely terrified. The look on her face made her companion burst out laughing. Deidre in human form had a large bulbous nose, a receding chin, a skinny neck and hair that came in fluffy grey tufts. She still looked every inch like herself. She was even making anguished, strangulated Dodo noises as the plane caromed through the night. It ascended through layers of cloud and falling snow into unfathomable heights of deepest blue. Maude drank in the ancient stars with a sigh.

'Oh, how glorious.' She encouraged her friend to look.

Deidre was dumfounded by everything for the full duration of their journey. The flight passed in a delirious flash and suddenly they were landing and disembarking and being ushered through customs quite smoothly. (Eric was a marvel! He'd magicked up passports and crisp new Euro notes stashed in their handbags like the lining of a plush nest.) 'He's most thoughtful, that crab spider,' Deirdre said, following her friend onto the travelator and the escalator to the railway station, where the Paris train was waiting.

'Isn't he just?' Maude smiled, watching her own reflection in the train window as it sped through the concrete suburbs. Their carriage was packed with all manner of people bound for the city. Some were clearly heading home for the holidays, laden with parcels and bags. Others were in their finery, looking forward to an evening of fun.

Deidre sat squashed close to her more worldly friend. She wasn't used to being out in the world at all. If she was honest, Maude, too, was finding it all quite bewildering. Everything had moved on so much since the last time she had roamed abroad. Everything was lit up and automated. There were electronic voices coming out of the very air, and all the humans had telephones they communed with as the train rumbled along.

And yet the skyline of Paris as they approached seemed very much the same as ever. The pale form of Sacre Coeur on the hill over there. The Eiffel Tower, all shimmering gold. Everything seemed more or less as Maude remembered it.

All of a sudden they were beneath the centre of the city and there was the crush and the confusion of the Metro station. They were hurrying up tiled stairs with hundreds of human beings and then, all at once, they were out in the open. It was snowy and dark and they were by the river. The air smelled different and delicious. Deidre was just about keeling over with excitement.

'We've made it! We've actually made it all the way here! Look at us, Maude! Just look at us! Look how far we've come!'

Maude was standing halfway into the busy road, yelling for a taxi.

7.

Eric had really excelled himself. He had organized everything so that this was a proper holiday for the two ladies. There was a reservation at a boutique hotel near Notre Dame. Here Deidre became giddy with excitement, running herself a bath that lit up with rainbow colours and churned all the water into bubbles. Maude thought it was a bit much, but Deidre was delighted.

'I've never had a bath before!' She flung off her clothes with abandon. 'What am I saying? I've never been human before.' Indeed, sitting in water was a terrifying idea to her everyday self, as it was to all stuffed animals.

They ventured out into the Latin Quarter for dinner, where restaurant owners stood in busy doorways and called out to them, trying to tempt them indoors. They opted for fondue, sitting in a bistro window, and a waiter brought chunks of raw meat for dipping into hot oil. Maude had ancient hunger pangs stirring inside of her, and Deirdre was happy picking at a salad. The Dodo became happily sloshed on Cote du Rhone.

When they realized it was coming up to midnight they left a wad of notes on the table and dashed out in search of another taxi, this time demanding to be taken to the Jardin des Plantes.

Of course it was, as their driver had tried to warn them, locked and bolted for the holiday. When Maude thrust money into his window and growled at him he hurriedly drove away. Then, without a second thought, she took a run up and leapt easily over the metal gates. Deidre gasped and applauded. She was gobsmacked with admiration.

The gates squeaked open, Maude let Deidre in and together they hurried to the main entrance of the bulky shape of the Natural History Museum.

'Righty-o,' said Deidre, gulping hard. 'This is where I find out if they turn me away at the door.'

'They won't,' Maude said, steadfastly.

'They'll know at once I'm not quite... you know... the real thing.'

'You've been worrying too much,' Maude said, though she was worried too that Deidre was heading for an upset.

'I must be brave,' the Dodo said, and marched towards the front of the building.

It looked lifeless and dark in the snow. It looked like there was nothing at all happening within.

But all kinds of things were happening inside.

Even a hundred feet away, if you listened very carefully (and if you had the right sort of ears) you could hear the strains of a band playing a very elegant tune. You'd hear the reckless timpani of a rhythm section at work on the ribcage of a suspended blue whale. And you'd hear the trembling and thrumming as a thousand stuffed party guests jitterbugged, foxtrotted and freestyled any way they wanted across the polished wooden floors.

The place was swarming with endangered animals from the whole world over. All of them were having a fantastic time. This was their only night out in the whole year and they were intent on having a ball.

At the reception area Deidre's eyes were out on stalks.

'A Barbary Lion! A Great Auk! A Snow Leopard…! And there's a whole bunch of Axolotls skipping in a ring! Oh, Maude..! I say…!'

So entranced was Deidre she hardly noticed the bouncers giving her the once-over. One was a Californian Grizzly Bear and the other a Chinese Salamander. They waved Maude through no problem, and spent only a few seconds staring intently at Deidre and her shiny beak.

Her shiny beak..!

'Maude! We've been transformed back… into our everyday selves!'

'Of course,' smiled Maude broadly. 'How else are we to join the jamboree, if not as our natural selves? Come along, Deidre. These gentlemen have no objection to letting you come inside, do you, lovies?'

The hulking great bear and the salamander shook their heads and waved them through.

'Oooh!' squealed Deidre.

They were in!

8.

What a fantastic pair they made – Deidre waddling with her chest puffed out, and Maude slouching calmly – into the heart of the party.

A cheer and a ripple of applause for the long-absent Tigon! A whoop and a carillon of welcoming laughter for the ungainly Dodo! Also, perhaps, a not-unfriendly gasp or two. Even in this gathering of the rarest beasts on Earth, there was a range of rarity and a spectrum of the seldomly seen and both Tigons and Dodos were among the most infrequent of attendees.

A space opened up in the middle of the floor.

'Shall we dance?' asked Maude, with a purr.

'Why not?' squawked Deidre and slapped her turkey feet on the floor and shuffled her bottom and twitched her tufted wings.

'We're dancing! In Paris! On Christmas night!'

Around them swept a mad jumble of birds, beasts and reptiles. She caught glimpses of Japanese Sea lions, Leopards, Forest Turtles, Bactrian Camels, Sumatran Orangutans, African Penguins, Volcano Rabbits and Tasmanian Devils. There was even a Steller's Sea Cow – huge and lousy at dancing – bobbing its grinning head high above the crowd. Dead for more than two hundred and fifty years and game as anything.

And could that possibly be a unicorn?

Deidre blinked in surprise.

'Are there completely impossible animals here as well?' she honked at Maude.

'Oh, I think so!' the Tigon chuckled. 'There certainly seem to be. Look there, by the buffet. A Minotaur! I thought he was a bison, but look at his sexy legs! Goodness! And working at the bar – see! A nattily-dressed faun. Oh, how lovely!' She grinned. 'Things have changed since I last attended this Christmas Jamboree. The committee have clearly loosened up their membership rules. Well, and so they should.'

'Fancy that!' Deidre clucked with relief. 'I'm very glad.'

'Things have worked out very nicely. They're letting in creatures from legend and myth, and I suppose we're almost that ourselves...'

'They're letting in made-up beasts of all kinds!' whooped Deidre, and they danced with a great deal of brio and vim, until they were completely worn out, and went to check out the buffet.

'What a wonderful spread!' Deidre gasped. Marshmallows in every colour, popcorn, puffed wheat and cakes made of multi-coloured rice crispies. Everything was guaranteed to make one bloat up and swell. It was just the kind of food stuffed animals love to eat at parties. All the drinks were bubbly, too.

There were a few snide comments at the buffet table from a nasty-looking Nonesuch – a fake mermaid from a museum in South London. She had taken against Deidre at first glance and muttered something about her head being obviously modeled out of papier-mache. Maude came at once to her friend's rescue, roaring one, twice, three times so loudly that the glass eyes of the Nonesuch almost fell out of her awful, withered face. And the spiteful ersatz mermaid slunk away.

Everyone else they met that night was very nice to Deidre.

'And so they should be,' Maude said, when the Dodo expressed surprise. 'I think you belong here as much as anyone. More than most, in some ways.'

'Really? Me?' asked Deidre. They were lolling on deckchairs on an upper gallery, eating marshmallows and sipping champagne, watching the party in the atrium below.

'Yes, you,' said Maude. 'You're the original and most obvious of the extinct creatures. I'm just rare and unusual. But you're really extinct, aren't you? Not a single scrap of you exists in the world. Well, apart from that daft beak of yours. You are the essence of this gathering of the lost. The epitome of gone-forever. And yet here you are. Having a lovely time. And I think that's pretty good going, don't you?'

'I do,' beamed Deidre, and burped.

Later, when the party was winding down and it was the early hours of Christmas morning they went up to the museum's rooftop to watch the snow falling on Paris. They stared at the frosty river and the towers of Notre Dame. And they watched as little groups of stuffed animals took to the air to float back home to the museums of the world. Off they went in fabulous dribs and drabs.

'If it's all the same to you, dear Maude, would you mind if we travelled back to Manchester the way we came? I was quite enjoying that hotel. And that wonderfully swooshy rainbow bath that lit up. And then, of course, there's breakfast...'

'Ooh, yes, breakfast,' rumbled Maude. 'Breakfast in Paris on Christmas Day. Caviar and salmon and strawberry jam. Oh yes. Let's not hurry home just yet…'

And so they stood together watching the extinct and rare creatures twirling away from the party. Light as snowflakes, fading in the dawn.

Klacky the Christmas Dragon

That Christmas dragon was useless because a) it was made out of cheap stuff, you could tell, and it only had two legs and b) dragons had very little to do with the Christmas spirit anyway.

From the weird hurdy-gurdy of the music you could tell those two guys were Eastern European or whatever, plus the way they were dancing (which Jeff said was a bit gay, too, laughing at them) so maybe they didn't know our customs, Mandy wondered? Anyhow, they'd got them all wrong.

Plus, she was being forced to watch them, stood out in the freezing drizzle while her mother dithered about inside the store, supposedly buying some kind of fancy biscuits that her friend in the Sheltered Housing Veronica liked. In a minute Mandy would tell Jeff to go in and fetch her (what were they even thinking of, letting Mum go drifting by herself?) but Jeff was in thrall to the Christmas dragon now, clapping his hands with the rest of the crowd gathering by the festive windows. The dragon was drawing a crowd, rubbish as he was.

Mandy sighed.

She'd definitely missed her works lunch by now. Here she was all togged up in the middle of the day. Her dress with the black and silver glitter (she had bauble-type earrings in her bag – she wouldn't be putting them on today.) The whole day had gone very awry and she was trying not to be furious.

'They're good, actually, aren't they?' Jeff was laughing and turning to her. First smile on him she'd seen all week. Now the dragon – really just some bloke in a red velveteen cape with ropes of tinsel flaring out from his neck – was twirling around and hopping about on one leg. Mandy urged him to slip and fall and break something. Let's see them all clapping along then, she thought.

Clack, clack, clack went his snakelike jaws. What were they made out of? It sounded like wood, as they clacked along with that disturbing music. And, under his tinsel antlers and his strange hat you couldn't even see his eyes. She shuddered. She hated the thing. And she hated his little gay mate, dancing alongside him with the fez full of money they'd collected and the ghetto blaster.

Did people still have ghetto blasters these days, or was it just beggars in the street? Come on Mum, she seethed, find those flipping biscuits.

*

It had been a long morning in the X-Ray department. Mum wasn't in pain anymore, or she didn't seem to be. In fact, it was like she was quite glad of all the attention as they sat there in those grey waiting rooms, one after the next, deeper and deeper in the hospital building, with nurses calling out her name every now and then and her perking up, 'Here!' and hurrying off with them to have her arm looked at and be generally fussed over.

Yes, she seemed to be quite full of herself today, did Mum, perched there in the natty white cardigan she'd been knitting herself (finishing it just in time for coming out today), The *People's Friend* splayed open on her lap and her ear cocked waiting to be called.

All morning Mandy had felt like slapping her. How dare she go clambering about in the attic while they were all out? How dare she go poking about through their things? She was a liability, is what she was. (She'd been living with her daughter and easy-going Jeff since August and it was a wonder she hadn't killed herself on the unfamiliar gadgets she liked to have a go on or with all her poking around where she shouldn't even be.)

And now, with her broken arm, she was mucking up Mandy's Christmas lunch with the girls from work. All the arrangements had gone to pot. Had the appointment taken only the half hour Mum's letter suggested, everything would have been fine. But it wasn't turning out like that and, as time swirled on, Mandy realized that the likelihood of her making it to *Sauce* in time had reduced to almost nothing.

At least she was already in her party dress and her hair and make-up were done.

She kept looking at her watch, which had been last year's present from Jeff. Not bad, actually. He must have had some advice. From a woman, probably. He wouldn't have picked this out by himself. It was too stylish and slinky to have caught his eye.

She watched him going through the Daily Mirror as they waited for her mum. What woman would have advised him about a watch? What women did he know? There was Cheryl on the phone at the garage, but that was about it. Mum didn't count, she had no taste for things.

Now Jeff was reading the problem page. Mandy saw the headline: 'He Prefers Porn to Bed Romps with Me.' What the devil was he reading that for? She coughed and spoke in that tight-lipped way she thought was appropriate for a waiting room like this, where you didn't want everyone knowing your business. 'I reckon she's got it wrong, you know, Jeff. You know what she's like.'

'Huh?' he emerged blinking from Dear Deirdre. Mandy wished he'd taken his anorak off before sitting down. He looked so hunched up.

'What she said before the nurse took her away. About that other doctor wanting to see her before she goes away today.' Mandy picked up her mother's magazine and started flicking through. 'She never gets anything straight. I'm sure they meant that she should see her doctor next time, not straight away. Later on, when it's settled down. What would be the point of seeing her twice in a day? Doesn't make sense.'

He shrugged. 'It's what she said.'

'She gets things wrong,' hissed Mandy, noticing a grumpy woman in a hajib paying close attention to their conversation. Mandy turned slightly to block her view and lowered her voice. 'She won't have understood what they were telling her.'

'We can check with the nurse at that window,' muttered Jeff.

'And,' Mandy went on. 'She's on about us taking her to Veronica's after she's done here. And picking up something from town beforehand. Biscuits or something. Our morning's gone.'

'Probaby,' Jeff said.

'She gets it all upside down. What was she even looking in our attic for, anyway?'

'Your old decorations,' said Jeff. 'From when you were little.'

'She told you that?' Mandy snorted, picking at the glitter on her dress. 'They're long gone. Why would she even think they were up there? She gets it all wrong. Everything's upside down. She confuses everyone with her going on. It's like these people here today. She's gone for her X-Ray now, and what's the point of that after they've already put the plaster on her? It's all the wrong way round and it's bound to be her fault. And it isn't because she's old. She was always like that. Watch out, here she comes.'

The old woman returned, smiling, fresh from her X-Ray. Her new white cardigan was really getting on Mandy's nerves. The way one sleeve was rolled to the elbow to accommodate the new pot on her wrist seemed to be deliberately drawing attention to the injury she had suffered in Mandy's house. Next thing there'd be social services banging on their door, claiming she was being maltreated.

Her smile was so brave and gentle Mandy felt herself growing incensed. She glanced at her watch with the elegant chain.

'I am to see the doctor again,' Mum announced. 'I didn't get it wrong, Mandy. He wants to look at me before we leave.'

'Never mind,' Jeff said, rolling his paper. 'Do we need to go back to the first waiting room?'

Mum nodded, wincing at the weight of the plaster.

'I don't understand why he needs to see you again,' Mandy said, as they shuffled out.

'He just does,' said Mum.

Jeff winked at Mandy. 'I think you can whistle for your works lunch, love.'

'Works lunch' sounded so common. They'd booked a table at *Sauce*, for heaven's sake.

*

Now it was way too late.

She had passed the point of being hungry and her mood was ruined by all her mum's carry on. Also, she had freezing drizzle in her hair and she could feel rain dripping down the back of her Christmas frock.

And Jeff was clapping even more heartily at the antics of that ludicrous dragon. They all were. Egging him on. Cheering and hooting.

Even more ridiculous, one of the store managers had emerged with a tablet he was holding up, video recording the proceedings. He was standing quite close to Mandy, fiddling with the buttons of his machine, shaking with laughter at the clacking dragon.

It wasn't *that* funny, was it?

The tinsel and baubles on the dragon's outfit were cheap ones like she remembered from being a kid. Nasty, sharp, old-fashioned things. Now she could see his eyes, after all. Revolving, spiral eyes, just like a snake's.

There was a new volley of cheers and laughter then, as the gathered crowd noticed something Mandy hadn't yet. Jeff was nudging her and going, 'Look! Look!'

It still wasn't hilarious, she thought. Even when she saw that the window display behind Klacky and his friend was filling up with shop workers.

At first she thought they were fiddling with the window display – the fake emerald trees and the angular shop dummies – but they weren't. The staff members were wearing party hats and they were walking along jerkily.

Mandy realized they were dancing. They were doing the same dancing as Klacky and his friend.

'Hahahahaha!' went the manager from the shop, trying to hold his tablet computer straight.

Jeff was laughing just as loudly. 'Look at them! They're joining in! Hahahahaha!'

Mandy still didn't see what was so hilarious.

'It's great, isn't it?' the manager called across to Jeff. 'That dragon thing has been there since the start of Christmas. Klacky, they call him. This is our tribute to him and his mate.'

More staff members were climbing into the window display and copying the dragon's dance moves. A great roar of approval went up from the crowd of shoppers, who stood watching, grinning in the rain.

Mandy thought it might offend Klacky, actually, and his mate. Really, the shop staff were taking the mick, weren't they? They were mocking the gay way those two were dancing and making it look stupid. It was probably their traditional dancing, from the land of wherever Christmas dragons belong...

Just at that moment she saw the dragon's snakelike head and his whole body freeze on the spot and do a sudden double-take. The man inside the outfit stopped prancing and flouncing for a moment or two, and so did his chum.

They were riveted by the sight of the shop display.

At least twenty staff members were crammed inside there, doing the Klacky dance and beaming, being filmed by their manager. There were even some customers in there too, joining in.

Klacky gave a little hop, and then a hoot of pleasure (Yes, definitely foreign, Mandy thought.) Then he started dancing even faster, more ferociously, whirling around, flaring his cape with extra vigour. His friend did likewise.

It was clear they were over the moon at the tribute from the department store staff.

'Hahahahaha!' went Jeff.

Mandy thought they all looked insane, those shop people: wearing party hats and strings of tinsel round their necks; dancing like Klacky the dragon. Worst of all were the customers in their heavy coats, still clutching their bags of shopping, thinking they were having a good time and being amusing.

It was at this precise moment that Mandy saw her mother. There was no mistaking her. She was right in the middle of the window in her white cardigan, one sleeve bunched over the end of her plaster cast. She was kicking up her legs along with everybody else and waving her good arm in the air.

Mandy's mouth hung open like the mechanism inside her had snapped.

Soon enough the moment was over and the staff left the window and went back to work. Their boss filmed the chuckling crowd filling Klacky's fez with coins, and then he too returned to the store.

Jeff turned to Mandy. Her voice came out, when it did, quite high-pitched, 'Did you see that..?'

He shrugged and smiled and glanced at his watch. 'If we hurry maybe you can make it to *Sauce* in time for the sweet course?'

Mandy's mum came flying out of the store, breathless and brandishing a box of fancy biscuits. 'Got them! We can go! Come on you, too. Stop dawdling! We need to get a shift on!'

Behind them the jaunty music came back on, even louder, and Klacky started dancing all over again.

The Nightingale of Planet 12

There wasn't much to listen to on Planet 12.

It was mostly a howling wilderness and the settlers stayed inside protective domes most days. Not because it was deadly, but because it was deadly dull.

The atmospheric conditions crackled and buzzed, filling everyone's ears with harsh static. Communications anywhere beyond the valley were sporadic and dreadful with interference.

The distant mountains were beautiful, though, and the skies were spectacularly colourful. Scarlet and golden.

But pretty skies and gorgeous landscapes didn't keep you fed and they couldn't make you happy forever.

The settlers were bored.

Their captain – he called himself Emperor Smith these days, just to cheer himself up – became an impatient and tetchy old man.

'Why did we come here? Why did we ever volunteer?'

His wife scowled. 'Stop going on! Shut up! Stop talking!'

His wife had had the most awful headache, ever since their arrival on Planet 12 thirty-three years ago.

Everyone – even the Emperor – tiptoed around her.

Then... one day...

They heard the nightingale.

*

They knew there were birds on this world but no one had ever seen them. Long-range sensors showed that there were verdant forests and woodlands on the other side of the planet, far away beyond the gorgeously craggy mountains... and presumably that's where all the avian life was concentrated.

The settlers had plonked themselves down in the least hospitable spot, of course.

'I know, I know,' the Emperor sighed, when someone pointed this out for the millionth time. 'But how were we to know? We decided on this valley because of the mineral deposits.' All the fuel they'd ever need was concentrated here, and it came in the form of many-hued jewels littering the valley floor.

Their Starship had been irreparably damaged in landing, and it would never lift itself into the skies again.

Parties had set out on foot from this valley, in an attempt to spread out across Planet 12 to explore… but they had never been heard from since.

All in all, a bit of a mistake, landing here, all that time ago. They might have enough energy, and lots of pretty jewels, but it was boring. They scraped along, merely existing… getting on each other's nerves. Two-hundred and twenty human beings… having a terrible time on a barely-habitable alien world.

Occasionally they got messages from Earth, where things were much worse. But even dreadful news cheered up the Emperor only slightly.

*

Then one day the nightingale came to sing outside his private dome.

Emperor Smith raised his head from his silken pillow and his eyes bulged out in amazement. 'What is that..?'

It was a whisper of music. A gentle, fluting breeze.

He got out of bed and followed it...

It was a bubbling, mellifluous stream of music. It was like nothing the Emperor had ever heard... At least, perhaps, he had once heard something like it a very long time ago. Back on Earth, maybe, when he was a child...

It was a still, warm day. It was safe to emerge from the dome.

The Emperor Smith stepped into the private garden that had been built in order to please his wife. Such a lot of careful, dedicated work had gone into creating this garden of jeweled stones. Pathways and rockeries had been carefully arranged and tended. But the Empress rarely bothered to sit out here, even when the weather was fine. She preferred to stay indoors listening to old recordings of what life had been like on her home planet. She locked herself away wearing a huge set of earphones, pining for the life they had left far behind.

The Emperor rather enjoyed the peacefulness of the little garden, however.

And, so, it seemed, did the nightingale, who had, for some reason, chosen to pay a visit.

*

The Emperor dashed and fluttered around his closest advisors. 'Come and see, come and hear... You won't believe it...!'

None of them had seen their leader as excited as this in years. He shuffled and twitched and beetled about.

'Come with me... out here! Out in the garden..!'

His most trusted team of advisors. There were three of them, each almost as old as he was himself. They had been together so long. They had dreamed and hoped together. They had despaired in deep space and shivered together through meteor showers and solar flares. They had braved long nights on an alien world when they had no idea if there'd be a new dawn for them to greet. Gradually they had grown old together, getting used to the idea that their adopted world was a let-down. They had already exhausted all the novelty it had to offer.

'But listen to this...!' urged Emperor Smith, and they went out into the pleasant morning, crunching over the gravel lawn.

A single, leafless tree. Gnarled and twisted. It was rare and precious in the valley. It was a wonder it was even alive.

It was the only perch for about a hundred thousand miles in any one direction.

And the nightingale had found it.

The bird blinked at its audience.

'Please,' said the Emperor, and his advisors were surprised by his pleading tone. 'Please... sing for them, like you sang for me.'

'It's such a dowdy, drab little thing,' thought the Emperor's chief advisor. 'Why, if we cooked and roasted it, there'd be slim pickings indeed...'

And the bird opened his beak to sing.

*

'Sweetheart, sweetheart,' gabbled the old man. He reached out and tried to take his wife's headphones from her ears.

She shrieked like he was stabbing her. 'What are you doing?' She batted him away. 'Get off me, you old fool!'

'You must come and hear...' he gasped. 'Come and listen to this bird...'

She seized hold of her headphones and sighed. What was he talking about? Why was he angling for her attention now? She glared at him, up and down.

How strange. She'd never seen him looking so animated in years. Something had clearly happened.

Which was very odd. Because nothing ever happened on Planet 12. They had spent thirty-three years absorbing this fact.

'A bird is singing in our garden... so beautifully...!'

'A bird?' she said, and the idea was so intriguing that she left her Earth recordings behind, for just a few minutes. Probably the old man had it all wrong. His mind was addled, obviously.

*

But he was quite correct.

The Empress of Planet 12 stood there in raptures.

'Oh, listen! Just listen...!'

None of them had ever heard anything quite like it.

Trilling. Warbling. So high, so pure. It made them feel heavy, debased. It made them feel claylike and cloddy. That something so delicate and airy and perfect could exist within reach of their ears. That it was happy to sit there and air its song for them like this... for nothing. Just for nothing. It wasn't gaining a thing. It was simply passing on delight.

The Empress stood there for some minutes with her mouth wide open.

Then her eyes blazed and she sprang into action.

'What are you doing? All of you? Are you all frozen? Are you dumbstruck?'

The advisors and lackeys looked at her.

'Recording equipment! Fetch it at once! Bring out the very best equipment we have! Get this wonderful music onto tape! It's wasting away! It's leaking into the air and will soon be gone forever! Oh, quickly! Quickly! Before it's too late..!'

The men hastened into action, and the bird went on singing, and the Emperor Smith was in two minds about what his wife was saying. All her panic and kerfuffle was disturbing the mood somewhat. She was agitated. She was flummoxing. He'd asked her to come out here and listen, quietly, just as he was doing. Surely they could stand here, listening quietly together? Why was she being so noisy?

*

Minutes later the advisors returned, all of a-stumble, with recording equipment on a squeaking trolley. They came lumbering and lurching. Shoving each other. All of them were keen to please the bad-tempered Empress.

Hmm, thought Emperor Smith vaguely. Time was, everyone tried to please me.

He shut out all their hullaballoo, and turned back to look at the nightingale.

The bird had paused in its song.

The noise had alarmed it.

The bird blinked at the Emperor once.

And then it took off.

It shot into the beautiful skies and was gone.

'Gaaagghhh!' shrieked the Empress. A very ugly noise. She whirled round and accused the advisors. 'You took too long! You scared it with all your noise! Did you record any of that? Did you get a single second of it?'

They shook their heads and mumbled.

'Typical!' she roared.

*

The Emperor kept listening.

While the rest of his people went about their daily work, he kept patient and somehow he knew that if he was quiet the bird would come back again and sing for him.

Not for the others, though. He had seen the startled look in the nightingale's eye when the others were carrying on...

The Empress went back to her room and put her headphones back on, transporting herself back into the crackles and murmurs that hailed from many light years away.

The Emperor sat in his garden of stones, waiting.

Days passed.

Comments were passed.

Questions were asked.

The Emperor... could he possibly be losing his marbles, sitting outside the domes at all hours?

The Empress was past caring. They didn't share their lives any more, not really. That spark had gone out, a long time ago.

But she thought about that snatch of song she had heard.

It played upon her, even as she immersed herself in otherworldly sounds.

She asked the advisors... could there be... somewhere... in all the many thousands of hours of recordings in the archive... just a snippet of nightingale song? Or something like it?

She couldn't sleep. She was agitated. It would soothe her, she thought. Just that little bit she had heard in the garden of stones... it was the most lovely thing she had ever experienced. It made her feel calm. Made her feel less disappointed in everything.

And meanwhile her husband sat quietly listening as the nightingale came back and sang to him.

His heart leapt with joy when it did so.

A fine reunion.

He hardly dared breathe as he watched it alight on the branch beside him.

It trilled, it sang, it unfolded a song so bright and perfect it made the old man weep silent tears.

It was just as beautiful as the first visit.

Somehow... it was true... and the Emperor never quite knew how this was so... but the nightingale was telling him about the world beyond this pebble garden, beyond these plastic domes and far beyond this valley of jewels.   Somehow the bird was telling him about the whole of Planet 12.

Lands. Cities. History. Fables.

Whole vistas opened up before the Emperor.

Not a word was spoken.

Tears streamed down his face.

How long did he sit there?

No one came to interrupt. No one dared.

At length the nightingale broke off, and flew away.

The Emperor jumped to his feet: 'No, don't... not yet! Not yet...!'

There was never enough time.

Never enough song.

*

That evening. Eating rubber cubes of artificial food in their dome. Emperor and Empress chewing away, as on so many nights before. Drawing sustenance, sharing what might have been quality time. But he was in another world. Thinking of all he had experienced. And she was eaten up with furious envy.

'It came back, didn't it? It sang to you?'

He looked at his Empress and nodded.

'Why didn't you tell me? Why did you sit there alone?'

He had no answer for her. There was no answer. Only: I didn't want to share that little bird's song with you. I wanted it for myself alone.

*

So his wife made other plans.

They were talented people, those who lived in the domes. They had talents going to waste in the hardscrabble of everyday endurance on Planet 12. What about art and artifacts? What about fashioning stuff of exquisite beauty? What about making something lovely for a change?

She asked her subjects to make her a nightingale of her very own.

'But don't tell the Emperor,' she warned them. 'He doesn't like to think of anyone else spending time in idle pleasures...'

And so the robotic experts and the geniuses with tiny, tricky bits of electronics set to work… and they created her a perfect bird of her very own.

Bigger, flashier, more gorgeous than anything that had ever set foot in the garden of stones.

They encrusted it with jewels of every colour, handpicked from the valley.

It was all gold and silver and sparkling crystals.

And it trilled and it sang…

Endlessly.

Perpetually.

Forevermore.

Some clever soul in the Empress's staff had found a recording of a nightingale from Planet Earth. A bird that had been dead for many hundreds of years. And yet its song was just as bright and colourful.

And when it was piped through the open beak of that artificial bird… Why, how convincing it was!

The Emperor didn't think so, though.

'That thing? Pitiful!'

He laughed hollowly and walked away. He shook his head and tutted.

The Empress fumed.

The Emperor sat in the stone garden and waited for his real nightingale to return. There could be no simulacrum. Only the real thing would do.

But nights were colder now, as the seasons of Planet 12 were changing. Ice crept into the garden of stones. It wasn't wise to stay out of the domes too late. But the Emperor wouldn't listen to his advisors.

His nightingale still came. Less regularly, and staying fewer minutes each time it visited. It seemed distracted, eager to be off, perhaps.

Its songs spoke of warmer climes elsewhere. The songs were about travelling farther afield on Planet 12.

The Emperor hoped that his bird would stay close. He hoped and hoped, but he knew what was going to happen.

And whenever he stepped back inside his domed palace all he could hear was the mindless, chiming nonsense of the Empress's artificial bird.

How hollow. How callow.

How wrong.

And then, once day, his nightingale failed to show up.

And the next it didn't appear either.

And the next.

An awful, chilling thought plagued the Emperor. The nightingale has heard the false song within the dome. He has learned that my people are enthralled by the Empress's ersatz nightingale.

And it was true that they – with their cheaper tastes – seemed to prefer that gold and silver bird with rubies, sapphires and diamonds stuck all over it. A bird that sang to order. Who sang the same sweet song again and again, never tiring, never flagging. Never taking it upon itself to fly away.

A biddable bird, who sang with cloying sweetness.

Of course they preferred such a wondrous toy.

The Empress was most satisfied.

Her husband wept privately over the loss of his drab, exquisite visitor.

Then he took to his bed and felt like dying.

And he almost did.

*

His wife saw what was happening to him. He was losing hope. He was giving up the ghost. The thought that she might lose him filled her with remorse.

'I have neglected him,' she confided to her nightingale. 'All these years I have let us grow apart. I have let my impatience show. I made no secret of the dissatisfaction I have felt in our shared life… And now I feel ashamed.'

The old man was listless. He lay on his satin pillows in his little cabin and nothing could tempt him out.

The Empress's nightingale listened to her woes with its head cocked. But it didn't suggest anything. It didn't have any ideas. It just sang its song. The same song over, endlessly, exactly.

The Empress commanded that the rarest and fanciest of their food supplies be opened up. She would tempt her husband into eating again. Real food. Tinned stuffs from earth. Meat and vegetables. Pickles and brine preserving all kinds of wonderful delicacies. 'What were we saving all this for, anyhow?' she wondered. 'A celebration on a happier day? What was it all for?'

He was fading away. His skin was translucent. She tried to count up on her fingers how old he was, and she was and how old they all were. But they had been through space warps and time wefts and all manner of distortions on the way to Planet 12. The Empress didn't understand any of it. Perhaps they were all too old, now. Perhaps their time was over?

Another winter advanced and came calling on their cluster of plastic domes. The Earth people battened down the hatches and sealed themselves tight. The stone garden was raked away by the claws of the freezing winds.

The Emperor woke in the night, screaming and sobbing. He clung to her when she went to calm him down. He said he would never be warm, never feel safe. He would never know peace again. All he could hear was the screeching of the wind through the mountain passes.

The advisors tutted and shook their heads. Emperor Smith was in a bad way. The should have seen this coming. That strange attachment he had, earlier this year... listening to that bird. Sitting in the garden. Why had none of them realized? His mind was gone.

But the Empress wouldn't believe that. She thought they were ungrateful.

'None of us would be alive without him,' she reminded them. 'His leadership. His knowledge. His determination... We all owe him so much...'

And she went to sit by his bedside as he turned over and over, gibbering and moaning.

She took her false nightingale with her and wound it up so it would sing to the Emperor.

He sat up, staring in wonder at the gorgeous effigy.

'How very kind you are,' he told her. 'To share your toy with me. To let me hear its music.'

His eyes and voice were earnest. There wasn't a trace of sarcasm there.

'I do like it,' he told her. 'I do. It's a lovely song. It's really delightful.'

She smiled. She was glad to have pleased him. 'Then I'll leave it with you through the night. Perhaps its song will drown out the howling wind and the noise of the storm...'

He smiled at her. How strange and wonderful. For the two of them to be kind to each other like this, so late in the day. Kinder than they had been to each other for years. She tiptoed away and he listened to the chiming and ticking of the toy bird's song. He watched its crystal feathers gleaming as it twitched and flinched. Not a single thought in its head.

'Forgive me,' he told the nightingale that belonged to his wife. 'I know you're trying your best. And so is she, perhaps.'

He got out of bed shakily, unsteadily making his way out of his room and through his private dome.

No one was about. No one stayed awake in the night.

Sensors monitored the storms, raging outside above the mountains.

The million separate, delicate instruments of the domes quivered and traced every particle of what went on outside, and collated the information into wonderfully colourful graphs. Someone might look at them in a few days' time, and pass a jaundiced, expert eye over them. All very interesting. Chilly and noisy and not very hospitable.

The dome dwellers would see the winter through by popping on their headphones and listening to recordings from home. There were many thousands of hours to get through. Someone had done the sums. Even if you lived to be one hundred and seventy-three, you'd never run out of recordings from Earth.

It just so happened that was almost exactly Emperor Smith's age.

What if I let myself out of my dome, he wondered? What if, when no one was watching, I opened this door and slipped away into the storm?

How long would I last?

The wind might tear me apart. The noise of the storm might deafen me.

I'd surely perish on the mountain slopes.

But somewhere north, over the mountains, we know there are woods. We've seen them. We've detected them. Even if we've never actually been there.

Why didn't we ever go there? When we were younger and strong and capable? What stopped us going to look?

He couldn't even remember why that was.

We should have gone.

'Sweetheart..?'

It was the Empress.

She'd not called him that for a long time.

'It's all right,' he told her.

'W-why are you standing by the door?'

She thought he was going to leave. She thought he was going to act on his impulse and totter out into the storm.

'Nowhere, my dear. Honestly. I just had to get up for a moment... but now, I'm ready to return to sleep.'

'Let me help you,' she said, leading him away from the doors and danger. 'Let me put you back to bed. And let me wind up the bird. Let's hear his song again. It seems to calm you... it seems to make you happy...'

'It does,' he smiled and nodded. 'It really does. You know, I think it's just about as good as the real thing...'

Mrs Frimbly's Festive Diary

1

21ST December

I've been putting together a few festive treats, just in case You Know Who comes back.

The past couple of Christmases I haven't heard from him, but he's bound to return soon, isn't he? Happenstance Village was where he loved coming home to at Christmas, he always used to say.

I've been across the green to the village store and I bought some nuts. Just a plain bag of mixed nuts. And some satsumas. I'm toying with the idea of doing my special stewed prunes again. He did admire them.

That Deidre Whatsit stopped me on my way back. Full of the joys, as per usual. Her face all aglow. She says she hopes I'll join them for some eggnog on Christmas Eve. Just like last year. She and Tish Madoc, her snooty so-called cousin (who lives in with her) haven't seen much of me lately, says she. Yes, I thought, and there's a reason for that.

I've kept out of their way since Tish published her silly novel about us all. 'Romance in the Milky Way' indeed. I'm only relieved no sensible publisher would touch it and I'm not forced to see the ghastly thing when I go to the library or peruse the paperback carousel at the post office. Tish Madoc had absolutely no right to novelise our strange adventures in space and she knows it. It caused a proper rift between Mike and her. Put the kybosh on their blooming romance, or whatever kind of ménage was going on next door. Well, naturally it did. He's military, isn't he? Signed the official secrets act back in 1971 when they found lizard men living under Wenley Moor, did Mike, or so he told me. Everything's on a need-to-know basis with him and he doesn't want it all written about and published as an e-book, does he? We've seen neither hide nor hair of him in Happenstance since Tish's launch at the village hall.

What's that funny buzzing? I've been hearing it all day. Something electrical. Not insects. Definitely not hornets. No, it's like a hairdryer's been left on in a distant room. Or the speakers on a faulty gramophone.

A deep humming note.

Oh, but the cottage is quiet.

Funny, I've felt all day like someone's watching me. I've been scrubbing out my smalls and it's like someone's looking right over my shoulder. My hackles have gone up.

2

22nd December

Snow on the green today, and all over the hedgerows. I put on a festive record to cheer the place up and wondered about trimming a tree. I never bothered last year. All the decorations are gathering dust in the attic and if that's not symbolic I don't know what is.

Saw the vicar on my way to the butcher's. I've put my name down for a big bird. In a fit of optimism I plumped for a whole turkey. Surely there'll be surprise company this year. Surely there will?

You know, I think there will be. I can feel it in

my water.

The vicar asked if I'd be coming to the pantomime on Boxing Day. He's wearing that woebegone look, like I let them all down by not taking part this year. Well, they can lump it. Fenella Frimbly can't be at everyone's beck and call. I had to stay here, didn't I? I couldn't be out gallivanting and rehearsing every night and running up costumes for Sleeping Beauty. My duty is to be here, at the cottage. Waiting for the call to arms. Sooner or later the Master's going to turn up, out of the blue, and need me. I just know it.

I gave the vicar short shrift and came home to get on with my rough puff pastry. That got rid of a few of my frustrations, walloping that lot about. I made two dozen mince pies. Far too many. I imagine they'll all go stale like last year's did.

Strange. I can hear that electronical noise again. And a smell... there's a smell like burning wires. I went round checking all the sockets and fuses, but I can't see anything amiss. Then I went to sit back by the fire and poured myself a little sherry. I've been knitting the longest scarf you ever saw. Just in case.

3

23rd December

There was a thump at the door very early on. I was up and mopping the floors. I heard the letterbox rattle and thought: that's curiously early. I never went running. Let them wait.

I forgot about it and later, passing through the hallway I saw there was a little card shoved under the door. Another takeaway opened up, I thought. Or hate mail.

But it wasn't. It was like computer print-out lettering. It read:

'Mistress. I knocked but you were out. This unit will call again.'

This unit, I thought? What the devil's that about? And why are they calling me mistress?

I felt a bit cross and – I must say – rather

nervous. I've reached a point in life where I don't want
or like new and unexpected things.

4

24th December

I surprise them all at The Hollyhocks next door. And I
actually turn up. I even put a nice dress on for them,
and a bit of lipstick.

Tish Madoc opens the door and her eyebrows
go up. 'We didn't think you would, my dear!'

'Well, here I am,' say I stiffly, and push a half-
empty bottle of Tio Pepe into her arms.

It's ever so festive in there. Deirdre Whatsit is
wearing a summer frock and everyone's got party hats
on. It's very noisy and jolly and they're full of talk about
the pantomime and other goings-on around
Happenstance. I start to regret being so distant of late.
I've been cutting myself off.

There's a lot of talk about that curious occasion, two Christmases ago, when the whole of our village was transported to a far distant planet. And then it got brought home again at the start of the new year. People talk about it in hushed tones and eye me through the press of bodies in Deirdre's living room. I can see them doing it. They think they're space travelers. They know I know more about the whole business than they ever will.

See? I stand apart from everyone else. My adventures in the universe make me different to them all.

Tish Madoc brings over some nibbles from the buffet and corners me. She wants to know all about the other adventures. The ones I never talk about. She's avid for impossible details. And I think, well I'm hanged if I'm telling you anything. Just so you can write another of one of your silly e-books. I've seen her sitting in the conservatory at the back of Deirdre's. You can see right in from the back of Baker's End. Tish Madoc at her electronic typewriter, writing e-books and smoking e-cigarettes.

Is it her electronic typewriter I've been hearing, I wonder? Has it become louder, somehow? Or is it... and this seems absurd even as I think it... is it somehow creeping round my door of its own volition and trying to get in? Is her typewriter as keen as she is on getting hold of my stories of outer space?

They all wish it had been them. The villagers all saw a little bit of adventurousness in Time and Space that Christmas and, even though they were terrified and thought they'd never get home, they still want more.

But that magic has gone. Those chances have fled.

I slip out of the party at the Hollyhocks as it starts getting rowdy. Deirdre cranks up the sound on her stereo and they roll up the rug in the living room and they're starting to dance.

Jitterbugging about.

And I go home.

I go in through the back kitchen. As soon as I'm in there, clicking on the light, I know I'm not alone at Baker's End.

If my hair wasn't in this bun it would all be standing on end, I can tell you.

I know what having intruders is like. I've had aliens and ghosts and metals trespassing in here. I keep a cricket bat under the sink, ready to wallop them. As I hug it to my chest I move carefully towards the main sitting and dining room. I can hear that queer electronical noise again.

'Regrets, mistress,' pipes a high, tinny voice. 'You were not in and so I had to melt the front door lock.'

I stare and stare and still the thing doesn't make any sense.

It's a metal dog on the flagstones in front of the stove. Looking up at me with glowing eyes.

'Keep back,' I brandish the cricket bat at him.

He seems to frown and take a step closer.

'Mistress, violence is not necessary. I mean you no harm.'

'What are you? Who sent you? And where do you come from?' But even as I bark out these questions I realise I already know the answers.

5

Later

It's Christmas Eve and I am alone. I draw all the curtains and shut out the noise of the warbling, awful carol singers on the Green. I light the fire and microwave myself some scrambled eggs.

He won't have a dish of water or any kind of food. He says he doesn't need it.

I sit down in the chair by the hearth and stare at him. 'Well, then. How is he?'

'Do you mean in the time period relative to the Mistress or to this unit?' says the dog-thing, and I don't know what he means.

'Is he well? Since he was last here, I mean...'

The dog looks helpless. 'I don't know,' he says.

All night the dog roves about the house, sniffing in cupboards and hunting through drawers. When I lie in my bed up in the attic I can hear wooden doors crashing, and then the unearthly buzz as he floats up the staircases. He's prying into every room. Before I went to bed he wouldn't tell me what he was looking for.

He showed some interest in the old books my Master keeps in his study. Those lurid books he had delivered from Ebay. 'Ah, not just ordinary Ebay, Frimbly,' he beamed at me as the curious-looking postman came up the garden path. 'Ebay in a different dimension, slightly tangential to this one.'

Those are the books the dog unit set about scanning with his red laser eye. Took him a good couple of hours. I left him to it and went to bed. Happy Christmas Fenella, I thought.

6
LATER

I'm sitting up in bed and at first it's like the devil himself has come into my room. I let out a shriek before

I realise it's that blessed metal dog.

'Forgive me, mistress,' he says in that strange, polite voice, and then, all of a sudden it's like he's reading my mind.

No, more than that.

I can see my past floating out in front of me. Like ectoplasm.

Long time since I saw ectoplasm. All that floaty, nasty stuff, like candy floss but with a supernatural aspect.

Not since the days of Mr Frimbly. Not since him. And his blessed peripatetic spiritualist church.

And I can see him now. High up in the cab of that van, with me at his side, chugging through the winding roads of Norfolk, visiting each small village in turn. I was his unwilling helpmeet. I wanted nothing to do with all that dark stuff. Turning up in villages and calling up the dead. Scaring the locals out of their skins when all they wanted was a bit of peace and reassurance.

He was a devil, Mr Frimbly. I've tried for so long to forget him.

Why's this metal dog reminding me?

He's perching on the bedclothes. He's resting on the candlewick bedspread. Somehow that impassive face of his looks regretful. He's sorry for making me relive moments from my dreadful past.

I see the day that I left Mr Frimbly. That terrible day when the old man tried to stop me. When I smashed his crystal ball and he howled like all the demons in hell were after him. He went running into the sea and I never stopped him.

When they dragged him back up the shingle the next morning his eyes were gone. The Cromer police were horrified.

I knew already though, that Mr Frimbly had never had no eyes.

Not in his head.

The metal dog shows me – pictures coming through that glimmering, pinkish cloud that hovers over my bed – how I found happiness of a sort. Living in that little town. Finding a job in that museum. How it became like a palace to me. I was so proud of being in charge of all the Curiosities.

This creature must be a spirit to know all of this. And to know about the eyes of Mr Frimbly. Mechanical or not, he must be a hound from hell. Made of minerals and metals forged by the spirits down below.

'Get out! Get out!' I shriek at him and the dog stares at me sadly.

Then he turns and glides out of the attic room.

Dawn's coming up. It's Christmas morning out there but I find myself still stuck inside the faraway past.

7

Christmas Day

Even with all the goings-on in the night I'm feeling unusually festive when I go downstairs on Christmas morning. I shall treat myself to hedgerow jam on my toast and cream in my coffee. Let's push the boat out.

In a way, it would be nice if there was a knock

at the door and someone was calling. It would be lovely to have a surprise.

Down in the dining room before the hearth that strange devil dog is waiting to greet me. Cheery tone as he wishes me a Merry Christmas. Taking me aback somewhat.

I make coffee on the stove and when I return he's looking at those books again. I sit and watch him. He uses a fuzzy kind of torch beam that comes out of his nose to turn the page and memorize everything he sees.

They look like kids' books to me. Lurid illustrations. Very peculiar stories. They remind me of the only book I had as a child – The Wonder Book. I haven't thought of that in years. Its cover was black and gold and I used to polish it up, I was so proud of having a book of my own.

'Shall I read to you?' asks the metal dog.

'Why not?' I smile and sip my cooling coffee. The Master used to sit here and tell me outlandish tales, whenever the mood took him. Outrageous things he claimed had happened to him on the journeys he

made into the Omniverse in the days before he knew me or the days when he slipped off and left me here to mind the cottage.

The dog tells me about a queer kind of place. A world the Master once visited with his young friends. A world where the men went off to live in the jungle. They actually lived within the fleshy leaves of huge cabbages. They were hiding from the women, who had turned rebellious and noisy, having fallen under the influence of a terrible yellowish-green monster. It was a cloud of vapour that approached from the horizon under a sky the colour of tomato soup.

'The Sinisterest Sponge!' I interrupt excitedly. And then I roll my eyes. 'Oh, I know all about that awful old thing. The Master brought one back in his infernal space machine and kept it in the downstairs bathroom for more than a month. He was supposed to be returning it to its own dimension, somewhere or other. Then he forgot all about it and the ghastly thing just hung there behind the shower curtain in a horrible mood. I had to clean up after the wretched monster. Even after it had tried to take over my mind…'.

The fire crackles and the grandfather clock ticks. It must be telling the wrong time. Surely it's later than six in the morning. Outside it's light, but a very muzzy, unclear sort of light that sparkles the frost. There's no one out and about. The windows around the village green are all dark still.

The dog is telling me a tale about a world of spiders. They were bigger than even the spiders of the sapphire world. And what's worse, these spiders of Perigross had large, staring eyes for bodies. They built webs inside intricate, slime-filled jungles and they lured their victims by mesmerizing them with their spiraling irises. Their victims walk straight down a dark, all-seeing tunnel into the mind of the spider itself... And there they find – rather unusually - a sofa and a television set. And on the television set plays a series of films encompassing their whole lives and everything they ever did wrong...

'Yes,' I murmur. 'I think I've heard of them... I think we even went to see the Eye-Spiders of Perigross once, the Master and I...'

But the dog has moved on and he's describing

the shrieking Sko-Cat: a creature made of bricks that floated through space boasting on many frequencies. And the Master's friend Swee, who'd gone to the bad. Like so many old friends who've gone to the bad. And wasn't it me – Fenella Frimbly - standing in that alien desert, looking up to see the face of a Sphinx and realizing the thing was alive? Then it woke and looked down at me with the oldest eyes imaginable and I felt so tiny, having these adventures in space.

Do I remember these things because I was there, or do I just remember the Master's voice telling me all about them? We were sitting in front of this fire when he told me improbable stuff and I always scoffed, though I knew there was a germ of truth in everything he said. But maybe I actually was there in the psychic jungle with his friend who looked like a cheetah? And I was in the Neuronic Nightmare world ruled by the man whose face was on fire. And the blue baboons who flew about the place on ships that looked like spoons and I laughed at first when I saw them and the Master said: hush! We're at the very edge of the universe and those are the Thousand and One Doors to Elsewhere, Mrs

Frimbly.

Or was I just here at Baker's End? Peeling spuds, carrying out the rubbish and feeding the rabbits?

All at once the dog jerks into life. He's off. The books he's spread out on the floor slam shut of their own accord and he reverses across the stone flags, back into the hall. He bumps into the elephant foot umbrella stand and opens the front door wide.

'Mistress Frimbly!' the dog calls me, and I hurry to catch up as he sets off down the garden path into the crisp morning. I'm on his trail, into the lane, and my slippered feet hardly touch the ground.

'Dog? Where are we going?'

Now he's running across the Green and the frost crackles underfoot

'He's back! Our Master's back! On Christmas Day, as well! And he's come back for us in his space machine..!'

The Dog is gliding and I'm accelerating too… Nothing aches. Nothing breaks.

I'm running and laughing just like I used to

when I was a girl.

The Christmas Trilobite

Knock knock.

Scritchy-scratch.

Thump thump thump.

It's 5.15 am – who *is* that?

Can't be the cat. He's already pushed his paws
into my face and clicked his claws on my pillowcase.
He's already woken me up and made me go
downstairs to feed him. So *who* is this, knocking on
the bedroom door?

There's a hard frost outside. The first dark
morning of December. White Rabbits! Open the first
little door on the calendar.

Oh no! It's the Christmas Trilobite.

What? There's no such thing.

Is there?

He comes skittering into the room on his long
insect legs.

'Hey, Paul! Remember me? From when you
were a kid? Wasn't I your favourite? Get up out of
that bed and talk to me!'

This is what it's like when something takes hold of you before it's even light. I go through to my study, pulling on my dressing gown. The house is chilly and I sit at my desk.

He jumps onto my laptop and preens beneath the spotlight of my anglepoise.

There can be no doubt about it.

He's definitely a Trilobite.

He smells funny – crabsticks? Lobster bisque?

'Look, kidda,' he says, being serious. 'You remember me. Now I'm calling on a favour from you. I want my very own Christmas story. Make it happen, can't you?'

*

As it happens, I *do* remember the Trilobite. He was in one of the first books I remember reading.

When I was very small we lived in Peterlee, in an estate of boxy houses set upon a hillside. Every time we went to the grocery shop my mam would buy me a new book. She couldn't afford it, but we loved reading them together.

For some reason, the Trilobite stood out for me in the book about Prehistoric Life. There he was, back in the Early Cambrian period, 521 million years ago, when the sea was azure and gorgeous. All the other deep sea creatures looked like twirly sundaes and items of gaudy jewellery with tentacles and suckers. But down on the sandy sludge of the ocean bed was where the Trilobites were hanging out and flourishing in their own little way. Scuttling about in two dimensions only: back and forth, left to right.

They were around for quite a long time in the story of the Earth and, even as a small kid, I felt that they were written out of the narrative quite brutally. Flashy fish came along, and fangy sharks and then things with arms and legs. Amphibians went sashaying out of the water onto the beach and soon they grew scales and feathers and then they were dinosaurs.

Later on they grew fur, etc.

And what about the humble Trilobite then? Who cared about his trials and tribulations?

*

We know lots about them. That's because they left lots of evidence about themselves with their Easily Fossilized Exoskeletons.

But, unlike many other creatures, even squishier ones, they didn't have many adventures. There aren't actually very many stories about Trilobites.

'That's what I want putting to rights,' he tells me, cavorting up and down my desk. 'I'm bursting with ideas!'

How about Red Riding Hood and the conniving, vicious Trilobite who disguises himself as Grandma, having eaten her first? 'Oh, Grandma! What great big feelers you have! And what a beautiful Easily Fossilized Exoskeleton you have!'

But wouldn't that only work if Grandma was plankton?

'I can act! I can be a villain! What do you think..?'

Or what about Beauty and the Trilobite?

Goldilocks and the Three Trilobites?

Snow White and the Seven Trilobites?

Ali Baba and the Forty Trilobites?

*

Could I really put him into a fairy tale?

Maybe he's the son of a nobleman, the youngest of three Trilobites, who sets off to make his fortune?

Or to slay a jellyfish?

Maybe he's a venal, bossy character who gets his awful comeuppance at last?

Or perhaps he's a princess and she's waiting for a beautiful fate?

A Trilobite who's been cursed by a goblin, an ogre, a wicked witch...

Or is it a fable in which he falls in love with some unsuitable creature? A Pteradactyl? They come from such different worlds…

The winged one has to resist dreadful hunger pangs in order not to devour his beloved. Snap snap. Love can be gone in a flash.

Especially slippery seafood.

'Oh, come on,' he groans. 'There must be a fairy tale ideally suited to one with my talents…'

Three lobes, three segments, lots of spindly, waving legs and feelers. They dominated the seas for many millions of years.

Not bad, considering.

Once upon a time…

But what did he *do*..?

*

'I would love to be a figure in history, having adventures…' he suggests. 'And I could teach children all about the key roles I might have played in the past, perhaps?'

He taught primitive man how to make fire.

He set off into the East with Alexander the Great and Richard the Lion Heart and Marco Polo.

He was seduced by Cleopatra and he burned down the library at Alexandria.

He was one of the few schoolmates who didn't mock Napoleon, and was rewarded by the Emperor and attended his Coronation in Notre Dame.

He was the only explorer to return from Scott's expedition to the South Pole.

We could fake the fossilized record to say that he was there for all these things. We could say he was there when the atom was split, and the computer was created, and even when clocks and time were invented.

'All that's great,' he nods. 'But what I really want to be in is my very own Christmas story...'

*

What generally happens in a Christmas story? Is there mystery and romance? Often there's a great journey... and flying.

The Trilobite can't fly, but he can scuttle, and he's marvellous underwater.

But that's not very Christmassy, is it?

Well... let's see. Maybe Santa has a disaster on Christmas Eve? He's streaking through the night sky with his sleigh and all his reindeer, crossing the ocean, when he has a disaster...!

And he has to be rescued by... a Trilobite..!

An especially nimble, heroic and handsome Trilobite!

One who fixes his sleigh and drags all the drowning reindeer back aboard. Santa is astonished and very grateful. 'I've never met one of your kind before! Though I know all about you, of course, from your Excellent Fossil Record. How can I reward you? How about a trip to the North Pole..? Would that do..?'

The Trilobite's eyes widen at both Santa's idea, and at my suggestion. 'I think I like it. Suitably heroic. I like the Santa angle. Maybe there's some magic..? Maybe I get to actually help pull Santa's sleigh? And I have a marvellous time helping to deliver toys all over the world?'

Then the Trilobite is picturing himself scuttling over snowy rooftops and squeezing himself down chimneys. Wouldn't he love dashing around in strangers' dark houses, filling up stockings... and occasionally giving early risers a wonderful surprise..!

Could the Trilobite even become one of Santa's little helpers on a permanent basis?

Santa isn't sure. His elves are quicker. They've got hands. They can carry things.

The Trilobite isn't such a great assistant.

He drinks all the sherry left out for Santa and makes high-pitched excited noises.

Maybe this isn't the right story for him, after all?

*

Is this just evolution? A natural process of exclusion?

There is no Christmas story about the Trilobite because he simply doesn't fit in? He's not the kind of creature who gets to be in such a tale?

Santa and I have to break it to him gently…

Look here, you've got a marvellous fossil record… Look at it! Not bad for one who's been extinct for hundreds of millions of years! That brittle exo-skeleton of yours has stood you in good stead – and that's why people remember who you were! How about that? They still remember you – up until this very day!

The Trilobite looks forlorn. Then he turns peevish.

No, it isn't enough. He is ambitious. His feelers are restless.

'I want a Christmassy story starring me! Something to teach everyone the true meaning of everything! Oh, do write it for me..!'

*

There were many different kinds of Trilobites. Twenty-five thousand different types. That's diversity for you. And they never fought amongst themselves. They respected each other's business and went about their prehistoric days very contentedly. Peace on Earth and good will to all invertebrates.

Not much tension or conflict in that story. So they had the perfect society for millions of years…? Huh. But where's the drama? Where's the excitement? Where's the sexy stuff?

'But we ruled the seas!' the Trilobite gasps. 'And in those days that meant we owned the whole world, because what else was happening on land but volcanoes going off and lava spurting everywhere? We were among the first living, sensible things on the Earth and we were the very first to realise that we were rocking it!'

*

The Russian Trilobite Asaphus Kowalewski had eyes perched on stalks that were two inches long.

'Is it that we just weren't pretty enough, by your modern standards? We would never be chosen to star in a festive adventure of our own because we aren't attractive to your human eyes? Is it true that when you see us you can't identify with creatures who look like this? Are you having trouble relating to us?'

*

There was a Trilobite from Morocco – Walliserops Trifurcatus – who had a three-pronged fork – a trident! – coming out of his head. Right out of his cephalon! I've no idea why!

'But maybe there's a story in that, eh? Maybe?'

The Asaphellus Cuervoca even had wings! He could guide himself better than most, cruising about on the ocean floor. 'He also had very large eyes, and maybe you humans could identify with him and all his struggles?'

And Dicranarus Monstrous had handlebar moustaches! As well as long, flowing, rather elegant legs. He went sweeping through the darkness of the ancient seas... What if Santa Claus was rescued by *him*?

Santa, caught up in a turbulent time storm, with a blizzard raging all around, and only this Trilobite can lead him back to his own time and place?

Santa glances at the picture of the moustached creature. 'He'd give me the absolute screaming ab-dabs.'

*

Strange-looking, funny-looking.

Sinister, even.

'We look like aliens now. Even to ourselves,' the Trilobite laments. 'Before coming out tonight I caught a glimpse of myself in the hall mirror and thought: "Crikey! Is that really me..?!"

'You see humans everywhere, and you imagine fitting in... and then, all at once, you're brought up short. When you notice your own mandibles. Catch a glimpse of your feelers. And you think: "Oh, yes. I'm a Trilobite, aren't I? I'll never blend in.'

'It's not even that I want to pass by unnoticed. Not really.

'I was used to fitting in. I had two hundred million years of fitting in.

'It might be rather nice to stand out in the crowd. I'd love to be remembered as, say, The Trilobite Who Saved Christmas. Or the Miracle Trilobite. Or the Trilobite in a Trillion.

*

'My story could be about my visiting a family of Flat-Earthers? A dynasty of dinosaur-deniers? I could slip down their chimney one Christmas Eve and terrify them at first? Then I could win them over and steal their hearts? The whole dopey, fundamentalist, bigoted lot of them could come to love me slavishly and believe every word I said!

'I would teach them – with infinite care and patience, perhaps through the medium of song – all about the fossil record?'

*

'I can't be cute,' says the Trilobite. 'Not a flopsy bunny or a kitten or a dewy-eyed, lonesome pony. How would I make myself cute?

'Fur. Big eyes. Helplessness.

'All that mammal stuff. Urrggh.'

But what if you pushed the lonesome angle, eh? He's the very last of his kind? And he's somehow survived hundreds of millions of years and now he's alone in a very strange land?

'Yes, I'm liking this,' he says (using the continuous present, which is his favourite tense, being an immensely long-lived creature.) 'Yes, yes, make me a miraculous survivor! People love those! A mysterious beast from antiquity! A lovely antediluvian animal!'

*

Santa glances at the top of the tree in his workshop. What's that horrid-looking thing standing in for the fairy?

It's the Trilobite, feeling fantastic. 'Look at me!'

Well, he's happy. Who can argue with that?

Mrs Claus rolls her eyes. She's seen it all before. A Trilobite at the top of the Christmas tree? A Trilobite helping with Santa's Christmas deliveries? Well, whatever. These aren't the craziest ideas Santa has ever had. Live and let live is Mrs Claus's mantra.

The fairy is livid, naturally. Supplanted and replaced. She's plotting revenge on the creature from the dawn of time. It curdles her tiny, glittering heart, this furious resentment she feels, and it turns her to the bad. She gets her closest elvish friends to take the

Trilobite captive. They sneak up on him and lash his feelers to his sides and though he struggles, he's no good at fighting, and he can't resist.

They take him off to the kitchens and pop him in the pot! They cook him in a seafood stew, which Mrs Claus is brewing on the stove for Christmas Eve's supper. Now it's a prehistoric broth.

A primordial bouillabaisse.

Of course, the Trilobite was very old. Well past his sell-by date. And you have to be very careful with shellfish.

Christmas Eve is the worst night in the year for everyone in Santa's household to come down with food poisoning. What a to-do. It's not a pleasant sight. All deliveries are cancelled. Christmas is called off, the whole world over. No presents for anyone, on account of the Christmas Trilobite in the pot.

It's not very festive at the North Pole this year, though the fairy is jubilant in her own bitter way.

The Trilobite frowns. 'I'm not exactly loving this story,' he says. 'I'm not sure I want to be eaten up, or to ruin Christmas for everyone! That's not the kind of thing I want at all..! Try again!'

Try and try and try again. It's the writer's eternal mantra.

He snaps his mandibles at me and glares across the desk.

'I want a magical Christmas story! A lovely one! How hard can that *be*..?'

*

What about a kind of quest thing? They're always popular. Something grand and sweeping and mythic. Perhaps set back in antiquity?

'Everyone loves the dinosaurs!' cries the Trilobite. 'Perhaps I could crawl up onto land and warn the dinosaurs they're about to be made extinct? I could lead them all to safety? It could even be a musical. Can I sing? Well, no. But I can hum. Is that no good?'

I'm picturing Busby Berkeley routines on the ocean bed, with rudimentary life forms in frilly shells cavorting in formation.

Even single-celled organisms joining the dance in geometrical displays, with lovely precision.

Fishy fractals.

'And I could be the glorious star in the centre of it all!' trills the Trilobite. 'Not tap-dancing exactly. More doing a soft-shoe shuffle. I could be twiddling my feelers elegantly...'

*

What about a disaster movie? An ocean cruise at Christmas time? A huge liner sinking to the bottom of the sea and everything looking hopeless. But look who comes leaping to help out the passengers! He's saving the lives of the most interesting characters and leading them to safety (shirtless, six-pack on show, flexing his steely antennae.) A friend to all mankind!

But I'm a feisty beast as well as a hero, he thinks. I can at times be filled with vengeful thoughts. All those years of neglect and obscurity...! I feel hard done by, if I'm honest...

'So, what if I was starring in a fantastic monster movie..?'

Somehow blown up to ninety feet tall.

Trashing the skyline of Tokyo and lashing about and stomping on humans. Reclaiming the earth for his own humble kind.

Except... his arms, though numerous, are not particularly strong. They are frondlike and ineffectual. He can't quite destroy the metropolis. He's simply flapping around, stroking skyscrapers.

His thoughts turn glumly to apocalyptic stories. Earth in ruins. Radioactive wilderness. Mutants and nuclear winter storms and sheer awfulness. And the only living creature is the earliest and hardiest of them all.

There he is!

With his proud and darkly-glittering exo-skeleton, dashing about on the dry-as-bone sea bed... Our friend the Trilobite!

He's celebrating Christmas all alone at the end of time.

*

What if he was a time-travelling crustacean? And he went back to witness the birth of Christ?

'I could smuggle myself among the sheep on the hillside and gate crash along with those dopey shepherds. They'd never notice...'

Or he could be with the oxen, lowing in the stall.

'I could disguise myself as a tick, maybe. Shush, Mrs Moo. Or I'll nip your udders. Don't tell them I'm here. The Trilobite at the Nativity.'

Or what if he was one of the gifts brought by the Wise Men?

Gold, Frankincense and a Trilobite?

That could work.

'Then at least I'd have an excuse to be at the stable. I'd be a part of that most famous of tales. Kids in school plays would one day dress up as me! They'd be proud to be me! They'd be like – "I don't want to be a shepherd or an angel! I don't even want to be Mary! I want to be the Christmas Trilobite!"'

*

'Oh, here's a lovely thought!' the Trilobite cries. 'What if I was among a whole bunch of pop stars who get together to make a charity record for Christmas? We put aside our egos just for one day and create a festive classic? Maybe it was all my idea and I'm the hero for a day?'

*

He still likes the idea of flying to the North Pole, though.

And he still thrills to think of himself scuttling about on the desert sands on the way to Bethlehem.

Following that twinkling star. A star that glimmered its first, way back in the days when he lived underwater with all his trillions of chums.

He's hoping to get a ride on a camel. He's hoping to make it in time.

He's thinking about sitting in Santa's sleigh and saving Christmas for everyone and being a miraculous crustacean.

He knows he can do it. He can do anything. He's come this far, after all.

*

Couldn't the Trilobite fall in love?

'Love often features in Christmas stories!' he points out, hopefully. 'And learning a special lesson about selflessness and kindness to fellow creatures. Well, I can do that! I can do any of these things! I can be anything from any of these stories!'

'But... why?' I ask him. 'Why do you particularly want to be in a Christmas story?'

'Because… because… it will mean that you remember *me*. Paul, do you remember..? On Christmas Day, 1972? The year that you learned to read… do you recall? You were reading your book about Prehistoric Life. Volcanoes were erupting. Earth existed in a state of primordial soupiness and flux. It was cataclysmic and all history was beginning. You were three years old and the words and the pictures were starting to make sense to you. The book was in your Christmas stocking. Early in the morning. Reading by lamplight. In your own room, staring at pages.

'Staring at the page with the Trilobite on. You realised that you weren't just staring at the lines of words. They were sweeping you along just like the grand surges of the tide.

'The words were moving you to understand and you weren't even trying.

'As the Trilobite and all his friends flickered into life and danced on the seabed you realised that you were reading, and all these little creatures were going to leave their footprints - and an excellent fossil record - inside your head forever.'

Party Like It's 1979

Some Christmases were snowy and so snowy that it
felt like our little town was going to be cut off from all
the main roads. We'd be snowed in and the holidays
would just go on and on. Our school often closed
because pipes burst and parquet floors flooded and
froze over like ice rinks and ceilings fell in with the
weight of snow.

Most of our teachers lived out of town, in the
surrounding countryside, and they couldn't get
through. We were given extra days off, and how we
loved it: skidding and sliding and skipping away
down the school drive, clutching worksheets hastily
distributed by the school secretary. Snow Days meant
being able to work from home, using sheets printed
in purple ink, turned out on the bander machine.

All the work I can remember doing consisted
of a few easy sums and a lot of nature study. We did
the shapes of trees and the silhouettes of woodland
creatures and birds. Nature meant going out down
the Burn and ploughing through drifts of snow and

crashing about in the frozen undergrowth until it grew dark.

Working from home also meant some serious writing. Schoolwork mostly seemed to be about writing stories (or maybe that was just the bit I paid most attention to?) There would be prompts and opening sentences printed in smudgy, purple ink and we had to continue these tales in our own time, in the extra days of holiday at home. Sometimes I think that – now I'm entering my fiftieth year – I'm still continuously writing one of those endless stories, begun with a sentence printed in purple on a worksheet given out on an abandoned school day in 1979. I've just never finished the sentence and got to the other side of that blizzard.

So – the Christmas holidays always seemed to be long, long, long. We stocked up our cupboards at home with Swiss rolls and corned beef and custard and tomato soup. Mam would put in an order with the shop in the precinct for extra fruit and veg. A van would pull up and we'd have a small wooden crate to unpack. The potatoes would be cloddy and mucky, the cabbages leafy and bright, the red apples so shiny you could see your face in them. The satsumas still had green leaves attached and their scent filled the whole house. You could smell them for days after the delivery of Christmas fruit and veg, until the last one was eaten. We liked the very softest ones, whose skins peeled off in one loose piece.

A string bag of nuts would be emptied into a dish on the coffee table. The silver nutcrackers would come out of the wall unit drawer. Most nights a sheet of newspaper would be laid out and we'd take agonizing, effortful, hilarious turns cracking Brazils, walnuts and hazelnuts. Little bits of nutty shrapnel shooting everywhere.

Much of our shopping we would fetch on Friday night and Christmas was no exception. We didn't have a car just then, but what we did have was our very own shopping trolley. Not a little pully-along trolley like old ladies had. Not just a piffling bag on wheels. No, this was an actual metal supermarket shopping trolley on four castors. Someone had nicked it from the Fine Fare superstore down town and –

horrible vandals that they were – sent it rolling down the steep hill of Burn Lane into the stream at the bottom. There we had found it and fished it out, one day last summer. It had been a little project: cleaning up that shopping trolley, yanking out tatters of mouldy lichen and slimy weed. It took some doing. I even rubbed some wire wool on the bits that had rusted and soon the wheels were turning round, good as new.

Lo and Behold – our family had its very own shopping trolley. I wondered briefly if Fine Fare would give me a reward for returning it, but I doubted it. They had updated their trolleys since this one had gone AWOL. Now they had ones where you had to put coins in.

So what we did was push it all the way to the town precinct every Friday night. We would push it down Burn Lane and through the estates on the other side and then into the town centre. We'd push it through the futuristic, automated doors of Fine Fare, quite brazenly. Here we are with our very own private trolley. We'd fill it up to the very top, pay for all our stuff and not even bother with carrier bags or boxes. We left all our shopping in the trolley and simply pushed it back home again.

Looking back, it's kind of crazy and absurd, the way we were almost proud of that trolley. At least, I was. Even in terrible, snowy weather I'd take that shopping trolley on a ride round our estate, sitting backwards and scooting it along with my feet. All the other kids went about on skateboards and bikes, and I'd be swooping about in long, backward loops in my own private shopping trolley. I'd had my own skateboard and bike, and I'd even had roller skates, but for some reason my favourite thing was that shopping trolley. Sometimes our golden retriever, Duke, could be persuaded to sit in the thing with me as I paraded about the estate. He would get over-excited, though.

The further away in time I get away from it all, I'm amazed by how chuffed we were by simple stuff like having our own trolley or running about in the snow down the Burn with Duke. In 1979 the whole of Christmas was exciting.

Mam loved to buy us presents. She liked to spoil us and overwhelm us with all these things she'd be up all night wrapping. The opening of gifts seemed to be endless. She always said it was because she and her sisters and brother had never got much at Christmas when they were kids. They were so poor back then, though my Big Nanna did her best for them. They'd get a handful of sweets, a Disney Annual, and Mam would have to share a present with her twin sister – a doll or, one year when they were teenagers – a Dansette record player that had its own carry case.

So, Mam liked to buy us lots of things and see us enthralled and amazed. Christmas Day would begin with the lights out and the door closed on the living room, and we'd assemble outside in the hall while she counted down. Then she would open the door and quickly put the lights on and then we would see in a flash: Santa had been! The room was filled – completely filled – with brightly-coloured wrapping paper. There would be presents on every chair and every surface in the whole room. There'd be sacks and sacks of them.

One year in particular she had a craze on getting stationery. It seemed like she had bought up everything you could ever need to fill a desk, furnish a home office and to supply a writing career. I was awash with pens and books and pencils and sharpeners and pen holders and bulldog clips and elastic bands and felt pens and Tipp-ex. Every year I'd start a new Page-a-Day Diary from Boots and the first few entries were always lists of all the goodies I'd been given and all the TV shows we had watched together. Very little in the way of reflection and few of the glimpses of everyday life I'd love to read all these years later. Just endless lists of *stuff*.

We watched a lot of telly together. We would sit on the settee with a continental quilt over our laps because it could get quite chilly. We'd have snacks at the ready – Aeros, Lion Bars, Topics and Glees. Monster Munch and Space Raiders. We'd have frothy milky coffee brewed up by the new percolator that was one of the fancy new purchases of recent times.

It was almost as good an innovation as the Toastie maker, the products of which were the best treat during late night TV viewing. Cheese and onion toasties – blistering hot and delicious. You'd scald your insides with melted cheese and then go to bed and have horrible nightmares.

We'd work our way through long nights of viewing, circling our choices in the Radio Times and the TV Times Christmas issues, cross-referencing and squabbling in the days before Betamax. Every quiz show, every sit-com and every serial drama. The big movie on Saturday night. The old black and white films in the afternoons. Strong female leads and sentimental songs. Most vintage films I encounter nowadays trigger a memory of having watched them before, with my mam, long ago on a snowy holiday afternoon.

The tree would have been up for a month by the time Christmas came. Artificial and silver, glass baubles and a fairy that had been bought the year I was born. In 1979 she was ten and the gauzy lace was turning yellowish and her glitter was dropping off.

Yards of tinsel were swagged on every wall, displaying all our Christmas cards. Black tape turned our windows into Victorian leaded panes and we'd sprayed them liberally with this sticky fake snow out of a can. That snow smelled wonderful to me. It's a smell as essentially festive as those oranges in the crate, or the pine fresh scent of the cleaning stuff Mam used in the bathroom and on all the floors. She set to work cleaning every corner of our house, because we had to be shipshape and sparkling for when Santa came.

In my living memory we'd always lived in council houses – blocky and square with no chimneys or fireplaces. From very early on I'd fretted over the question of just how Santa would get in. I remember going to aunties' houses and both Big and Little Nanna's and being told: 'Oh, look! Santa's come early to this house!' and watching dumbstruck – the week before Christmas – as boxes and parcels were produced and handed over to Mam. So, Santa went out more than just the one night in the year? So he did an extra shift, especially for aunties and grandparents? My mind ticked over the logic of all this.

Only very recently I've had a memory come back to me, of glimpsing a mysterious heap on top of Mam's wardrobe well before the Christmas holidays. It was only partially covered by a striped sheet. It had slipped, revealing a tell-tale corner of Christmas paper. That, I think, was the very moment I started having serious doubts about the literal truth of Santa and his so-called marathon dash around the world, visiting good boys and good girls. (Also, I knew some very bad children. Real stinkers. And they seemed to get presents, just the same as everyone else, so where was the fairness in that?)

Once, when I was very little – about four years old – I finished unwrapping gifts and said, 'Is that it?' And Mam was upset and furious. She dragged me across the road to the home of the family from Glasgow. They were known on our street for being very poor. Her idea was to show me how little their little boy was being given, in order to teach me a lesson I'd never forget. We said hello and were invited in and there wasn't very much Christmassy going on.

We stayed a moment but before we left the mother presented me with a hastily-wrapped gift. It was in a scrap of crumpled paper, not even taped together. When we went back home I was delighted. It was a Ladybird Book of Dinosaurs. Mam took it off me and found the scrawled dedication on the title page: 'To Michael from Mammy and Daddy for Christmas 1973.'

The little lad over the road had only just been given that book and they'd felt obliged to hand it over to their unexpected guests. I think I was ashamed and upset, just the same was Mam was. Also, I knew that I really wanted to keep that dinosaur book.

We couldn't take it back. Mam said it would make everything worse if we returned and tried to give it back. We would be flinging it back in their faces. After that, there was always a sensation of horrible shame attached to that book for me. Any glimpse of a dinosaur in a book can revive that sickening guilt, even now.

It was a lesson about not growing up to be a spoiled little bastard.

The next year I remember sitting on my new sledge and opening a Dr Who Paint-by-Numbers kit and Mam was saying that she was sorry I didn't have so many presents this year. I remember telling her that I thought I had loads, and I was so happy with those I had. I remember really being sincere and feeling sad because I couldn't make her believe me. She always wanted us to get more; to be happier than we were. She wanted us to be impossibly happy, and it was hard to be that.

I think I always knew that it was Mam who was the one marshalling her resources, putting money by each week, pinching the pennies. For all my trying to work out the logic and truth of Santa's magic, I knew it was always down to my mam.

In Aycliffe we did, however, have a kind of Santa. He appeared each Christmas Eve after it got dark, and he made an appearance on every single street in town. He was the Council Van Santa and his lorry was an old dust cart; his elves were all dustmen.

There was a wooden house on the back of his van, all strung with fairy lights. The Council Santa's itinerary was the same each year, evolving gradually as the town expanded with new estates. The list of ETA's was printed in the Newton News and his van would roll around promptly from street to street. We'd hear his handbell ringing from some distance away and we'd dash excitedly to put shoes and coats and scarves on.

Outside we would cluster round and wait for the Council Santa to come round the corner and into our cul-de-sac and throw sweets at us. The Council Santa was fat and reasonably jolly and when he talked his local accent gave away the fact that he came from round here. He chucked boiled sweets over the sides of his van and we caught them. People offered up new babies for him to hold, and everyone talked to him like he was the real Santa Claus, asking him questions about the busy night he had ahead of him.

Older kids would chuck snowballs at his little house, trying to knock his fairy lights out. We all loved the Council Santa, though, even the older ones – the Goths and the hard girls and the bad lads and the older brothers and sisters who moaned about coming to stand in the cold. They would still gather with everyone from our street. It was the only time in the whole year – unless there was a fire – that you'd see the inhabitants of the street all out together, saying hello and Season's Greetings to each other.

I liked that slight formality of everyone saying Happy Christmas to each other, because I was something of an old-fashioned little kid. I liked it when adults spoke to me properly and expected me to speak sensibly back. I never really liked the way that kids carried on. To me, it was the kids who spoiled school. Apart from other kids, I thought school was great. Especially at Christmas, when it was mostly making stuff out of tissue paper, glitter and glue. And putting on school concerts where we did Ibsen's Peer Gynt as an improvised dance piece, dressed as trolls.

And now, nearly forty years later, I'm sitting in a café and I've filled twenty-two pages of my current journal with this stuff, without even thinking. I'm looking back at a time when I'd fill twenty-two pages of an exercise book brought home from school at the end of term. We were always allowed to take home our unfinished books and most kids chucked them over the hedge or into the Burn on the day we broke up. But I went home and filled up all the pages just for fun.

Weird kid, I know. My favourite Christmas thing involved filling up pages and pages...

I wish I'd kept them all. I wish I could see what I'd noted down. But I do remember quite a lot of detail from that time, and that's just as good. I can remember all the details that made up the best of our Christmases.

I remember that Christmas only began properly once we'd had all our groceries and deliveries. We'd been to Fine Fare with our shopping trolley, and filled the fridge and the cupboards and fruit bowls. We'd trudged home from the last day of school and no one needed to leave the house again until Christmas was over and the sales in Darlington had begun.

It was Mam who ceremonially began Christmas each year. On Christmas Eve she'd put a certain record on that tall, stacked hi-fi unit with the smoked glass cabinet. From that futuristic stereo system would come the squeaky voices of two pigs singing 'Santa Claus is Coming to Town.' It wasn't really Christmas until we'd all sung along with Pinky and Perky.

Then we could have a glass of ginger wine – the sweet, hot, non-alcoholic sort that my Big Nanna brewed up and bottled and brought to us when she visited with her best friend, Deaf Olive. Mam had the recipe now – it was black currant jelly dissolving in boiling water, bagfuls of sugar and a bottle of spicy ginger essence. It steamed aromatically in a giant mixing bowl and it was so hot you had to water it like whisky.

Tomato soup for tea and then Disney Time and a visit from the Council Santa. Back indoors for the big film, maybe, but you could never concentrate for excitement. It was the one night of the year an early bedtime seemed preferable. I would sit up in bed reading last year's annuals by torchlight. The Beano, Cheeky, Whizzer and Chips. Very nearly sick with minty chocolates, satsumas and ginger wine.

It was all about egging time on and wanting time to go faster and faster and for all the hours and the days to go flashing past. That seems the craziest and most marvelous thing of all when I look back now: that there was ever a time when I wished time away.

But I did. Faster and faster. Bring Christmas faster.

I was a long way off trying to master the knack of making happy times slower. I was still far from hoping that the happy times might stay.

A Tingle of Happiness

She's doing something unusual.

She's completely focused on her task. I've never seen her looking so absorbed, pen in hand, making little notes and drawing rings around certain titles.

Effie's sitting alone in the café. She's wearing a bobble hat and a black jumper with diamante appliquéd stars. Her shopping basket is pulled up close to her table and her brolly's hooked over the handle, dripping melted snow onto the carpet. She's got a tray of tea things but she's not even poured herself a cup out yet. She's so intent on the magazine in front of her.

From what I can see it's a TV listings magazine for the Christmas period. It's very odd. As far as I know, Effie's never been a big TV watcher. Certainly not one for marking up pages of the Radio Times.

'Hello, there,' I interrupt her and she jumps – actually jumps – in her seat. She looks almost furtive.

'Oh, Brenda. Fancy seeing you here…'

It's our usual café on our usual afternoon. The Walrus and the Carpenter, three o'clock on a Saturday. She looks dazed like she's been off in a world of her own. With one quick movement she picks up her garish magazine and stuffs it into her shopping basket.

I sit down heavily, glad to be off my feet.

'How's tricks?' I ask.

'Oh, you know,' she shrugs. 'Same old, same old.'

Why does Effie look so shifty this Christmas?

*

Whitby is beautiful in December.

Perhaps it strikes me as more beautiful than ever because this year we have had so many disastrous situations and near-death experiences? I find myself filled with zestiness and gratitude for still being here at the end of another year. I race out into each new day, hurrying down to the harbour, togged up against the freezing wind and I greet these clear blue skies like I can't quite believe I'm still alive.

How old am I now? I've actually lost count of the years, and that makes me think I must be happy and contented at last.

At twilight I hurry up the 199 steps to watch the sun go down. I've been up here in the churchyard most nights this week, simply because the skies are gorgeous and I don't want to miss them. Hot pink and gold, brightening impossibly until you think it all might burst.

I sit on that bench on the cliff and watch the dark come rolling in from the sea, along with the mist. I wish I could gather up all that beauty and all that colour in these two great hefty arms of mine…

I feel like I could gobble all of it up, like an ogress in a fairy tale.

I sound crazy, don't I? Effie would tell me I'm going doolally. Except Effie isn't with me on my jaunts around town these days. She isn't sitting in the graveyard at sundown watching the skies. Lately she's gone a bit quiet. My best friend is keeping herself to herself.

Oh, I don't take offence. We've spent an awful lot of time together this year – all the adventures and escapades we've been embroiled in – and now that it's holiday time, perhaps she just wants a little peace. Away from me.

Funny. But I've never known her to make much of a fuss about Christmas.

And yet there are twinkling fairy lights up at her windows. I've looked. Tasteful white lights are draped everywhere.

Oh, that sounds like I'm peeping and spying on her. But you can't miss them, the decorations she's been stringing up inside her place. Downstairs in the junk shop there are baubles and trimmings over the bottles and clocks and cabinets and funny old gee-gaws. It's all over her private upstairs rooms, too. There's a very dramatic tree, all gold and black, in her private sitting room.

Effie really has gone to town this Christmas. She's even baking. The last time I was round there she was stirring up sticky fruit and spices and talking about cakes. Not like her at all. That day she didn't even offer me a cup of tea, she was so intent.

I must admit, I feel a little bit pushed aside.

I've put up my small, artificial tree and the little wreath on the front door of my B&B. Business is ever so slack this season. I don't have much to do. There isn't even anything much in the spooky or supernatural line to investigate recently.

At least, that's how it seems this Saturday teatime… just before the start of the Krampus Run.

'The what?' Effie frowns, leaning over the café table. The waitress brings me cinnamon toast and tea. 'What did you say?'

'It's a parade this afternoon,' I tell her. 'For Christmas. Demon Santas and so on.'

She frowns. 'I'm not sure I like the sound of that.'

I ask her if she knows the old legend of the Krampus?

She professes not to. Her expression goes dark. I fill her in with as much as I know.

'It's the tradition of the anti-Santa Claus, really. He's a kind of horned god, all furry and nasty and dragging chains behind him. He comes before Christmas to take away all the bad children and punish them. It's an old, old story from Europe, and they're bringing it back here… the tradition of the Krampus Run… '

Effie tuts. 'As if Goth weekend wasn't bad enough. Whatever will they think of next? I suppose it's all about tourism, isn't it? Anything to keep everyone visiting and to keep us all buying touristy rubbish.'

She's in a right mardy mood, I realise. 'Are you okay, Effie?'

Her eyes blaze at me, just for a second, like she thinks I'm being too personal. 'I'm perfectly fine, Brenda.' Then she changes the subject, asking about my Christmas plans. I tell her I'll be happy with my own company, all day long. I'll have spicy tea, a racy novel and a pound of fancy chocolates. I won't see another soul again until teatime on Boxing Day, when

I wander over to her place for our traditional glass of sherry.

'You still want me to come over to yours, don't you?' I ask, pointedly.

'Oh, of course,' she says. But Effie is still looking shifty.

*

After that we wend our way onto the cobbled, uphill slope of Church Street, where a crowd is already gathering to watch the parade. I don't know why, but a strange shudder goes through me, as soon as I see the first of the slightly maleficent Santas.

I know they're just locals dressed up, but the costumes and the masks are so good, you could be forgiven for thinking that real demons are walking amongst us this bright and frosty Saturday afternoon.

They've got horns and spiked ears, crowns and forked tails and livid, nasty tongues. There are Green Men and Ice Kings and shaggy blokes who look like yeti. There are women in furs and wreaths of tinsel, garlands of ivy and mistletoe. They hand out bitter sweets and sickly candies to the cheering crowds.

'I don't think I like it,' Effie says, stepping back from the passing parade. Horns blow and drums are bashed. There's a hollow jollity to it all. A macabre glee…

'It's just a kind of pantomime,' I tell her.

'I know that,' she snaps. 'But it isn't funny, is it? How many times over the years have you and I faced real monsters and evil entities who've manifested themselves here in Whitby? Doesn't it make you feel peculiar, Brenda, to see the locals capering about like this? In celebration of such wicked things?'

I frown. I hadn't thought about it like that at all. I just thought it was a bit of fun, like when they have the Goths running about. But Effie doesn't care much for that kind of thing, either.

I realise then that she's fallen quiet. She has locked eyes with one particular person in the parade. A subdued figure near the back, shuffling along, bashing a tambourine and bringing up the rear. He's a little bloke with smallish horns sprouting out of his forehead, woolly furry legs and a bare chest. He's carrying a pile of parcels and winking mockingly at my friend.

'I've got to get away from here,' Effie gasps.

A witchy young woman in a leotard leaps in front of us starts doing expressive dance moves, preventing Effie's crossing the road. The man with the hairy haunches cracks out laughing.

'Excuse me, please!' Effie cries out. 'I do believe I'm being triggered!'

What's she talking about, I wonder? And before I know it, my friend has dashed away, across the street and down an alleyway.

There's definitely something funny going on with her.

*

When I dream that night I see the weird Krampus parade once more... I'm standing there with Effie and her disapproval is still radiating off her like heat waves. Bringing up the rear of the parade come that faun and the girl in the leotard once again. This time they have something to say.

The girl is all spiky and jabby with her elbows and knees. She's got stardust or snowflakes in her hair. It's all crimped like I used to do to mine in the Seventies. I forgot how I used to do that!

As she dances round us waving a branch of mistletoe the faun comes sidling up. He whispers in my ear.

'She's being a fool, Brenda,' he tells me. His voice is so delicate and fluting. There's a sweetness to his breath, like he's just been eating something delicious. 'Effie, I mean. She's holding out hope. But it's a ridiculous business. It's dabbling in the dark. It's stirring up bad forces. The silly old fool ought to know better...'

I try to grab his arm, but he slips out of my grasp, dancing past on those delicate hooves. 'Wait! I don't understand! Come back...!'

But the young man with the furry legs is whispering into Effie's ear by now. My friend looks absolutely livid as he finishes and bounds away from her.

The girl in the leotard laughs at my consternation and she goes whirling past, as well. The two of them hurry over the cobbles and through the crowds, catching up with the parade.

Effie is giving me a funny look. 'What did he say to you, that silly creature? You shouldn't listen to anything a faun says, you know.'

'Oh... er... nothing,' I say. I just know I shouldn't tell her. 'Why, what did he say to you?'

Effie fixes me with one of her basilisk stares. A real humdinger. 'He says that you, Brenda, had better look sharp! Look sharp and think on..!'

*

The next day I'm wondering how much I dreamed, and how much was real. Did that faun really say anything at all to us both? And surely he wasn't a faun, anyway? He was just some fella, wasn't he? Some bloke with beardy bits and false horns stuck on his head...

Yet when I close my eyes at the breakfast table, with buttery toast halfway up to my mouth, the image of him in my mind is very vivid. Very real. And I think: maybe he really was a supernatural creature. Maybe he really was giving me a warning about the way that Effie's carrying on?

She was definitely hiding something yesterday. That's what I think, as I hasten myself along, getting ready to face the day.

Circling things in the Radio Times, indeed!

*

I've found over the years that it's best not to tackle Effie head on. You'd think she'd appreciate direct questions. Her who's all Yorkshire good sense and bluntness. In the past I assumed that she'd appreciate a friend who just came out with things and laid it on the line.

Apparently not.

You have to deal quite carefully with Effie. She's a bit like a funnel web spider, in many ways. One wrong move and up she shoots, back into her webby, sticky enclave. Mortally offended. It has to be softly, softly, catchee Effie…

So that morning I nip out the back, into the shared tangle of brambles that borders both our neglected gardens. Ow, owww, nettles and thorny things. Why aren't either of us better, more attentive gardeners?

My idea is to creep up to Effie's back windows. Have a little peek inside her downstairs rooms without her knowing.

It's quite a simple plan, I know. I'm not denying that. But sometimes simple is best, isn't it?

Well, blow me, but I was right before, when I said I thought she'd gone overboard with her decorations this year. And it's not just one tree she's got up in gold and black tinsel. Oh, no! There's a tree in every room!

And, do you know… (though it's hard to tell from outside) but I believe she's even dusted. *Dusted!* Effie has *dusted!*

Every lamp and chandelier is switched on, blazing with rainbow light. All of her antique dolls and toys have been brushed and straightened up and are sitting in attendance. There is music coming from the vast green trumpet of her gramophone player. I think it's the Nutcracker. Yes… that's what it is… The Sugar Plum Fairy, if I'm not mistaken.

I duck sharply then, beneath the frosty sill of the back window. There she is! She almost saw me! What would she even say if she knew I was spying on her? She'd think I'd gone bonkers. Or worse, I'd become untrustworthy. Fancy spying on my very best friend!

But you must admit… it *is* rather queer, isn't it? She's making this old palace of hers into a fantastically welcoming Christmas wonderland. But she's doing it only for herself! She's selfishly doing it all up, simply for her own sake! What's all that about, eh?

*

'She's probably going to have a *man* in!'

This is a little later in the morning, when I've taken a walk up the hill to stretch my legs and sat down for coffee. I'm at the Miramar hotel at the top of Pannet Park and I'm sat down with Robert. He boggles his eyes at me speculatively.

'Oh, I'm sure if she was… seeing a gentleman friend, then she would have told me all about it,' I say. 'We don't keep secrets from each other about things like that.'

Robert shrugs and offers me Turkish Delight. I like it, but I do find it a bit claggy.

I'm surprised to see that my young hotelier friend is wearing his elf costume once again. Of course he wants to be festive, but surely this green felt ensemble can only serve to summon up memories of his terrifying time working at the Christmas Hotel on the West Cliff? When he was in bondage there, and a slave to the monstrous Mrs

Claus, he and all his fellow workers had no choice but to dress as elves every single day of the year. I find it strange that he'd willingly put the old uniform on again now, when he's free of that old monster's malign influence.

But what do I know? People – even your best friends – can surprise you by acting strangely, any day of the week...

'She is! She's having some man in over Christmas!' Robert bursts out, scandalized and enjoying every second. 'And she's keeping shtum about it all. So I suppose that means it's someone terribly unsuitable. Maybe somebody rough and from the wrong side of the tracks..!'

'Nonsense...' I take another piece of Turkish Delight, spilling icing sugar on the table and down the front of my cardy. 'There's bound to be a harmless explanation. If she wants to start keeping secrets from her nearest and dearest friend, there must be a very good reason...' Even as I say it, I know I'm sounding miffed. I'm sounding peevish and petulant about the whole business.

And do you know why? It's because I'm jealous. I'm completely jealous that Effie's got things going on that are worth keeping secret.

How shallow of me!

I feel a very brief stab of shame.

'I bet she's having absolutely brilliant sex,' Robert says.

'Shut up!' I gasp. 'Don't say that!'

He laughs at me. 'Why? Does it horrify you! Brenda, I'm shocked! You should be glad for her.'

'She should be more careful,' I mutter. 'She's not the woman she was. We don't want ambulances coming out in the middle of the night during Christmas week. They have an awful job backing down our steep alley…'

Robert is still laughing. 'What's so awful and shocking about Effie having a nice clandestine affair over Christmas? It might do the old sourpuss some good. And don't worry, I'm sure she'll divulge all the spicy details afterwards…'

I shudder, spilling more powdered sugar down my front. 'I'm sure I don't want to hear any spicy details. That kind of thing has never interested me.'

'Oh, rubbish!' he chuckles. 'Don't you go all prim, dearie. If you do, I shan't tell you all about my little dalliance with this fella I met from the Krampus parade...'

'*You..?*' I burst out. My goodness, has everyone gone sex mad round here lately?

'Why not me? What's wrong me? I'm not completely ancient and hideous, you know!'

'Sorry, I didn't mean that...' I shake my head and reach over to squeeze his hand. 'It's just that Effie and I watched a little of the Krampus parade yesterday, over on Church Street. And it was so creepy and strange! It fair put the willies up me.'

'Well, yes,' he says. 'Quite!'

I stare at him. 'And you're saying you... *met* someone involved in the parade?'

'Later last night,' he nods. 'Some of them came over to the Miramar for a drink. All done up in their furs and horns and all their spooky gubbins. They gave the regulars quite a turn. Anyhow, I met this young fella... he was done up rather fetchingly as a kind of faun. You know, with the little horns and the furry legs...'

I gasp. 'I met him! I talked to him earlier! He was the one... who whispered in my ear... warning me about Effie... about her getting involved in something awful. He implied that she was biting off more than she could chew!'

Oh, but hang on. Had that really happened in the real world? Or was it only in my dream? When he took me aside and whispered into my cold ear..? And then he'd trip-trapped over the cobbles to say something sotto voce to my friend as well and she had looked absolutely furious with him. And how he'd laughed!

But that had only been in my dream, hadn't it?

'Oh, yes. That's the fella,' Robert says, a little mistily and dreamily. 'There was only one faun in the parade. One sexy bare-chested faun. With woolly hair and gorgeous hot pink nipples. He didn't take his horns off you know, or his fake little hooves. And his legs were really almost as hairy as they seemed. There wasn't much that was fake about him…'

'Might he be… a new boyfriend for you?' I ask hesitantly. I don't really know if Robert is looking for someone new or not. Perhaps he's happy on his own these days? Perhaps I have touched upon a sore point? But I'm interested, and concerned for his welfare.

Also, I think he might have had a sexy encounter with a supernatural being and, in the past, that hasn't always gone well for our Robert. He does let his libido draw him into some very spooky areas.

'Oh, no, not really…' he says airily, looking rueful as he pops the wooden lid back on the box of sweets. 'He was here and gone. He came and he went in a shower of Christmas fairy dust. I woke up in the very early hours and he'd vanished. Seriously, I even wondered if I hadn't dreamed the whole thing. The window of my room was flapping open and the wind was blowing snow indoors. He'd slipped out down the drainpipe, like he'd had to escape from me…!

Story of my life, eh? So I don't suppose I'll ever be seeing Mr Tumnus again…'

*

I set off back down the hill to home.

Honestly! This festive season, it seems that everyone I know is having adventures! Everyone I know but me!

I pop into the butchers and the green grocers and pay off my accounts and make arrangements for deliveries on Christmas Eve. Then I head home and wonder what I ought to do with the rest of my day. Every room in my B&B is sparklingly immaculate. There's nothing at all to do but relax…

But somehow I don't feel like relaxing.

And lo and behold! What's this? When I arrive home! Here are guests! Here are actual, unexpected visitors! They have arrived unannounced and they need putting up!

*

Of course, I sweep straight into action.

I hadn't even realized how much I need to work. Inactivity isn't good for me. When I've got no work on – that's when I start to brood.

But this afternoon there's such a crowd! A queue down my stairs and into my side passage!

'You'll fill up all my rooms at this rate! Where have you lot all come from?'

All seven of my rooms are going to be bursting at the seams, all through Christmas week. There's a little family, with small children. A couple of young couples. One or two solitary souls.

If I thought on a bit more I might be wondering: it's a bit suspicious, this. All these folk turning up at once. But I don't. I'm just glad of the business. They're polite and quiet and one young man is apologizing for not booking ahead. 'That's quite all right,' I assure him, with a flourish of my fountain pen, scattering droplets over my ledger. 'There's always room at Brenda's B&B!' Which isn't strictly true, of course, but I want to sound welcoming.

All seven rooms! All Christmas! We are going to be snug as anything. And more to the point – I'm not going to be at a loose end! I'm not going to be lonely!

I get them all settled, one party after the next, in the Red Room, the Blue Room, all the rooms of the rainbow. And at last I come to the last person waiting by herself at the end of the queue.

She is an eccentric figure, bedraggled and clutching a moth-eaten carpet bag. She isn't quite elderly, but there's something timeless about her. I recognize the look. There's something about her eyes when she looks straight at you.

But she is dressed like a jumble sale, I have to say. Layers and layers of fabric and all kinds of ill-fitting garments. On her head she's got jammed a wide-brimmed hat crowned with exotic feathers.

'I'm afraid you can't smoke in here,' I say, rising up and folding my arms.

'Oh, yes, yes, of course,' she mutters, and stamps out her tab end on the concrete before scuttling indoors. When she signs my book her writing is indecipherable. She rummages through her carpet bag for her purse and tries to pay with a number of very strange-looking currencies. At last she manages to find a paper bag that contains a brick-thick wodge of five pound notes. 'Will this do?'

There is something about her that makes my heart go out to her. She seems crushed somehow, as if something awful has recently happened in her life. I decide that I'll keep a special eye on her, to make sure she's all right.

'Will you be here all of Christmas week then, Mrs...?'

'Ms,' she corrects me sharply, and then smiles. Such a warm, wide smile she has. Suddenly all that crumpled sadness melts away. There are dancing sparks of happiness in her eyes. What colour are they? Lilac? Green? Gold? I can't really tell. 'Oh, yes, lovey. I'm here for a few days. A quiet festive break by the sea. I need a rest. Oh dear me, but I need a little rest and recuperation, after the things I've been through!'

She laughs then, and it turns into a coughing fit.

I ask her, 'Will you be all right in the Orange Room? It's right at the very top of the house...'

'Ahh, don't worry about me, lovey. I'm fitter than I look.'

The Orange Room is the latest refurbished room in my B&B. It's up in the attic, right next to my own private corner of the house.

'Come on then. I'll help you with your luggage...'

She swings her battered carpet bag. 'This is all I've got! It's all I need!'

Oh help, I think. I've brought in some bag lady for the Christmas season... I hope she's not going to be any bother. When she follows me up the first flight of stairs I can definitely hear bottles clinking in that solitary bag of hers...

But who am I to judge anyone? I wonder. Live and let live. That's my watchword.

'I couldn't make out your name in the guest book...' I say, as we thunder up the stairs.

'Wildthyme,' she calls after me. 'Iris Wildthyme.'

'What an unusual name!' I say.

'It's completely made up,' she says. 'It's my nom-de-plume. My alias. My stage-name. My real name... well, you'd never be able to pronounce it. No one would. So you can just call me Iris...'

Hmmm. A woman of some mystery, then! I ponder. Well, I know how that feels, don't I?

When I fling open the door of her appointed room she gives a happy little sigh. 'Oh, it's lovely!'

It's a symphony of orange. I was wondering, when I finished doing it up, whether I hadn't gone a bit far with the décor in my seventh rainbow room. But Iris totters in with a look of dazed rhapsody on her face. 'Oh, I feel like I'm getting all my vitamins just by standing here in this room!' she laughs. 'Suddenly I feel so much more... *zesty!*'

I leave her to get settled in.

And I spend the rest of the afternoon making teas for my other guests, and doing a spot of baking. Some scones, I decide. And a nice sponge cake. The radio in my little kitchen is playing Christmassy tunes. And... do you know? I might be starting to feel a little bit festive at last...

This is what I need! Good old work to get on with. It'll stop me obsessing over whatever bother that daft Effie is surely getting herself into.

I'm singing along with Roy Wood and Wizzard when my phone goes. It's Robert.

'I've seen him again..!'

'You what..? You've seen who..?'

'The faun! Mr Tumnus! The one who ran away last night and left me in the lurch...' Robert sounds breathlessly excited.

'Oh, yes?' I turn down my radio and concentrate on the receiver.

'Yes, well, I took a little walk around town this afternoon. Just a little bit of last minute Christmas shopping, you know...'

'Yes..?' I frown because all of a sudden I can hear thumping and banging coming from the Orange Room, just across the landing. Is that Iris woman moving all the furniture around..?

'And I was on Silver Street, peering into shop windows and... blow me, but then I see that someone's reopened the bookshop. The Spooky Finger is open again for business!'

Now, at the mention of that place – which has been derelict for a few years – I can't help but repress a dreadful shudder. There is no way I want reminding of the awful events that went on because of The Spooky Finger. I shouldn't think Robert would want to dwell on them, either.

'It's under different management, of course.'

'Well, naturally...'

'And it looks rather nice, as it happens. Much more inviting and cosy than it was before. I ventured inside, thinking I need to stock up on some new books... and I found that it's been taken over by this young couple. Well, not a couple. Brother and sister, that's what they are. I met her – Fenella. She's young and very bonny, really, with masses of crimped dark hair. Sat there in a leotard with a kind of witchy look about her. 'Welcome to Whitby,' I tell her and start to introduce myself. Well, before I know it I've been sat there for half an hour, sipping fennel tea and gassing away with Fenella…'

I'm starting to wonder where this tale of his is going, and why he saw fit to phone me so urgently. And still there's banging and clattering emanating from Iris's room.

'Anyway, to cut to the chase, I was chatting away with Fenella about our mutual interest in the Unexplained and Mysteries of the Unknown, when in walks her brother. He comes bustling in with a pile of parcels and snow on his shoulders and all in his curly hair. When he claps eyes on me he does look surprised! Because it's him! My faun from last night! He's Mr Tumnus – or Timothy, rather. Fenella's twin brother.'

'Oh, they're twins, are they?' I ask distractedly.

'The point is, Brenda – I was glad to see him again. I was cockahoop, actually. And – not to flatter myself – I believe his eyes lit up at the sight of me, too. Fenella gets up and moves with lissom grace towards him, kissing him on the frozen cheek. 'Well,' she laughs. 'I guess you two have met each other already?' And we two stand there, looking embarrassed and shamefaced. And Fenella chuckles again, as if she understands in an instant what's already passed between us...'

Thump! Crunch! My goodness! Is the woman smashing things up in there? What's going on?

'Robert, I'm sorry... but I'll have to go. There's...'

He's miffed to be cut short. He clearly wants to go into much more detail about his romantic bookshop moment. 'Listen,' he says. 'The upshot is, I'm taking them both out. I've got a night off, and I found myself inviting them both out with me tonight. I'm going to chuck these two newcomers to Whitby straight in at the deep end!'

'Oh yes?' I ask worriedly.

'It's cabaret night at The Christmas Hotel. I get ex-staff discount. Fenella and Timothy are very keen. What I want to know is, are you coming out with us, Brenda? Will you come out tonight for a bit of a Christmas bop?'

'Me?' I gasp. 'I was going to sit quietly with my book and my chocolates…'

'Nonsense!' he jeers. 'Go and give that Effie a knock. Get her out as well! We'll get her a bit drunk and pump her for information about her mysterious goings on…'

'Well,' I say musingly. 'That's not such a bad idea… All right. I will.'

Because all at once I really do feel like an evening out. It's funny how the desire creeps up on me some nights.

Yes, I shall venture out! I shall sally forth!

And it gives me an excuse to bang on Effie's door, too.

First though, after putting down the phone I step out into the hall and drift closer to the Orange Room. All the banging and thumping has calmed down now, thank goodness. But as I step closer, and before I've even got my ear jammed against the paintwork, I can hear voices coming from within. Voices, plural!

There's the woman, Iris herself, gabbling on in that raucous, wheedling voice of hers. Where's that accent even from? Somewhere in deepest, darkest Lancashire, maybe. I can't quite place it. Sounds to me like an unholy blend of Gracie Fields and the Pendle Witches...

And... what..?! What's *that..?*

There's definitely a second voice!

A low, rumbling, rather cultivated voice. An urbane and slightly gruff voice. It's a man's voice! She's got a *man* in there with her!

And she's only been in the place for about an hour!

I can't make out a single word.

Except... for a sentence or two. In that gruff man's voice.

He says: 'Are you sure she's the one, Iris? Can you really be sure?'

And she replies: 'I'm sure of it, chuck. It's definitely *her*.'

*

I don't go bursting in. I don't make a grand to-do. It's none of my business what Iris Wildthyme does in her room. She can have a whole platoon of the Coldstream Guards in there with her, and it'd still be nothing to do with me.

I leave well alone, and concentrate on dolling myself up – as best I can. I fluff out my favourite wig, smarm my make-up on – great dollops of the stuff. Then I wriggle my way into something vintage and gaudy by Ossie Clarke. And I look fabulous. Really, I do.

I use Christmas tree baubles for earrings. Just for a laugh. Just to show that I'm in with the swing of things.

Then I take a last look around my B&B to check all my guests are all right, and I dash out into the night.

It's absolutely freezing, and my heels feel perilous on the frosty cobbles. What am I doing running about in heels? 'I don't know why you torture yourself,' Effie said recently. 'You hobble about like no one's business and they make you look about eight feet tall.'

'But I feel like a glamorous lady when I wear them,' I told her.

She shrugged. 'If you say so, ducky.'

Sometimes she can be quite unpleasant, but I do love her. The old ratbag.

Next door. Effie's Antiques Emporium. Well, all the downstairs rooms are as dark as you'd expect, this time of night. But the upper rooms are a blaze of light and colour. All the rich curtains are drawn against the night and it would all look ever so inviting, if it wasn't for the fact that hardly anyone ever gets invited into Effie's home. It's her sanctuary and her safe space. Even I only venture there on special occasions.

Banging on the front door is a fruitless task tonight. Either she can't hear me, or she's studiously ignoring me. She wasn't picking up her phone earlier, either. The funny old dame has retreated into her shell for the season.

Well, I'll let her get on with it.

I knock one last time. 'Effie? *Yoo hoo..?*'
But she doesn't come down.

*

Now, I feel like I must have explained all this to you
before? So forgive me for repeating myself – I'm an
addled old lady who's been round the block far too
many times. But the thing about the Christmas Hotel
is this: it is owned by the monstrous and peculiar Mrs
Claus, and for years she has maintained her vast,
clifftop hotel in exactly the way she fervently wishes
it to be. IE, Christmas every single day of the year.
The place is lousy with tinsel and tacky decorations.
There's a party every night. An army of elves are
forever dancing attendance. And the place is jam-
packed with over-excited pensioners. It's a terribly
successful establishment.

Like many here in Whitby it's had its ups and
downs. Due to various shenanigans in the timelines
and the messing about with alternate dimensions
that have gone on over the years, Mrs Claus and I

have reached a kind of understanding. Once we were sworn enemies, due to her being utterly and irredeemably evil. However, she's been rejuvenated, reincarnated, possessed, exorcised, eradicated and even sent off into another world. Well, we all have, round here. You wouldn't believe half the things that have gone on. Anyhow, our shared spooky experiences have resulted in a strange kind of bond growing between us. In other words: there is a truce.

Which is just as well, because I really do enjoy a good night out at the Christmas Hotel.

Music is booming out of the long gallery of windows of the hotel frontage, all along the West Cliff. Boney M, if I'm not mistaken.

'Goodness me,' shivers Robert's new friend. 'It sounds very noisy in there!' That girl from the bookshop, Fenella. She's dressed in a floaty wrap over a leotard and she's got a wreath of mistletoe and ivy in her hair. Beside her strides her grinning brother, Timothy, with his hairy haunches, bare chest and little horns back in place. Linking arms with both, Robert looks chuffed to be out, showing off to his new friends. He's in a wine-red velvet jacket and he's had a sharp new haircut.

I must admit, we do look like a stylish group!

'It seems like a lot of fun,' smiles Timothy the faun. He stamps his elegant hooves on the frozen path to get warm. It's remarkable, really, how authentic-looking they are. Both bookshop twins have dressed up just like they did for the Krampus parade, and that gave me a bit of a shiver when I met them with Robert in the cocktail bar earlier.

I felt like asking them – I still do – about the warning that they seemed to plant in my head down on Church Street on Saturday. Warning me about Effie. About the danger she was getting herself into. But... that was just a dream, wasn't it? I'd only imagined the two of them whirling up to me, and whispering like that? But... it had seemed so real. And their voices really did sound how I had imagined then. So maybe... it really had been a warning, then?

We had vodka and gin in the busy bar and there hadn't really been a chance to ask them. We talked instead about their magical bookshop, and

Robert had been all lovey-dovey with Timothy. Really, it is nice to see him with someone who might turn out to be a new boyfriend. It's about time!

'Is it really a *magical* bookshop?' I asked them.

They stared at me. 'Magical as in… wonderful and lovely,' gasped Fenella in her breathy voice. 'Not as in enchanted..!'

'Oh, I see,' I nodded, oddly disappointed.

'Brenda sees spooky things everywhere!' Robert laughed, and I felt a bit like he was making fun of me.

Well, now, here we are at the Christmas hotel and ready to plunge into that heaving melee of festive carrying on. It's the very night of the solstice, and just a few days before Christmas Day itself. So there's a very special atmosphere inside the place. The Christmas Hotel is being timely and relevant for once! The whole tacky place is actually 'trending', as the youngsters might say. Mrs Claus's establishment is completely 'on brand'!

And here she comes: the old devil herself. Shunting along in her steam-powered bath chair. Slumped and dissolute. Crazed and goggle-eyed and all empurpled with broken veins. Attended by her tame elf boys, who protect her like she's a Roman Empress.

'Brenda, my dear!' she croaks. 'Those earrings..! How witty of you! And how beautiful you look. How you grace us with your company! Where's your mardy-looking friend, then?'

I make Effie's excuses for her. 'You know she's not one for a night on the razz.'

Mrs Claus pulls a face, because she knows that's not quite true. 'I've seen her up on that dance floor when she's had a few. Effie loves having a dance. We've all seen her black bottom, haven't we? We've all seen her bust a few moves, as the parlance has it. Now, who's this you're with..?'

Her face falls when she claps eyes on Robert.

'Hello there,' he grins at her warily.

To Mrs Claus Robert will always be the elf who got away. He abandoned her. He fled her hotel several years ago, in order to seek his fortune elsewhere. I mean, who can blame him? What, with that whole scandal to do with human flesh in the meat pies and elvish staff going mysteriously missing? Anyone would feel nervous working here at that time. But it's clear that Mrs Claus still feels betrayed by the lad. Silly old moo.

Robert introduces his new friends and Mrs Claus gazes at them coolly. 'Oh, you were on the Krampus parade, weren't you? We've got all your friends in tonight. They're all in their costumes again, all those devils and demons and fellas with horns. It's all very pagan in my ballroom this evening...'

'Oh good,' Timothy the faun winks at her cheekily. 'I'm glad to hear it!'

'Krampus, indeed,' Mrs Claus shudders. 'I don't hold with it, I don't. I think it's meddling, I do. I think it's meddling with dark things from a long-distant age. No good can come of it! No, indeed.' She slaps at her elves with her meaty palms. 'Here, set me going! Set me rolling again! I've had enough of talking to this lot. Let me circulate! Push me through! Let me meet all my lovely people!' As the elves get her moving again, shunting between the gaudy trees and noisy guests, she bellows back at me: 'Enjoy yourself, Brenda! At least you haven't got Effie holding you back tonight!'

*

Whatever Mrs Claus says, I do wish Effie was here tonight. It feels peculiar, being out on the town without her constant dry and acerbic commentary going on in my ear.

She'd have a thing or two to say about the ballroom, I know that much. Our little party all gasp when we set foot in there, for Mrs Claus and her staff have outdone themselves.

Everything is bloody red or black as a raven's wing. Mist hangs heavily in the boughs of all the many Christmas trees. And the trees are real, as well, because you can smell them. There's that genuine scent of pine, even above the stale Brut and Charlie of the dancing and whirling pensioners.

And yes! Here are the horned gods and grimacing dervishes and tall-hatted wizards from the Krampus parade. Horrid beings with claws and talons, tusks and shaggy whatnots. They look like they've been beamed in from another dimension.

Timothy, Fenella and Robert are thrilled, of course. The boys go straight off to join the dance, clutching each other's hands and hurtling into the middle of the floor. The young girl with the crimped hair accompanies me to the bar and we take our drinks to a little table. I'm happiest at the edges of things at first. I like to see how things are.

'Robert's told us all about you,' Fenella smirks as she sucks at a silver straw. She's got some kind of foaming potion. I've got a sweet sherry.

'All good, I hope.' I wince at my cliched reply, but there's something about the girl's expression that I find disconcerting.

'Good?' she titters. 'Good? Hardly! Good! Hahaha!'

I frown. What does she mean by that? She's being a bit cheeky, I think. 'What do you mean?

What's he been saying about?' Surely my lovely Robert can't have been slagging and bad-mouthing me behind my back..?

'*Infernal*,' she says. 'That's the word I'd have to choose for you, Brenda. Not 'good'. Not 'nice.' Not anything insipid or dreary like that. You're infernal! You're hellish! You're *demonic!*'

I gasp at her and fiddle with my bauble earrings. 'I'm no such thing..!'

She pulls a wry face at me. Sheer scepticism. 'Oh, really? You're just an ordinary old granny, are you? A simple old lady? A poor, boring old soul with no secrets at all..?'

I sit up straighter on my stool and glare at her. 'I don't know what exactly my friend Robert has been telling you, young lady. But I wish he wouldn't. An old lady's secrets and her past lives are no one's affair but her own.'

The girl shrugs lightly. She looks so carefree as she giggles and sips her awful-looking drink. How dare she sit there mocking me like this? 'Well, never mind,' she laughs. 'Perhaps I've got the wrong end of the stick. Perhaps Robert was just being silly and making it all up.'

'Aye,' I growl. 'Perhaps he was.'

She beams at me. It's a very insincere smile. I could fetch her quite a slap, I could. And that's not like me. I'm not a violent person. Only when my dander's up. And it's up right now. There's something about this young madam – this insinuating slip of a thing – that's getting right on my nerves.

I wonder if I've made a mistake coming out with these people tonight...

'*Oh..! Hello* there, chuck...! Hello there, lovey!'

Now there's someone yelling raucously down my earhole. I jump in my seat and swivel round in alarm.

And there she is! Standing there in what must be her gladrags.

She's looking a lot brighter and bushier-tailed than she was earlier, I must say. Her eyes are gleaming brightly and she's in some kind of silver lurex space outfit, complete with cape and thigh-high boots. Her hair is bushed out in a lilac frizz.

The woman from my B&B! Whom I last saw, looking lost, forlorn and frazzled in my Orange Room.

'Ms Wildthyme..!' I smile at her. I'm surprised to feel a tingle of happiness at the sight of this strange person.

'Oh, call me Iris, chuck,' she cries. 'Let's not stand on ceremony. How lovely to see you. Is this where it's all happening then, eh? I asked around and everyone said – this is *the* hotspot to be at! The Christmas Hotel..!'

I nod. 'It is indeed.' Then I turn to Fenella from the bookshop, ready to politely introduce her to my house guest. But guess what? Fenella has slipped away. 'Oh! I must have been boring her,' I pull a face.

'Here, let me join you,' grins Iris. 'What do you want from the bar? My shout..!'

I try to demur, and to tell her, one little drink – the tot of sherry I've already got – will be quite enough for me. Quite enough to be going on with. But Iris won't hear of it. 'We're out. It's Christmas. And you and I, lovey – we're going to have ourselves a fine old time.'

And do you know what?

That's exactly what we do.

*

Of course we end up going home well before the young ones. They've got boundless energy, and so do the fervidly festive pensioners from the Christmas Hotel. When Iris and I decide that enough's enough and it's time to go home, the place is still rocking like mad.

Us two old girls stagger home through the dark, empty streets, quite happily, depleted and slightly dizzy on two-for-one cocktails.

It's not quite been like having a night out with Effie. Iris has insisted we dance to every single song. She's been grabbing hold of other people and swinging them round and at one point she was up on the stage! I lost track of her in the melee during an Abba medley and then suddenly caught an awful glimpse. She was up where everyone could see her, making a show of herself! Kicking her legs up!

Still, there's something refreshingly frank and straightforward about Iris. As we head home to my B&B I find myself spilling my guts, rather. It's unlike me, really, but I'm airing all my worries to someone who's just about a stranger.

'It sounds to me like this Effie of yours has a guilty secret,' is her considered opinion, as we lurch down Silver Street together.

We pause a moment outside the darkened window display of The Spooky Finger. 'I'm not sure about those twins,' I say musingly. 'That skinny girl was downright rude to me. And I'm sure Robert's getting himself in too deep with that little faun fella. Wouldn't surprise me if there isn't trouble brewing there.'

As I sigh Iris is chuckling at me. 'Tell me, Brenda. Is your life here in Whitby a constant round of hair-raising adventures and queer escapades?'

I frown at her. 'Well, yes it is, actually. Why do you ask?'

'Ha!' she gurns at me. 'I thought so. Mine is too, you know. Ooh, it's non-stop escapades and funny do's.'

I narrow my eyes at her. 'Hmmm. Well, I'm past the point of any more escapades tonight. Let's get ourselves home...'

It's the shortest day of the year, but we seem to have made it last bloomin' forever.

And it isn't over yet.

Now Iris is intrigued by the mystery of Effie next door. So intrigued that, when we return to Harbour Street, she gets all excited when she sees that there's a single light still glowing on Effie's second floor.

'It's her sitting room,' I say. 'She must still be up.'

A crafty look comes over Iris's face. 'You know what we could do, don't you, lovey?'

I'm not sure I'm going to like what she's about to suggest...

And next thing I know she's demonstrating a surprising amount of agility and wiry strength, jumping onto a pile of old crates and clambering up on top of them. She clatters about, giggling and shushing herself.

'Oh, come down from there! Come down at once!' I cry out. 'You'll do yourself a mischief, you daft woman…'

But a steely determination comes over Ms Wildthyme and I'm forced to watch, with my heart thumping in my throat, as she clings to the old drainpipe and starts shinning up the crumbling brickwork of Effie's house. She's like Spider Woman!

'Iris…!' I hiss, wishing I'd never told her anything about my friend next door. But up she goes, clambering and giggling, with her silver cape flaring out behind her. I suddenly think: this daft old woman has done this before. She's quite used to climbing and risking her life and sneaking about.

I watch, holding my breath, as she reaches Effie's parlour window. She hoists herself up to the gap in the curtains. She must have a splendid view of whatever is transpiring inside…

There's a dreadful, silent, empty pause as Iris takes in whatever she can see. Then she goes: 'Oh my giddy aunt!'

And in that very second her hands lose their grip on the windowsill and her feet start scrabbling at the drainpipe for purchase.

'Iris…!'

I dart forward, hopelessly, as she reels backwards through the air…

'Oh, *buggery flip…!*' she screeches, in the split second that it takes her to fall back all the way she's clambered.

She drops heavily onto the boxes and crates. Flattening them completely with a great big crash. Her arm is twisted beneath her and, as soon as I dash to her side, I can see that it must be broken.

'*Flamin' Nora!*' she howls at the night, as I try to shift her.

The two of us are making so much noise I reckon we'll have half the street awake. Iris sobs with pain as she gets to her feet.

But there's nothing from Effie. She doesn't suddenly appear. She clearly hasn't heard all of our hullaballoo.

'We'd best get to the hospital, if you've broken it...' I frown, putting my arm around Iris.

'No way,' she grunts, pulling away. 'If they get their hands on me, they'll turn me over to the Authorities. Wanting to discover all my secrets! They'll do terrible things to me... It's only sprained, that's all. I've got special medicine in my carpet bag, up in my room...'

So that's the end of that. She shuffles crabwise, wincing, to my side passage and waits impatiently while I fiddle for my keys.

She smokes a cigarette fiercely and says: 'Just you wait till I tell you! You'll never believe what I saw through your friend's window! Ha ha! It was almost worth falling for!'

*

Minutes later we're in the Orange Room and I'm watching her rummage through her carpet bag.

I must say, she's made a right mess of my lovely room in just her few hours of occupancy. There are numerous outfits strewn on each surface, as if she had tried on every item at a theatrical costumier's before coming out tonight. And books! There are books and scrapbooks of cuttings piled up everywhere. Also, complicated items of electronic gadgetry, linked together by dangerously-frayed looking wires and all of them hooked up to the mains.

Where has all this stuff even come from, I wonder? She couldn't have been lugging all this in her carpet bag, surely...

The dressing table has been cleared of its seashell collection I'd arranged so prettily and instead there's what looks like a space-age telly sitting there. She's connected it to the aerial wire and it's hissing and fizzing with static. I bet she's running up my leccy bill something awful!

I watch her necking a couple of bright blue pills and swigging brandy. 'Have a swallow,' she tells me. 'You'll need it.' As I do so, she's winding a multi-coloured scarf around her injured arm. 'The pain will fade in a few moments,' she nods, sitting heavily on the bed. 'Whew! 'Ell's teeth! I really did myself a mischief, didn't I? Just like folk always warn me I will!'

'I suppose you did,' I smile worriedly. 'Are you sure you're all right?'

She waves my concern away. 'Forget me. You want me to tell you about your friend, don't you?'

I nod. 'What did you see?'

Iris bites her lip. 'As far as you know, does this Effie person have any peculiar... tastes... or predilections... when it comes to her love life?'

'What?' Honestly, I dread to think what's coming next. I try to think. How can I even start in on the details of Effie's complicated love life with this stranger? 'Why? Who did she have in with her?'

'Well, I could only see the back of him,' Iris says. 'He was sitting facing away from me. But he were a big brute. Huge broad shoulders. She looked so dainty beside him. Well, not beside him. Lying across his lap. That's what she was doing.'

I'm not sure I want to hear anymore, but Iris goes on.

'He had her over his knee, Brenda. And he had a handful of sticks. Like birch twigs, in his hand. And he was… well, he was beating her on the bum with them. I could hardly believe my eyes.'

I stare at Iris in appalled fascination. 'But… was she all right? If she was being… beaten… surely… she…'

'Oh, she was having a lovely time,' says Iris. 'She looked like she was loving every minute. In fact, just before I fell off the wall, I saw her getting up and the pair of them switched around. He was too big and heavy to climb onto her lap of course, but she made him get down on his hands and knees so she could whip his bum, too. It was all very shocking! It was all rather wonderful! And wouldn't you know, but that's the very moment when I fell from my perch…'

*

Too much information.

That's what I've had.

Whatever Effie gets up to in the comfort of her own home after midnight, it's of no concern to me. When she was seeing old Kristoff Alucard on the sly, that was nobody's business but her own. When she had her brief lesbian dalliance with that ghost of the old Warrior Queen from the eleventh century – that was all to do with her and no one else.

But all of this being hit with twigs... I don't know. It sounds a rum do to me. If someone ever tried beating me with branches I'd rip their bloody head off.

But other people's love lives are always a mystery, aren't they?

Anyhow. I've work to do. I've a business to run and Christmas to enjoy. I don't want to be dwelling on the sado-masochistic doings of friends and neighbours.

The next day dawns beautifully and bright blue. Even after my late night I have to be up making breakfasts. Perfect fried eggs and rashers of crispy bacon. Foaming pots of strong coffee. My guests shuffle into the dining room looking rested and refreshed by a good night's sleep.

Only Iris is missing. During a lull in service I nip upstairs to knock on the door of the Orange Room. All I can hear from within are groans.

What if she's in agony? What if that arm of hers really does need medical attention?

I put my shoulder to the door and find it unlocked.

She's lying there, still in her space-age disco outfit and all her make-up on. Sprawled in the tangerine sheets and dead to the world. She's been drooling but at least she hasn't thrown up.

There are books open all around her head, as if she'd been reading several things at once before eventually passing out in her bed. A scrapbook catches my eye. Something about the yellowed clippings and the smudgy photos draws my attention. They are very old newspaper stories, I think. I peer closer... I can't help myself having a quick scan down the page… Very, very old, in fact… the paper is almost crumbling away…

And then the strange little telly on the dressing table hisses and buzzes. It's like an alarm has gone off. I jump up and almost shriek.

Iris mutters and stirs in her sleep, but doesn't wake.

The screen is fizzing with blue static. A shape is wavering and trying to form. A voice says: 'Iris? Iris, are you there, dear?' And it's that gruff and cultivated voice that I heard before, emanating from this very room. Ah! So she didn't have someone in here, after all. He was talking on her funny old telly. Talking straight to her! 'Iris! Are you all right?'

There's a silhouette on the screen. Someone with a very round head. Someone with very dark and boggling eyes.

I draw closer to the screen. I want to tell him she's okay. He sounds so concerned I feel I have to tell him that she's safe here. She's just unconscious with drink.

'H-hello..?' I stammer at the screen. 'Can you hear me?'

There's a crackling pause. 'Who *is* this?' demands the deep, growly voice.

'My name is Brenda,' I tell him. 'Listen, Iris is fine here. She's just been a bit drunk and hurt her arm a little bit after falling off a drainpipe...'

'*What?*' he gasps. 'Look, who is this speaking, please..?'

'It's Brenda...' I repeat. 'You don't know me, but I'm the...'

'Oh, bugger!' curses the voice and suddenly the screen goes dark. He's gone!

*

I leave Iris to sleep off her night of excitement and excess. I hurry to see to the rest of the needs of my other guests.

By ten o'clock I'm dead on my feet. Everyone's gone off to enjoy a day of shopping or walking or sight-seeing and I have some time to myself. I'm just brewing up a pot of my favourite spicy tea when there's a knock downstairs.

It's Effie come to call!

All at once I'm ashamed. I suddenly recall... in our drunkenness Iris and I thought it was a good idea last night, to spy on Effie during an intimate encounter! Iris actually saw her indulging in a strange and saucy activity with an unknown man! And what's more – then she was doing it back to him...!

I can barely look my friend in the eye.

I fuss with tea things, and a plate of biscuits, as she settles herself on my bobbly green armchair.

To be fair, she looks rather shifty, too. And, do I imagine it? She might even be sitting awkwardly because her bottom's slightly sore?

I pour the tea and marvel at the multifariousness of forms that human desire can take. I can't imagine how being spanked might feel nice. I'd be fuming if someone tried that on me. But like I always say: it takes all sorts. And Effie is a fathomless mystery, I've always thought...

When we've both got our tea she looks me dead in the eye. 'Brenda, I have to tell you, ducky. I'm afraid I've got myself into something rather deep...'

*

It all started at the beginning of December, she tells me. Just a matter of weeks ago...

'Have you seen that new channel on the telly..?' she asks.

Now Effie knows for a fact that I don't have much time for television programmes. I don't think they make shows for people like me anymore.

'Oh, but you'd love this station, Brenda. They show nothing but lovely films and TV shows from the olden days. Everything is black and white! It's ever so soothing...'

I sip my spicy tea and wait for her to go on.

'Crackling Images, this channel is called. You should look it up. I've whiled away many an afternoon tuning into shows from yesteryear. And sometimes I sit up in bed, through the wee small hours, absolutely revelling in nostalgia.'

I don't have much time for nostalgia, I must admit. Never look back! That's Brenda's motto. When you've got over two hundred years to look back on it can fair make you dizzy.

'So you've been watching vintage telly...' I prompt her. 'What's wrong with that?'

She bites her lip. 'This is the funny bit. The deucedly strange bit.'

'Go on...'

'Well, I was drifting off one night... watching these old movies... with all these old glamorous stars. All those sexy men in their smart suits and their slicked back hair. Musicals and war movies and everyone talking like they're at a Buckingham Palace garden party. And at the same time I was idly flipping through one of my Aunties' old books of magic spells...'

Oh help, I think. What's coming next?

'I just got to thinking... wouldn't it be lovely... just to live in that simpler world again, just for a little while? To spend some time with one of those wonderful romantic heroes?'

'Effie Jacobs... what did you do..?'

She bursts out: 'Nothing dangerous! Nothing wicked! I just... put my finger on a summoning spell. I thought... well, surely... if my aunties could summon up creatures from out of the ether using their old books and incantations... surely I could bring myself a little bit of gentlemanly company for during the holiday season..?'

I could picture it now. What kind of devilry had she been getting up to in front of her old, flickering telly-box?

'Who've you gone and called up?' I demand.

'I thought I had the choice of everyone,' she says, despondently. 'I was flicking through the Radio Times – you saw me, remember? I was putting circles around particular films. I was thinking... ooh, Dirk Bogarde. David Niven. James Mason... My mind was fair boggling...'

I purse my lips. 'Yes, I thought you were looking a bit distracted. I knew you were up to something.'

'Yes, well, I was a woman with a mission. I got all my ingredients together, as listed in Old Aunt Maude's grimoire – it was mostly spices and strange, wizened items out of jars. And I sat there with my Radio Times and the telly tuned into Crackling Images...'

'But Effie! You swore off ever trying out magic again! You said that your aunties had caused so much bother in the past with their spells that you've been put off forever!'

'Well, perhaps...' she mutters. 'But I was feeling lonely, Brenda. What with Christmas coming up. Long, lonely days. Just me and the four walls...'

'But... but you've got me!' I tell her.

She smiles. 'I know that, ducky. But... you know. I just wanted... a bit of romance. A bit of excitement.'

'Hmm,' say I. 'And what exactly happened when you cast your spell?'

She puts her hands over her face and shudders. Then she looks at me and says: 'I was watching an old Christmas movie from the 1940s. Bernard Baxter in 'What Ho, Santa Claus!' Have you ever seen it?'

I shake my head.

'Well, Bernard Baxter was a smart-looking gent, I always thought... So I decided that I'd sprinkle a bit of witchy-dust over the telly while he was on. I'd see if I could get him to manifest himself in my back parlour...'

'And did it work..?'

She trembles. She quakes. She sips her spicy tea. Then she looks me in the eye. 'Magic definitely happened, Brenda. It turns out that I can do those old spells, just as well as Aunt Maude ever did. The room went darker. The telly glowed brighter. There was a very strange atmosphere brewing all around me... and I was transfixed! I was staring dead ahead as a tall, broad, manly figure formed inside the old cathode ray tube. And he stepped right out! He broke through the glass like it was just mist and fog! He stepped out of the screen and onto my carpet!'

Oh, Effie. Will you never learn, I wonder?

'And who was it?' I quiz her. 'Was it Bernard Baxter?'

'No..! No, it wasn't...! It was... it was... I don't even know how to tell you this... but it was a... a...'

And at that very moment we are interrupted.

I jump up in my seat as the door flies open and Iris totters in. She's wearing a ratty old dressing gown trimmed with feathers and she looks half dead. 'Brenda, lovey. I feel dreadful – and it's all your flamin' fault, lady!'

Appalled, Effie stares at the newcomer. 'Who the devil is this?' she asks. 'Bursting into your sitting room without a by-your-leave? Looking like death warmed up?'

Iris's eyes widen at the sight of Effie. She rubs them, smearing last night's eye make-up till it looks even more horrific. Then she grins wickedly at my best friend. 'Ooh, it's Effie, isn't it? The lady from next door.'

Iris still has her injured arm wrapped in that colourful scarf. She's holding it awkwardly, as if suddenly reminded of the tumble she took last night.

'You have me at a disadvantage,' says Effie primly.

'I'll say!' Iris guffaws.

I step in: 'Effie, this is Ms Iris Wildthyme. She's staying in my Orange Room over Christmas.'

'Hello, there,' Iris grins at my cross-looking friend. 'What a pleasure it is to meet you, face to face, as it were.'

Effie narrows her eyes, as if she suspects that Iris is having a laugh at her expense. Which she is, of course. I just pray that Iris doesn't go blurting out anything about spying on Effie's having her bare bottom spanked last night. Surely she wouldn't? Effie would expire on the spot. She'd be mortified!

Oh dear. Is THIS what my life has become? Once I'd be fettling gods and monsters from other dimensions! I'd be wrestling with the great big questions of creation! I'd be solving mysteries and quandaries and pondering the impossible! Now I'm sitting between squabbling old ladies and thinking about their funny goings-on.

'Ooh, is that spicy tea?' Iris asks, peering at the pot. 'Can I have some? My mouth's like a budgie's bumhole this morning.'

Effie flinches at Iris's coarseness and she simmers with disgust as she watches the interloper help herself to tea and handfuls of biscuits. 'Well, here I am with the famous lady detectives of Whitby!' she grins, flomping down on my sofa. 'What's going on, eh? Are you investigating anything over the festive season?'

Icy fury flashes in Effie's eyes. 'Famous lady detectives? Where do you get your information from, ducky? Brenda and I are nothing of the sort!'

Iris sniggers. 'That a fact, is it, lovey? Well, you see, I have my sources. And I know all kinds of things. You'd be surprised at the things I know...' She slurps her tea in what I can only describe as an insinuating manner.

'As it happens we are investigating flip-all during this festive season,' Effie tells her frostily.

Then she stands up and straightens her tweedy jacket. 'Brenda, I shall talk to you later. Perhaps we can discuss my little… issue later in the day? When you are less discommoded by company, hm?'

'Oh,' I flummer, standing up to see her out. 'Well, yes, I suppose so… if you're sure you're all right?'

Steely eyes meet mine. I gather from her expression that Effie isn't about to tell me anything further about her magical adventures, what with madam sitting on my settee in her dressing gown.

'Charmed to meet you, Miss Wildthyme,' Effie tells Iris, staring down at her like she's something that's gone off.

'Aye, cheers, up yours, as well,' Iris mutters, and crunches up a custard cream. 'Brenda, is it too early for a little drinky, do you think..?'

Effie tosses her head. I've never seen her look haughtier. 'I will leave you to your sobering up. Goodbye, the pair of you.'

*

Later.

Iris is feeling a little bit brighter, and she's glammed herself up in a rainbow coat and what seems to be a pirate hat. I'm accompanying her into town so we can pay a visit to the new bookshop. It seems that both of us have some investigating in mind.

'I wish you and Effie had been able to hit it off a bit better,' I tell her. 'It's such a shame!'

'I know!' she chuckles. 'You could have cut the air with a knife, couldn't you? Is she always such frowsty old madam?'

'I suppose she is, yes, really. But she's my friend.'

Iris nods. We're yomping up a steep bit of hill besides the old church. 'I can understand that. I've got some funny, sometimes unlikable friends, too. But when you're close you see past their peculiarities, don't you?'

This reminds me of that moment last night, when Iris was passed out on her bed and her clunky old television set fizzed into life and that gruff voice was talking. 'What even was that?' I ask her now. 'Hey, you haven't been summoning up spirits on your television set, have you? Not another one!'

She shakes her head. 'Summoning spirits! Do I look daft? Spirits are for mixing and downing, not summoning. No, that's my Time Telly.'

'Your what?'

'My Time Telly. By which means I communicate across the decades and the centuries with my companions when we are separated by the time continuum.' While explaining this her voice has become quite lah-di-dah. When she notices the confusion on my face she cracks out laughing. 'Oh! I haven't explained yet, have I?'

'Explained what?' Honestly, I'm dreading what's coming next – knowing it can only be yet another complication in my life.

'I'm a Transtemporal Adventuress,' she says, very grandly, throwing out her multi-coloured arms and wincing at the pain.

'A what?'

'I travel in time,' she smiles, confidingly.

'Oh,' I say. Time travel, in my limited experience, is a right palaver.

Iris carries on: 'And I'm here in Whitby to investigate a very peculiar kettle of fish.'

'Oh yes?' My heart's hammering in my chest. It's me, isn't it? I think. She's here to investigate me...!

But Iris leads the way over the road to Silver Street and tells me: 'Them twins and their new bookshop. Fenella and Timothy Winters of the Spooky Finger. That's who I'm here to investigate.'

I'm hurrying after her towards the welcoming bookshop. I'm horribly relieved not to be the subject of her mission. 'Oh! I thought there was something... odd about them, too.' And I remember just how queer and horrible Fenella was to me, last night at the Christmas Hotel, just before Iris popped up at my table.

Before we enter the shop another thought strikes me: 'Iris, that person I saw on your Time Telly last night, in the wee small hours. Was it really a talking stuffed Panda?'

'Ha!' she bursts out laughing. 'Oh, probably, lovey! Probably!'

And then she flings open the door to the bookshop.

*

It's lovely inside. Just like I knew it would be. All the shelves are very orderly and even the vintage and secondhand volumes look tidy and well-behaved. There's not a feeling of jumble or rummage sale anywhere about this shop.

Delicate fairy lights are glimmering around the walls. Tasteful pictures are placed in just the right spots. I can smell home-baking. Something spicy and fragrant.

It's a lovely, fancy, welcoming bookshop.

But I know I'm not really welcome.

There's the woman who runs it. She's sat at that desk. And she's got a right face on her, soon as I step through that door.

'Iris... I'm not sure about this...' is what I try to say to my companion. But Iris looks quite set on being here. We're paying a visit to the Spooky Finger this afternoon. Here we are. We're here to buy books. Together. Two ladies. Hello! Here we are.

And that girl is staring at us from behind that desk. Fenella Winters. She's glaring. She looks at us askance.

'Oh! Hello, there!' Iris grins, hurrying over to the desk. I follow more reluctantly, as I remember Fenella's words to me in the ballroom of the Christmas Hotel. She said peculiar and insinuating things. Things that revealed that she knows more about me that I'd want her to...

'Is there anything in particular you're looking for?' Fenella asks.

'We're merely browsing and following our noses,' Iris tells her, looking the young woman up and down shrewdly. 'I've found it's the best way to go about these things. Now, what are those delicious-smelling cakes you're baking back there? We'll have two of whatever they are, plus some lovely coffee, if you don't mind. With cream and marshmallows and everything else chucked on. Ta!'

The girl goes off wordlessly into the kitchen alcove to do Iris's bidding and I marvel at the way this woman seems to be able to tell everyone exactly what to do.

'It's a knack, lovey,' she says, patting me on the arm. 'You see, I've got very winning ways. Now, have a scour about in the stacks to see if you can find something you'd like to read on a long journey...'

'I'm not going on a long journey...!'

She looks at me as if I don't know what I'm talking about. Perhaps I don't: I have the oddest sensation of my life slipping out of my control. Just then Christmas music starts playing through hidden speakers. 'I feel proper Christmassy this week,' Iris confides in me, looking very happy. 'That's quite hard when you zig-zag through time like I do, you know. So I guess I've got Whitby and you to thank for that, Brenda. You've made me feel part of everything here.'

This warms my heart a little, even if everything Iris says does tend to make me feel bewildered.

We scan through shelves and I find myself drawn to the thrillers and crime novels of yesteryear, as ever. For such a gentle soul as I am, I have surprisingly bloodthirsty tastes when it comes to my leisure time. Iris is hunkered down and flipping through bound volumes of ancient magazines. There's a kind of gurgling noise and, when I stare more closely, I realise that she's drinking from a silver hip flask as she searches.

Soon enough Fenella brings us our coffee. She slams a tray down on her desk and doesn't look very happy about being treated like a skivvy. 'Have you seen my brother?' she asks, snappishly.

'Beg pardon, lovey?' Iris asks.

'I've not seen my brother Timothy since we were all at that dreadful Christmas Hotel place last night. He took off with that young friend of yours, Robert again.' Fenella narrows her eyes at me. 'I'm not sure he's the right sort for my brother to be involved with. Timothy is very sensitive and sweet. He hasn't seen very much of this world...'

I rise up to defend my friend. 'There's nothing wrong with Robert! Your brother ought to be glad to knock around with him!' If anything, I think, it's her brother who I feel wary of. He looks like a little devil, doesn't he? I don't know how much of that look of his is real and how much is stuck on. 'Anyhow, I imagine they're both up at the Hotel Miramar, where Robert works and lives.'

Fenella shudders. 'Ugh, that place. Isn't that where Mummu Manchu used to live? Presiding over his empire of evil and skulduggery?'

'Years ago,' I agree. 'But it's been done up since then, and it's quite respectable now.'

Iris laughs. 'I once had a run in with old Mummu Manchu! Is he still going, then? He had a lovely young wife, Sheila...'

'I know Sheila!' I burst out.

'It's a small world!' Iris exclaims.

'Look, Fenella,' I tell the frosty young bookseller. 'I'm sure your brother is safe and well with my Robert. There's nothing for you to worry about.' I can see that under her touchy exterior she's actually a mass of nerves and fretfulness.

'Don't you patronise me,' Fenella warns. 'Mind your own business.' Then she turns on her heel and leaves us to our browsing.

'Huh!' Iris huffs. 'What a nightmare she is!' Then she beckons me over to look at what she's found. 'Look at this! You'll be very interested, I think…'

It's a heavy volume containing a whole year's worth of issues of an old story magazine. The pages are custard-coloured and almost falling apart. The paper is called 'The Queer Fandango' and I've never heard of it.

'It sounds like just my kind of periodical,' Iris chuckles, carefully turning pages. We both squint at inky, smudgy illustrations and columns of painfully tiny print. 'You know how the Strand magazine had Sherlock Holmes and other mags had other, famous heroes and detectives…'

'I suppose so…' I can't fix my eyes on any of the print on these pages. Everything's much too cramped. Even the drawings are too dark and indistinct for me to make anything out. They seem to be mostly pictures of people having punch-ups in dark, foggy streets…

Iris says: 'It seems that The Queer Fandango had its own particular brand of heroine…'

'Oh..?'

We peer at lavishly-drawn headings and ornate title pages.

'Oh..!'

'The Voodoo Queen and Brenda.'

'The Dance of the Whirligig: An Iris Adventure.'

'Brenda and the Psychic Sisters.'

'Wildthyme Ahoy!'

We both look up out of the ancient volume and gasp.

'But it's *us*…!'

Now, Iris's reaction is just as innocently flabbergasted as my own. I have no reason to suspect that she's not as gobsmacked by this moment as I am.

As far as I know, we're both having the same epiphany at the very same time.

It doesn't hit me that it might be a very strange coincidence that she's happened upon this mysterious book almost as soon as she started looking…

If Effie was here, that's exactly the kind of sniffy and sceptical thing she would point out…

I just stand there with my mouth open. I can hardly believe what I'm seeing. 'But… but it's *us!* Stories about us in the nineteenth century!'

Of course, I'm playing up my reaction just a little bit. Of course I know it's perfectly possible for stories of this vintage to exist about *me*. I just have to *seem* to be astonished. It's best that I don't give too much away…

'And there's something else,' Iris says. 'I found something stuck under the end papers of this book. It came away and fell into my hand almost at once…'

She slips a crackling, yellowed envelope into my hand.

'What's this?'

'It must have been waiting inside this book for more than a hundred and fifty years. Just for you to find it, Brenda!'

'Me?' I stare at the thing. And my vision reels for a second.

'See?' And now Iris is trying to cram the whole hardback volume up the front of her jumper and to pull her rainbow coat around it.

The envelope has written on the front: *For the Attention of Brenda.*

And it's in Effie's handwriting.

Now, it's one thing to catch a glimpse of myself back in Victorian times. That's fair enough. But *Effie*? There's no way on Earth she should be back there.

And, sure enough, when I open up the letter I find it dated October 1861 and the whole thing is scribed in Effie's distinctive copperplate.

'My Dearest Brenda,

If you're receiving this letter, I can only imagine that it's down to the machinations of that dreadful Wildthyme woman. Watch out for her – she's manipulated the lot of us! And I can also only assume that I myself have vanished off into the night. Have I? Have I vanished yet? Or am I in time with this letter? Have you received it in time to stop me..?'

I look up from the letter. 'Effie's back in 1861!'

Iris rolls her eyes. 'Silly cow. What's she doing there?'

Then Fenella is back with us, made suspicious by all our hissing urgency. 'You haven't eaten your seed cake.'

Iris shrugs. 'Those little bits in it give me the heave.'

Fenella's eyes flash and next thing we know, we are leaving the premises.

Iris looks ridiculous with that book up her jumper. How could the daft girl Fenella not even realise that she was nicking it?

Unless… unless the whole thing was a set up?

Now, this doesn't occur to me till much later.

What if Fenella and Iris are in cahoots? What if I am being stitched up?

I really wish that I had a more suspicious and cynical nature. I'm such a credulous fool!

But as things stand right at this moment, I'm dashing down Silver Street clutching Effie's ancient missive in my mitt, mad keen to get home to read it in peace. And Iris comes waddling after me with her purloined book trapped under her coat.

At this moment I'm assuming that we're both on the same side, and my head is filled with fear and anxiety for Effie and the idea of saving her. She can't be trapped back in the nineteenth century! She simply *can't*!

She would absolutely hate it there...!

*

Dearest Brenda (the letter continued...)

Yes, it was all my fault. As usual. I went too far and I wasn't honest with myself or with you about what I was getting up to. I was flexing my magical gifts and dabbling in things that ought not to be dabbled with. I should have come out and told you. As soon as I knew I was in danger. I should have begged you for help.

But all I could see was you knocking about with that awful Wildthyme woman. I saw green! I'm sorry! I should be able to rise above such petty reactions. But I can't. I'm human, just like the rest of us. (Correction: I'm not sure that either you or your friend Iris actually count as human. Do you? Don't take offence!)

Anyhow, I thought I could deal with my situation all by myself. That Christmas I had summoned up a being through the medium of my telly box and I thought I could deal with all the ramifications and consequences...

But I couldn't, Brenda! I just couldn't control him... I've never experienced anything quite like it!

Iris is reading over my shoulder and cracks out laughing when she reaches this bit. 'I'll say!'

I shush her and read on.

'Oh, I wish that I'd never heard of that TV channel, Crackling Pictures. It was my downfall, Brenda! Without it I'd never have been tempted to do witchcraft on my telly box and I'd never have summoned up that time-travelling demon…'

'Oho!' Iris chortles. 'Time travelling demon! That's what he is! Well, I'm not surprised…'

'Anyhow, ducky. I'm hoping this letter finds you well. I'm not really enjoying Victorian times very much. Everything's quite a bit muckier than you'd even imagine. So, if there's any way of you sorting everything out and rescuing me and getting me home for Christmas, I'd truly appreciate it. In fact, I'm begging you, Brenda. I can't stick it back here. I've been a stupid old woman and I need your help!'

And with that she signs herself off with a great flourish and a spatter of ink, which has faded to indigo over the decades.

'The address is in London,' says Iris. 'Bloomsbury. I wonder what she's doing there.'

I'm struggling to get my head round all of this. 'So, this is from eighteen-sixty-whatever… and she's been there a while. But, as far as we're concerned, she isn't there yet?'

Iris is taking a slug from her hip flask. Her breath reeks of gin. 'I'm quite used to these time-travelling conundrums, you know. It's all old hat to me. You know, really, there's no need to panic about any of it. Not when you have my expertise and experience to help you. 1861 will still be there tomorrow.'

I blink at her. I'm starting to wonder if I'm in the company of a complete maniac. 'But maybe we're not too late!' I cry. 'Maybe she's not been carried off yet! Perhaps we've still got time to save her from this time travelling demon of hers?'

Suddenly I'm back on my feet and grabbing my coat again.

Iris is peering out of the attic window. Dark has come down early over the town, and it's snowing.

'You might be right, chuck. You might be in time to prevent her. But, you know, I'm looking down at Harbour Street now... and isn't *that* her? Isn't that her leaving her place right now? And setting off determinedly into the crowds? Where's she off to, I wonder..?'

I rush to the window and yes, I believe Iris is right. That's Effie's stiff-backed walk and her familiar carriage. She's disappearing into the mass of people out and about enjoying the festive lights and atmosphere of town.

'We have to get after her..!' I gasp, grabbing hold of Iris's arm and dragging her with me.

'Hang on, lovey,' she laughs. 'Didn't you hear what I said? When you're a Transtemporal Adventuress like me, you never have to hurry! You never have to panic about time..!'

'Never mind all that now,' I growl. 'This is my best friend Effie we're talking about. I don't want her vanishing into bloomin' awful Victorian times! We're going after her - right NOW!'

*

Town is ram-packed tonight. Everyone's out in the narrow streets doing last minute Christmas shopping. As Iris and I pile into the melee, surging across the harbour bridge, I notice that there's something else going on.

The Krampus people are out again! The Krampuses? The Krampi?

Clearly they enjoyed themselves in their traffic-congesting devilment the other night and now they're out again! Snarling and waving and roaring at the crowds. Handing out candy canes and chocolate-covered Brussels sprouts.

'We don't have time for this,' Iris gasps. 'We're looking for our friend!'

Mind, I don't think Effie would be chuffed to be thought of as Iris's friend.

Someone's setting smoke bombs off! Noxious green fog spews out and floats around our ears. The snow's coming down thicker than ever, turning the cobbles under our feet quite hazardous.

'You know, if it wasn't a race against time, this would feel quite festive,' I remark, and Iris rolls her eyes.

'Look, you know your friend. Where's she likely to be going..?'

I confess that I really don't know. 'If she's bobbed out for a few bits of groceries, then I suppose she might be at the...'

A savage squawk from Iris interrupts me. 'Look! It's them again..!'

She elbows me hard until I clock what she's noticed: Fenella and Timothy Winters are dancing in the parade once more. She's in her witchy yoga outfit and he's resplendently faunish again. They're dancing around like whirling dervishes in the snow and colourful mist, and this time they're joined by a new friend! It's Robert! My Robert! He's wearing his red and green Elf costume, complete with pointed ears and rouged cheeks. It's almost like he's in a trance, the way he's dancing in the street!

'Oh, *Robert..!*' I call out. 'They've transfixed him with their pagan influences and strange ideas..!'

Iris urges me on. 'There's nothing more we can do for him now...'

'But what if something terrible happens to him..?'

Iris looks grim. Like she knows that a dreadful fate really does await my lovely Robert!

'You've brought us bad luck!' I rail at Iris suddenly. My temper gets the better of me. All that tambourine-bashing and drum-rolling hullaballoo has gotten on my nerves so that I snap at her.

'Me!' she gasps, cut to the quick.

'Everything was fine till you turned up,' I growl at the startled woman. 'We were all settled in for a lovely Christmas. A peaceful Christmas! But then you pop up and everything goes to hell!'

She cracks out laughing. 'Yes, that's often the way! But remember, Brenda – Effie had magicked up her mystery man before I even arrived! These events were underway without any prodding and provoking from yours truly...'

I have to concede that. 'You're right. I'm sorry.'

'Mind,' she shrugs and looks rueful. 'I'm not saying that my presence hasn't exacerbated everything...'

'No, no,' I hurry to reassure her. The dancing crowd is parting around us. They're blowing little horns and kazoos. 'You've been a great help, and a lovely friend to me this week. Really.'

She looks to crestfallen as she whips out her hipflask and gurgles down some gin. Then suddenly she's seen something over my shoulder.

'*It's her..!*'

I whip around and, yes: sure enough. There's Effie!

She's in the Krampus parade, wearing her normal clothes and clutching her shopping bag. Oh, but she's dancing in the most bizarre, almost lewd fashion. She can't be in her right mind at all, making a show of herself in the street like that! It's like the spirit of Mick Jagger has suddenly taken her over as she jerks her arms and legs and sticks her bottom out.

'Effie! *Effie!*' I yell at her. 'Stop it! *Stop doing that!*'

I hope no one's filming this impromptu parade. She'd hate seeing herself twerking outside the fishmongers.

When her head turns in our direction her eyes are chilly and blank.

'She's possessed!' Iris howls into my ear. '*Something's* got a hold of her!'

'She's got a *bloke* with her!' I cry. 'Is that the one you saw through her window, Iris?'

All at once Effie has been gathered up in the arms of a very tall gent.

'*Yes!* Yes, that's the bugger..!'

So this is who she called up through her telly box. He's about eight feet tall and just as wide. And if I know anything, I don't think he's some smoothie from a black and white movie.

He's a *Krampus*! With the head of an old goat and huge curling horns. He's got wings on his back: tattered leathery things. Effie has submitted to his arms and he's licking all over her face with his forked tongue.

'Ooh, oh! It's disgusting..!' Iris screeches. 'And do you know what, chuck? I think he's the real deal! He's an actual flamin' demon!'

I believe she's right. But what can we do? He looks unstoppable!

'This is who she let beat her on the bottom with birch twigs?'

Iris nods. 'It's traditional, apparently.'

I know the legends. The Krampus comes to carry away all the bad boys and girls…

And as we watch, the distance between us and Effie is growing by the second. The noisy music is becoming harsher and more grating and the parade is moving on. The Krampus creature has produced an old sack from somewhere and he's waving it around.

'Oh no! Effie! Get away! Run away from him…!'

But Effie doesn't hear us. She's beyond listening!

The Krampus picks her up and shoves her in his sack. She goes quite limp as he chucks it over his shoulder.

'Effie…!'

And then he's pegging it on his cloven hooves. He darts away from the parade, and up Church Street.

'*He's got her!* He's nabbed our friend..!'

And we go running after them. The Krampus and Effie. He's bounding three steps for every single one that we can take, picking our way over the icy cobbles.

He's got her and there's nothing we can do!

The crowd parts around him. Idiotic shoppers coo and applaud his realism.

By now Effie is struggling and wriggling inside the sack. Right at the last moment she has realised the danger that she's in!

'*Effie…!*' I call, to no avail.

Up and up the winding street… to the foot of the steps that lead to the church and the Abbey.

Iris is clutching her knees. 'Those bloody steps!' she pants. 'I'll never make it up there!'

But it's too late to give chase.

Look at that Krampus go! So nimble and lithe! Throwing back his devilish head and shrieking his triumph to the darkening sky. His muscular legs go pumping like pistons, taking the one hundred and ninety-nine steps three at a time!

And I can hear Effie now, crying faintly:

'*Breeennnndddaaaaa....! Saaaaavvveee meeeeee....!*'

Iris touches my arm and looks both sorrowful and knackered.

We've failed! We've lost Effie!

And in that second of realisation there is a flash of green fire. An infernal kindling in the snowy air!

And then... *they are gone*!

'They've vamoosed!' Iris gasps. 'They've shot off into time and space!'

I swear very loudly. 'That's it, then. We've lost her. We've failed!'

I turn to Iris and for a second she looks just as defeated and hopeless as I feel. But then... like air rushing into a hot air balloon, a new resolve starts to fill her up. She seems to grow several inches and a fierce look comes into her eyes.

'Bugger that!' she roars. 'We're not defeated! If we rush now… we can follow their Time Traces through the Maelstrom! Come on, Brenda, chuck…!'

I'm frankly baffled. 'We can follow their what in the what..?'

She's dragging on my arm. Suddenly she's got the puff to get her up the winding steps to the Abbey. 'Come on! You want to go after her, don't you?'

'But how? Where are we going? You said she'd been taken off into… into the past!'

Iris nods, looking much wiser and ancient than usual. 'Yes, and so she has. But we can get after her. Right this very minute. If we stir our stumps..!'

And so – entrusting myself completely to this wayward ratbag – I put all my remaining energy into clambering up those steps.

*

Oh, Effie! How many times have you and I ran up and down these terrible steps in pursuit of our enemies! And how many times have we been chased by monsters and villains, fearing for our lives every step of the way?

At least those times we had each other. I knew you were there and we had each other's backs. Only rarely were we parted!

As I pant and heave my way up the stone staircase I'm having wild thoughts: what if we've lost her forever to a time travelling demon? How lonely must she have been, deep down, to fall in with such a creature?

'Flamin' heck!' Iris screeches. 'The view's very pretty, but I'm done for! I feel sick as a dog!'

But we're almost at the top.

She's quite right. The view of the harbour and the West Cliff from up here is quite spectacular. We peer down into the winding, thronging streets where that pagan carnival is still underway. We can see right across the harbour, to where there's yet another party in full swing at the Christmas Hotel.

Iris takes in all of this vista and breathes out. 'This town of yours is absolutely bloody *mental*, Brenda.'

'I know,' I agree. 'But it's home.'

At the very top of the steps, at the edge of the graveyard, Iris whips some strange device out of a pocket in her coat. It bleeps and chimes and lights up different colours as she waves it through the air. 'Hmmmm,' she goes, thoughtfully.

'Look, what do we do now?' I ask her. 'This is where they vanished. Now you said we could follow them. You said it was possible. How do we do that, Iris? Is it with that thing?'

She stops waving her strange device around. 'This thing? Oh no. Not this thing. This is just a thing I use to take readings. This is a Time Tracer, this thing. And it's picking up the trail that Effie and her demon left behind in the ether. Yes... I've got it now...'

'Then what do we do now?' I ask her, and I know I'm sounding demanding and cross. I'm on the verge of losing my patience with her.

'Now?' she says, and she grins at me. That huge great grin fills up her whole face and you can't help but feel reassured and warmed by it. Even as you think she must be crazy. 'Well, now what we do is… we catch the bus..!'

I stop dead in my tracks. '*What?*'

She laughs. '*Oh!* You don't know yet, do you? I haven't told you yet, have I? Hahaha!' Then she's off, capering through the graveyard. Dancing between the ancient stones. Weaving her way past St Mary's church. It's getting darker now. Almost full dark and the snow and wind isn't abating. She's dancing us out onto the exposed flank of the East Cliff, with that wonderful view over the sea.

'Iris!' I call after her. 'What are you talking about? Where are we going?'

'Hahaha! Follow me, lovey! You'll soon see..!'

And indeed I do.

There's a double decker bus in the graveyard.

It's an old fashioned, bright red London bus. Somehow she's managed to drive it inbetween all the narrowly-packed gravestones right to the very edge of the cliff.

'But that's not possible…!'

'*Hahahaha!*' She's clearly enjoying every second of this. As she skips and jumps closer to the hulking vehicle all its lights flare into life.

It's no ordinary bus. It's got gaudy curtains drawn at every window and a wonderful, golden light emanates from within.

'*Oh…!*' I tumble closer, clutching the graves for steadiness as I approach.

There's a strange humming noise coming from the bus… as if its engines are warming up. Preparing for… preparing for what..?

What does it do – *fly..?!*

'Like you say, Brenda. Whitby is your home. But *this* is mine! My wonderful bus! The number twenty-two to Putney Common!'

I stare at her. 'But I don't want to go to Putney Common…!' is all I can think to say.

This makes her howl with laughter. Then the hydraulic doors spring open at her touch. 'Lovely

Brenda! We can go wherever we want! Now, hurry along! And step this way..! Welcome aboard my beautiful red bus..!'

Brenda and Effie, Iris Wildthyme and Panda will all return in:

Brenda by Gaslight

With huge thanks to Rylan for artwork and all
the help! And thanks to all of Fambles – and to
Jeremy, Panda and Bernard Socks.

For Mam